PRAISI
DHARMA KELLEHER

"Kelleher's characterizations and voice are fresh and new, the action comes fast and furious."

GREG HERREN, AUTHOR OF *BATON ROUGE BINGO*

"Dharma Kelleher has created one of the most unique characters in crime fiction. She takes readers on a thrilling ride that will have you turning pages into the wee hours of the morning!"

RENEE JAMES, AUTHOR OF *SEVEN SUSPECTS*

The action-packed scenarios don't quit, right up to the story's unexpected, satisfying resolution."

MIDWEST BOOK REVIEW

A MURDER OF CROWS

AN AVERY BYRNE THRILLER

DHARMA KELLEHER

dark pariah press

A MURDER OF CROWS: AN AVERY BYRNE THRILLER

Published by Dark Pariah Press, Phoenix, Arizona.

Cover design: JoAnna Kelleher

Ebook ISBN: 978-1-952128-35-6

Paperback ISBN: 978-1-952128-36-3

Hardcover ISBN: 978-1-952128-37-0

To my wonderful wife, Eileen.
After twenty-five years of being married to you,
it still just keeps getting better.
No one has stood by me and encouraged my writing like you have.
Every moment with you is a gift more precious than any treasure.
Thank you.

CONTENTS

2.
3.
4.
5.
6.
7.
8.
9.
10.
11.
12.
13.
14.

15.
16.
17.
18.
19.
20.
21.
22.
23.
24.
25.
26.
27.
28.
29.
30.
31.
32.
33.
34.
35.
36.
37.
38.
39.
40.
41.
42.
43.
44.
45.
46.
47.
48.
49.
50.
51.

CHAPTER 1

DEATH IN THE FAST LANE

"Boze, dude, what's wrong?" Hatchet wiped the blood-red cupcake crumbs from his hands and onto his grease-stained work shirt. He set the bottle of ginger beer he'd been drinking on a nearby metal tool cabinet.

The tall, older man shook his head as if trying to clear the cobwebs. "Feeling woozy. Must be the meds them docs got me on. Or maybe I'm coming down with something."

"You don't look too good, my friend," Fisch chimed in. "You need to lie down or something? There's a cot in the office we can set out if you need."

"Naw, I'll be all right. After all, it's payday," Boze replied with a tired grin. "Don't wanna be falling asleep for that. When's that guy supposed to be showing up, anyway?"

Hatchet gazed up at the old clock on the service bay wall. "Said eight. So half an hour."

Boze rose unsteadily to his feet. "Maybe I'll splash some water on my face."

He took two steps before he lost his balance and fell against the side of a 1955 Thunderbird that Classic Autos was restoring. His head clipped the side-view mirror on the way down.

"Fuck!" he groaned.

Hatchet was at his side in a heartbeat, checking his friend for injuries. Blood seeped from a cut on Boze's temple, staining his gray afro a bright red.

"Something ain't right, Hatch. Feelin' all kinda—I dunno," Boze said woozily. "Maybe I oughta drive myself to the ER."

"You can't drive yourself like this." Hatchet pressed a clean shop rag to Boze's wound. "Fisch, help me get him into the Blue Streak."

"Probably better if we call for an ambulance," Fisch replied.

"No!" Boze snapped, his voice shaky. "Don't need no damn ambulance. Got enough medical bills already. Blue Streak's faster."

The two younger guys helped Boze to his feet and, supporting him on their shoulders, got him out into the parking lot.

"Where should I take him?" Hatchet asked.

"Saint Joe's closest," Fisch replied. "On Thomas at Third Avenue."

"Sounds good."

Hatchet lowered his friend into the passenger seat of his 1965 Mustang convertible, pulled the seatbelt across his waist, and closed the door. The pale-blue paint looked silver in the golden glow of the streetlight.

"Just hang in there, brother. We'll get you taken care of."

"Should I follow in my car?" Fisch asked, pulling out his keys.

"No," Hatchet insisted. "Someone's got to stay here and collect the money. I'll call you soon as I know something."

"Okay. Be safe."

Hatchet jumped in behind the wheel and tore out of the parking lot, tires squealing. Engine roaring, they raced south on Seventh Street, using the suicide lane to get around cars in their way.

"Oh, man. Oh, man," Boze gripped his chest. "Hard to breathe."

Hatchet wasn't feeling so good himself. A wave of drowsiness hit him suddenly. He struggled to keep his eyes open and on the road, even as he wove through the obstacle course of vehicles in front of him.

Whatever was making Boze sick seemed to be affecting him now too. *The flu? In early May?*

As it became increasingly harder to focus on the road, Hatchet considered pulling over. He was looking for a parking lot to pull into when Boze slumped forward, held into his seat only by the seatbelt around his waist.

"Boze! Wake up! Hey!" He tried to shake his friend awake, but there was no response. Panic gripped him. "Fuck! Hold on, brother!"

Hatchet pressed the accelerator to the floor. His own drowsiness intensified. Suddenly, he was floating. His concerns for Boze dissolved into a cloud of euphoria.

"Shit!" Hatchet opened his eyes in time to see the utility pole flying toward him at bullet speed. A deafening metallic crunch was the last thing he heard.

CHAPTER 2

FALLEN CROWS

The HorrorPops' "Walk Like a Zombie" played on the Seoul Fire Tattoo Studio sound system. Avery Byrne bobbed her head to the beat as she inked a new design.

Her client, a white guy in his forties who went by the moniker Walrus, sported a bushy horseshoe mustache and a bit of a beer gut. The tattoo she was creating depicted a chef's knife running the length of the man's bicep, with the head of a crow reflected in the blade.

"You change your look?" Walrus stroked his whiskers with his free hand.

Avery stiffened at the comment. Since her girlfriend Sam's murder, she'd abandoned her usual '50s pinup style for a more trad goth aesthetic. "A little."

"Cause your girl got killed?"

"You heard about that?"

"Missed you at race night last few weeks. Asked around where you'd gone. Really sorry for your loss."

"Thanks." Avery tamped down the emotions threatening to erupt and tried to focus on her artwork instead.

Walrus continued, "Speaking of which, d'you hear two Crows died last week?"

The Sonoran Crows was a club of old-school hot-rodders with a reputation for street racing. Walrus had been the club's president until a member named Mendez defeated him.

Avery often attended their race nights, drawn to the beauty of the restored classic cars, the drama of the drivers boasting and throwing shade, and, of course, the excitement of the street races themselves.

Avery's hand trembled when she heard Walrus's news. She told herself it was just the vibrations from the tattoo machine. A deep cleansing breath steadied her.

"W-Who died? Somebody crash during a race?"

"Hatchet and Boze. But not at race night."

Her hand froze in midstroke, trembling all the more. Not just the tattoo machine. Raw trauma pressed hard against the barriers she'd erected in her mind. *Don't let your personal shit spill over into your work*, she chided herself.

"Hatchet was in here just a month ago, getting a tattoo in honor of his late sister. What happened?"

"Crashed his '65 Mustang into a utility pole on Seventh Street. Boze was riding shotgun."

"Shit! Hatchet's one of the Crows' best drivers. What caused the crash?"

"Phoenix PD claims he had fentanyl in his system. They both did. Listed their causes of death as a drug overdose. Not from the crash itself."

"That's unbelievable. Hatchet never struck me as a junkie."

"He wasn't. His mother was a dope fiend when he was a kid. Saw what a mess it made of her life. He hated that shit. And Boze was a substance abuse counselor and had been clean for over ten years." Walrus again stroked his mustache. "You ask me, somebody slipped 'em something. And when I find out who done it? I swear I'll bash their fucking brains in with a pry bar."

"Why would anyone hurt Hatchet and Boze?"

"Beats the hell outta me. Everybody liked Boze. He'd give you the shirt off his back, even if it was freezing out. And Hatchet was cool too. Sure, there are rivalries within the group. But no real enemies to speak of. Nothing worth killing over."

"Are the cops looking for who did this?"

"What do you think? They chalked it up to a couple of street racers dying from a drug overdose. Case closed."

"Fuck."

Was someone murdering Crows? And would they stop at just two? Just thinking about it made Avery want to join Walrus in beating those responsible to a bloody pulp. But she reminded herself that her days as Avery the Avenger were over.

You're no longer that street kid, protecting your friends from abusive pimps, dirty cops, and ruthless gangbangers, she told herself. *Avery Byrne is a citizen now. Not a vigilante.*

She had a career now, along with an apartment, a car, and bills to pay. And she had people who cared for her and depended on her.

And still, the reflection of the female Peter Pan tattoo on her bicep caught her eye. Pan the Avenger. The righter of wrongs. Slayer of pirates. Protector of the innocent.

"There going to be a funeral?" she asked.

"Funeral was a couple days ago. Immediate family only. But the Crows are having a memorial tomorrow night at Tailfins." It was a bar popular with the hot-rodders.

"I want to pay my respects if that's okay."

"Absolutely. The more, the merrier."

Again, she caught the reflection of the tattoo in her workstation mirror. Pan the Avenger appeared to be staring up at her. Calling her to vengeance.

Horrific memories buzzed in her mind like a hive of angry bees. Finding her girlfriend tied to a chair and tortured. Avery's desperate attempt to rescue her foiled by the gunshot that splattered Sam's brains on their kitchen wall. The killers coming after Avery, pursuing her all the way to Las Cruces, New Mexico, looking for the money Sam had so foolishly stolen from the Desert Mafia.

Sam's killers had paid dearly. Avery the Avenger had seen to that. But Sam was still gone. And five weeks later, the crushing loss ached like a gaping hole in her goth soul.

Would the cops punish whoever had drugged Hatchet and Boze? Doubtful. To them, the Crows were a bunch of reckless gearheads who endangered the good citizens of the Valley in their loud-as-fuck rat rods.

"Ow! Fuck!" Walrus barked.

Avery snapped back to the present. She'd been pressing the needles too deep. She wiped away the excess blood. "Sorry."

CHAPTER 3

APPA

A few hours later, Avery finished filling in and shading Walrus's new tattoo. It wasn't her best work. The lines could have been cleaner, the shading more subtle. Even as she struggled with the onslaught of emotions, she had to accept that this was the best she could have done.

Walrus stood and admired the tattoo in Avery's workstation mirror. "Fucking awesome, girl. You're a goddamn Picasso."

She forced herself to accept the compliment with a smile.

When Walrus sat back down, she wrapped the tattoo in cellophane and gave him the usual post-ink care instructions, though he'd probably memorized it after all the other tats decorating his body.

"I'll see you tomorrow night at the memorial," he said when he paid her.

"I'll be there. Have a good night."

She began cleaning and sanitizing her station, thinking more about Hatchet and Boze.

After most marathon sessions of working on a design, she felt drained mentally, physically, and creatively. Walrus's suspicions about Hatchet's and Boze's deaths only worsened her exhaustion, reopening raw wounds that had only started to heal. She wanted to crawl into a hole and disappear for a year.

Hatchet had been a bit of a goofball, but he had once intervened when some drunken sleazebag came on to her at one of the Sonoran Crows' street races and refused to take no for an answer. Hatchet had kicked the guy's ass and told him not to come back until he could keep his hands to himself.

He had also restored her car, a 1957 black Cadillac Coupe de Ville nicknamed the Gothmobile, to its former glory and only charged her for parts. He'd been a good man who didn't deserve to die so young.

She didn't know Boze as well, but he'd always been polite to her whenever she saw him. He didn't deserve it either.

While she cleaned, Bobby Jeong, the owner of Seoul Fire Tattoo, strolled over with an expression she recognized all too well. He was worried about her.

"Couldn't help but overhear, kiddo," he said cautiously.

Avery feigned an innocent look. "Overhear what?"

"Walrus talking about his buddies getting killed. You knew them?"

She sighed. "Yeah."

"Thought the names sounded familiar."

"Fucking sucks, Appa," she replied, using the Korean word for Dad. Back when she was a homeless teen living on the streets, he'd offered to be her foster dad. Despite only knowing each other for six years, she loved him more than she had ever cared for the family who'd kicked her out of the house at thirteen.

She focused on wiping down her station, refusing to meet his eyes. "Cops aren't doing shit to find the killer. Calling it an overdose. Not that I'm surprised. What do they care about a couple of dead Crows?"

"Maybe it was an overdose that killed them."

"Or maybe it wasn't. I've known them more than a year. They weren't junkies."

"You're not planning on…" He gave her a knowing look.

Her body stiffened. She knew what he was asking. "Planning on what?" she asked defiantly.

"Getting involved."

"What makes you think I'd get involved in finding out who killed my friends?"

Bobby pulled up a stool and sat so that she had to look at him. "Ave, this past month has been a rough one for you. Sam's horrific death and then you being forced to flee from those gangsters. Nearly getting murdered by that dirty police lieutenant. I don't blame you for being cynical. But you weren't the only one traumatized." He gripped his chest. "I'd never been so scared in my life, knowing my daughter was in such danger and not being able to help."

Avery said nothing. The experience of watching her girlfriend die in front of her remained seared in her memory. It was there every time she shut her eyes. Every time she ached for Sam's touch. The only thing that made it bearable was knowing she'd punished those responsible.

"Sorry I worried you, Appa."

"It wasn't your fault, sweetheart. But this thing with your hot-rod friends. Please don't get involved."

His beatific smile, sad and worried as it was, cut through her resolve like a switchblade through silk. The man truly cared for her.

"It's just…" She struggled to find the words.

"Sit." He gestured to her client chair.

She sat.

"A month ago, I feared I'd never see you again. I don't think my fifty-six-year-old heart could take it if you died. Not after losing Melissa a few years ago."

Avery recalled her foster mother's joyful smile, gone forever due to a terrorist's bomb.

Bobby continued. "Before we met, you protected your friends when you were all living on the street. The Lost Kids, you called them. And you were their hero—Avery the Avenger. Very admirable. Especially for a teenager."

"Just did what I had to. No one else was there for us."

"That's right. But then you learned a very hard lesson. Our actions, however noble and well intentioned, can often have grave, unexpected consequences."

Her mind flooded with the scent of blood. The horror of finding the Lost Kids' bullet-riddled bodies. The crushing realization that it had been her fault. The floodgates of her trauma broke loose, threatening to drown her in the bitterly cold and bottomless well of despair.

She wiped the tears from her face and swallowed hard.

"I don't bring it up to hurt you, kiddo. I know you blame yourself for their deaths. And I want to be clear. You are not to blame. You did what you could to protect your friends from that violent pimp when no one else cared. But actions can have unintended consequences."

"You think I don't know that?"

The two other artists in the shop, Butcher and Frisco, gave her silent looks of sympathy from their workstations.

"I know you do, Avery. And I understand that these hot-rodders were your friends. But do your old dad a favor and don't go looking for trouble."

"But whoever killed Hatchet…"

"Deserves to be punished. But that is a job for law enforcement." He tucked a lock of her hair behind an ear. "Not a job for a beautiful young woman with a promising future as a tattoo artist."

"But the cops wrote it off as an accidental overdose."

"Maybe it was."

"Hatchet wasn't a junkie. Neither was Boze anymore. The cops are just too lazy to worry about a couple of street racers getting murdered."

"You may be right. But I don't want to see you get into a dangerous situation again. If someone murdered your friends, that's the perpetrator's karma. They will suffer because of it. Best you stay out of it, or what happened to them could blow back on you or someone you care about."

"What if they kill again? How many of my friends have to die before someone does something?"

Bobby kissed her forehead. "I don't have an answer to that. But after all that's happened, I don't want you risking your life. Not over this. Please, kiddo. Promise me."

"Yeah, yeah, yeah."

“Not ‘yeah, yeah, yeah.’ I mean it. Promise me you won’t get involved.”

“I promise I won’t get involved. I’ll leave it up to the police.” She looked deep into his brown-black puppy-dog eyes. She didn’t want to worry or disappoint him. “I gotta get going. I promised to meet Kimi and Chupa for drinks at Johnny Heretics.”

Bobby J. nodded. “Give Kimi and Chupa my love. And be careful.”

She gathered up her purse and kissed his cheek. “Yes, Appa.”

“Also, you’re invited for dinner tomorrow night. I want you to meet Dana.”

A part of her cringed. She’d been avoiding meeting Dana Kim, Bobby’s new girlfriend, for a while.

On the one hand, she wanted Bobby to be happy. On the other, she still freaked out about the idea of him being romantic with anyone other than Melissa. It felt like a betrayal to her foster mother’s memory, even though she knew it wasn’t.

“Raincheck. Tomorrow night is the memorial service.”

He sighed heavily. “Fair enough. How’s Friday night looking?”

“You two are still getting to know each other,” she replied. “You sure you want to risk introducing her to your white goth foster daughter?”

“We’ve been dating for nearly six weeks. It’s time you two meet. I know she’s not Melissa. But it’s been three years. A man gets lonely.”

“Ew, Appa.” Avery tried hard not to imagine Bobby and this new woman getting hot and sloppy.

Again, those puppy-dog eyes met her gaze, and compassion softened her revulsion.

She nodded “Friday. I’ll be there, Appa. For you, not her.”

“Give her a chance. It’s all I ask.”

"I promise." She kissed him on the cheek, walked out the back door, and climbed into the Gothmobile.

She could still hardly believe Hatchet was gone. Just like Sam. Just like Melissa. Just like the Lost Kids.

Not for the first time, she wondered if she was cursed. Normal people didn't have so many loved ones murdered. She was only twenty-two, for goth's sake. Then again, most people hadn't committed murder, either.

Bobby J. had repeatedly insisted she wasn't cursed. But as more people she cared for died, she became more convinced she was.

CHAPTER 4

SET UP

Johnny Heretics was already bustling when Avery arrived. Normally, it was a punk rock club, but once a month, they had a goth night. The audience was largely Gen Xers who had embraced the music genre back in the early days of Bauhaus and the Cure, when much of it was still categorized as postpunk.

Avery also saw numerous millennials like her, who found meaning in the macabre themes and dark electronic beats from classic bands and more current groups. They also reflected more diversity than their older counterparts. In addition to the trad goths dressed all in black, the younger crowd included brightly colored pastel goths, futuristic cyber goths, and retro-styled pinup goths.

And then there were the tourists who showed up to gawk and laugh. Fortunately, there weren't many in this evening's crowd.

Kimiko Sato sat at a table next to her hulk of a husband, Marco Melendez, whom everybody called Chupa. Kimi wore a halter top printed with cheesy vintage horror film cover art and a leather skirt. Her hair was pinned into a cute updo. Kimi and Avery had been friends since before her birth parents kicked her out for being transgender.

Chupa sported an unbuttoned black shirt decorated with demonic jack-o'-lanterns over a white T-shirt. Even sitting down, he towered over his wife by a good six inches.

A tall, tomboyish woman Avery didn't recognize sat opposite Kimi. Her dark hair was cut short and spiky with a side shave on the left. Scarlet embroidered spiders cascaded down the front of her white western-style shirt. A bolo tie with a skull cameo slider encircled her neck. Avery's gaydar caught a serious lesbian vibe from her, along with the alluring scent of jasmine.

Kimi hadn't mentioned anyone else would be joining them. Avery felt a little awkward when she sat down next to the woman.

"Sorry I'm late," Avery said.

"No worries." Kimi reached across the table to give her hand a squeeze. "Glad you could make it."

"How are you feeling?" Avery asked Chupa.

"A lot better, especially now that the tour's over. And for the record, getting shot in the stomach hurts like a mofo. Do not recommend."

"I'm sorry that happened. I still have no idea how Bramwell's men tracked me all the way to Las Cruces."

"No worries. I'd take a bullet for you any day."

Kimi cleared her throat and gestured with her beer to the woman across from her. "Avery, I want you to meet my friend and a longtime fan of Damaged Souls, Rosalind Fein. She runs the Spy Gal shop on Indian School and Thirty-Second Street. Roz, this is Avery Byrne, my best friend since middle school and an award-winning tattoo artist."

"Hi," Avery said shyly, catching Rosalind studying her tattoo sleeves.

In a confident and husky alto, Rosalind greeted Avery and shook her hand firmly. "Nice ink. Is that Peter Pan and Wendy on your arm?"

"More or less."

"Is it my imagination, or does Peter look a bit… feminine?"

"I intentionally drew Pan female," Avery replied, finding it hard not to stare deeply into Rosalind's dark-honey eyes. "I reimagined them as a lesbian couple."

"Right on." Rosalind gave an approving nod. "Makes sense, considering Peter's often played by a woman. You've got some mad skills, especially to do it on your own arm."

Avery tried hard not to blush and failed. "How about you? What's Spy Gal?"

"Retail shop selling a range of surveillance and countersurveillance equipment—nanny cams and security systems mostly but also parabolic mics, bug detectors and similar spy tech. Used to sell signal jammers until the government outlawed them."

"Sounds interesting." It actually sounded boring as hell, but Avery didn't know what else to say. She'd never been good at small talk.

Avery caught herself being irresistibly attracted to this woman, which triggered pangs of guilt. *Sam's barely been dead a month. Have some fucking respect for the deceased, for goth's sake*, she scolded herself.

"We attract a unique mix of customers. People suspicious of babysitters or cheating partners, conspiracy nuts, parents worried about troubled teens."

"Just the place for Avery the Avenger," Chupa quipped with a laugh that always reminded her of Seth Rogen.

Avery shot him a scolding look, and Kimi nudged him. "Chup!"

"What's Avery the Avenger?" Rosalind's eyes twinkled with interest. "Sounds like a fascinating story."

"It's nothing." Avery glanced around the place. "They still have table service here? I could use a drink."

Kimi added, "Avery the Avenger was something from when she and I were kids."

"Come on. Spill," Rosalind pleaded. "Embarrassing childhood stories are the best."

"Really, it was nothing. I helped someone who was being abused." Avery stood and met Kimi's gaze. "You know, on second thought, I think I'm gonna head home. Been a long day."

Kimi knitted her brow. "Home? You just got here. Chupa, go to the bar and get her a drink!"

"No, Chupa, stay," Avery insisted.

"I'm sorry," Rosalind said. "That was rude of me to press the issue. Don't run off on my account."

"No, it's not you. Earlier today, I learned some friends of mine were killed. I could use some alone time to process it all."

"Where better to process death than goth night?" Chupa chuckled again. He'd clearly had a few and was feeling it.

Kimi clasped Avery's hand. "Ave, sweetie. I'm sorry Chupa brought up the Avenger thing. Please don't go now. I missed you when you left the tour. And after all that's happened, I think you could use some girl time."

"That's me," Chupa said. "Just one of the girls."

"I'm okay. Really. Just need to process."

"At least let me walk you to your car."

"Yeah, okay. See you later, Chup. Nice meeting you, Rosalind."

Rosalind's expression was one of regret. "I'm terribly sorry if I said something I shouldn't."

Goth, she's cute, Avery thought, which only made her feel worse. Like she was cheating on Sam. Like her abrupt departure was pissing on what could've been a fun evening for everyone. It felt as if there wasn't enough air.

Avery grabbed her purse and dashed through the crowd toward the front door. It wasn't until she stepped outside into the sweltering desert night, trying to remember where she'd parked, that she could breathe again.

"Ave?"

She turned to see Kimi standing there, looking worried. "You okay?"

"I'm fine. Just trying to remember where I parked the Gothmobile." She scanned the lot frantically. Her hands were shaking again.

Kimi's fingers entangled with her own. "Hey, it's me you're talking to. Your sister from another mister. Don't shut me out."

Avery faced Kimi, her heart pounding. "I know."

"We both been through a lot of shit recently—Sam's death and Chupa getting shot."

"And me in the middle of it all."

"How are you holding up?"

Avery felt the pressure behind her eyes, but she refused to let the tears flow. "I miss her, Kimi. I miss her arms around me. I miss her silly laugh. I miss her crazy, impulsive ideas. I know that she worked for the Desert Mafia and that all this happened because she stole that money from them. But goth, I fucking miss her."

"Of course you do. Who wouldn't? Girl, you've lost a lot of people in your life. But all of that's over. Now you get to live a normal life. Well, semi-normal. Goth normal."

"Do I? Someone just killed a couple of my friends. They were members of the Sonoran Crows."

"What happened?" Kimi asked. "Who killed them?"

Avery shrugged. "They crashed into a utility pole. The cops claim they overdosed on drugs. Only they weren't junkies. Well, one was an ex-junkie, but he'd been clean forever. And my friend, Hatchet, wouldn't have taken that shit in a million years. Someone must've slipped them something."

"You're not getting involved, are you, Ave?"

Grief, anger, and fear hammered Avery. "I don't know. The cops don't give a shit about a couple of hot-rodders. But they still deserve justice."

"Avery the Avenger. I get it. But you barely escaped from the Desert Mafia."

"Yes, but they're gone now, thanks to me."

"Yeah, I saw the news footage. All those bodies hanging from the bridge. Scary shit."

"Not my fault they snitching on the Mexican cartel and getting their shipments seized at the border." Avery stared down at her feet.

"You gave the cartel proof that the mafia was double-crossing them."

"The Mexicans would have figured it out eventually. All the people Bramwell and his cronies hurt, decent people like Sam and Chupa and Bobby J., deserved justice. I did what I had to do. My friends, Hatchet and Boze, deserve justice too."

"Avery, look at me."

She met Kimi's gaze and could see the worry. The same worry that was in Bobby's eyes.

"I love you. We're family. And while your hot-rodder buddies deserve justice, you don't need to be entangled in anyone else's shit. You've dealt with more than enough for one lifetime. If you get involved, whoever killed those guys could come after you. And I don't want to lose you."

"I…" Avery didn't know what to say.

"Promise me you won't get involved."

"Yeah, okay. I promise." Something niggled in the back of Avery's brain. "Hey, this Rosalind chick. Was this whole thing a setup? Like a blind date?"

"What? No. Chupa and I were just getting together with old friends. Not *old* old. Longtime friends. No setup." But mischief glimmered in Kimi's eyes. "Although she *is* single."

"I'm still grieving Sam."

Kimi pressed her forehead against Avery's. "Of course you are. Give yourself time to grieve and heal before you jump back into the fetid swamp they call the dating pool."

"Yeah, right. Even if I was ready, it probably wouldn't work out. I always pick losers. Even Sam, I hate to say it."

Kimi leaned back and met Avery's eyes again. "You sure you don't want to come back in and join us? I really missed you after you left the tour."

Avery considered it. "I missed you too. But I need some time alone tonight."

"Just don't isolate too long."

"I won't. I promise."

They hugged, and Avery spotted the Gothmobile across the parking lot. The streetlamps reflected off the Caddy's twin bullet taillights in a way that made them look like gawping faces.

"Love you, girl," Kimi said when they parted.

Avery walked to her car. "Love you more."

"Call me tomorrow."

"Will do."

CHAPTER 5

SAMARITEEN

On the drive home, Avery couldn't wait to tell Sam about Hatchet's death, forgetting for a moment that Sam, too, was gone. Never again would Avery run her hands through Sam's strawberry-blond locks, go on one of Sam's crazy last-minute adventures, or feel Sam's deft fingers inside her.

Why did she have to work for that psycho gangster Theodore Bramwell in the first place? And why did she think stealing two million dollars from him was a good idea?

But that was Sam—impulsive, reckless, and at the same time, sweet and tender. She had wanted to get out of that life and run away with Avery to Seattle. And it'd gotten her killed, leaving Avery alone and heartbroken.

Avery stopped at a red light. A nearby billboard promoted the Samariteen network of shelters for homeless youth. The image of the distressed teen on the billboard ripped open a flood of half-forgotten memories, filling her with disgust.

Nine years earlier, she'd wandered into the Samariteen shelter on Monroe Street in downtown Phoenix after her bio dad kicked her out of the house for being transgender. Other kids had warned her to steer clear, but surely it couldn't be worse than sleeping in Civic Space Park, doorways, or bus shelters when outside temperatures barely dipped below the triple digits, even at night.

It looked like an ideal place to get a good meal and a night's rest. The staff members were kind and welcoming. And even though her spiritual beliefs leaned more toward Wicca than Christianity, she could deal with all the crosses and Jesus talk.

She woke the next morning on a cot and covered in a stained, but comfortable blanket. Someone was shouting that breakfast would be served soon. She sat up, rubbed her face and gasped. Her blue backpack was gone.

Panic squeezed her chest like a vise. She glanced around at the nearby cots but didn't see it anywhere. All of her remaining belongings were in that pack. Without it, she had absolutely nothing.

After wiping away her tears, she shuffled to the manager's office, clinging to the thinnest thread of hope.

Paul Andrews, the manager, was a white guy in his fifties, with graying blond hair and coffee-stained teeth.

"Mr. Andrews?" she said shyly when she opened his office door.

"Come in. Most people call me Pastor Paul. Please, have a seat. What's your name?"

"Avery Byrne." She sat in a guest chair across from his desk.

"What can I do for you, Avery? You look upset."

"Someone stole my shi—my belongings."

"Oh, I am so sorry." Concern creased Pastor Paul's brow. "We do our best to maintain a secure environment. Was this your first time here?"

"Yeah. Seemed better than sleeping on the streets with it being so hot. Now I'm not so sure."

"Well, we have made an awful first impression, haven't we? What all was stolen?"

"Everything. My clothes, my makeup, my phone, my wallet."

"Was it in a bag or suitcase?"

"A blue backpack."

"How old are you, Avery?"

"Thirteen. Why?"

"And pardon me for asking, but are you a girl or a boy?"

"I'm a girl," Avery snapped, remembering her last conversation with her birth father.

"But really, you're a boy, aren't you? You just like to play dress-up."

"What's that got to do with my stolen shit?"

Pastor Paul seemed to study her for a moment as if trying to work something out in his head. "I have some good news, Avery. I can help you get your belongings back."

The panic seemed to lift. "Really?"

He nodded. "But, as you'll soon learn, everything in life comes with a price."

A jolt of fear shot down her spine. "What do you mean, a price?"

"Shut the door."

"What? Why?"

"You want your stuff back, don't you?"

"Yes, but□—"

"Then shut the door."

She did so, her heart hammering in her chest. Something was wrong. She just wasn't sure what.

When she turned back to face him, Pastor Paul was standing behind his desk, his erect dick sticking out of his fly. "I assume as a thirteen-year-old, you're familiar with what a blowjob is?"

"This isn't right. This is rape."

"No one's raping anyone, Avery. This is just two people providing each other a favor."

"How do I know you can even get my stuff back? Did you take it?"

He grinned and shrugged. "I promise you, I can get your stuff back. But first, you do me a favor."

"I could report you."

"But you won't. Because no one would believe the word of a queer street rat over an esteemed, generous pillar of the community."

Ten humiliating minutes later, after complying with his demands, she asked, "Now, where's my shit?"

"Just a moment." Pastor Paul zipped up his fly and opened the office door. "Mike, could you see if there's a blue backpack in our lost and found? Thank you."

A man in a Samariteen polo shirt walked in a few minutes later with her pack in his hand. “This it?”

She snatched it out of his grip. “Yes.”

“I’m so glad we could help you out, Avery,” Pastor Paul said.

Avery didn’t bother looking at him. Instead, she stormed out. A sweltering night on the streets and eating food scraps out of dumpsters had to be better than this bullshit.

A year later, when she and the Lost Kids were squatting in the vacant house, Delinda brought home a new girl—a twelve-year-old named Rayna, who’d been through the same thing with Pastor Paul.

“Fucking asshole,” Avery spat. “I’m sorry he did that to you. You’re safe here. We watch each other’s backs. No one will mess with you here. I promise.”

“Thanks.” Tears trickled down Rayna’s face.

“Somebody should do something about that guy,” Delinda said.

“Maybe somebody will,” Avery replied.

“Avery the Avenger.” A smile crept across Delinda’s face. “Avery here’s our hero. She blackmailed the owner of this house into letting us stay here. With utilities, no less. And she got that cop busted who planted drugs on T.J. Maybe this time, justice will find that sick bastard Pastor Paul.”

“You should cut off his fucking dick,” Rayna suggested.

Delinda added, “Or better yet, blow his fucking head off.”

Avery considered her options. No doubt the asshole had been doing this to kids for some time. He deserved to die screaming. But after growing up with an abusive father, violence scared her. She had no interest in buying a gun and only carried a pocketknife for self-defense and more practical uses.

“He says the cops won’t do anything,” Rayna said. “No one will believe us street rats over him.”

"Maybe they will if we do it right."

Avery's appearance had changed considerably in the past year. Her hair had grown out. And the hormone blockers and estradiol she bought off the street had softened her features so she looked less like a feminine gay boy and more like a girl.

Still, it took a week of staying at the shelter before Pastor Paul took the bait. This time, she'd kept her phone on her person rather than leaving it in her pack. So when she walked into his office, looking for her missing stuff, she had it tucked into her shirt pocket, recording.

"You're new here, aren't you?" Pastor Paul asked when she sat in the small chair in front of his desk. "What's your name?"

"Annie. I've been staying here a week. I didn't have anywhere else to go." Avery channeled her anger into her performance, summoning up tears. "Now my stuff is gone. Everything."

"How old are you, Annie?"

"Fourteen."

He nodded solemnly. "Not a very good first impression of our facility. I am truly sorry about that. We work hard to provide a safe place for youth with nowhere else to turn."

"I don't know what to do," Avery insisted.

"Well, I've got some good news. I can help you get your belongings back."

And then he made his salacious pitch. Avery had debated about whether to take him up on his offer or tell him she'd recorded him soliciting her. But she needed proof that he wasn't just a creeper but a full-blown pedophile. And so she did the deed once more, trying hard not to gag.

When she was done, Pastor Paul miraculously once again found her stuff in the lost and found.

She stormed out and threw up on the sidewalk. When she finally quit heaving, she pulled up the recording on her phone. She had him dead to rights. In a perfect world, she could send the video to the cops, and they would bust his ass. But she'd learned that most cops couldn't be trusted.

She grabbed a free copy of *Phoenix Living*, the weekly alternative newspaper that frequently published stories exposing corrupt politicians and businesses. On the page-two masthead, she found the email for their editor in chief. This story would be right up their alley.

She sent the editor an email explaining what had happened to her, Rayna, and countless other teens. Her message included a link to the video. She also posted the video on several social media sites. She knew it would eventually be taken down for violating so-called community standards, but hopefully not before it garnered national attention.

The story went viral. Within a week, Pastor Paul had been arrested. Soon after that, he was found hanged to death in his jail cell while awaiting trial. Whether he did it himself or had help, she didn't care. He would never hurt another kid again.

A car horn from behind her roused Avery from her memories of teenage vengeance. The stoplight had turned green. She continued driving to her empty apartment.

The news about Hatchet's and Boze's deaths still ate at her, even though she'd promised Bobby and Kimi she wouldn't get involved. And for all she knew, Boze could have had fallen off the wagon and taken Hatchet with him. Maybe the police had gotten something right for a change. But the nagging feeling that someone else was responsible wouldn't go away.

She needed to know for sure. Maybe if she talked to the detectives handling the case, she could get a sense of whether it was genuinely an accidental overdose or if they were sweeping it under the rug.

Normally, she wouldn't step foot inside a police station. But a few weeks ago, she had finally met a cop who seemed like he really cared. Not just a cop but a senior homicide detective. Detective Pierce "Hardass" Hardin.

When Avery got home, she sent him an email.

I need to speak with you about something. Call me.

CHAPTER 6

PARTY'S OVER

As tired as Avery was, sleep refused to come when she crawled into bed, despite taking the trazodone that her primary doctor had prescribed.

The walls of her apartment echoed with loneliness and desolation. Not because there were no pictures on the walls or because she had only a minimal amount of furniture. She didn't care how the place looked.

Without Sam, her life felt empty and bereft of life. The nights were the worst. The meds did nothing to ward off the horrific nightmares of Sam's battered body strapped to the kitchen chair, followed by her head exploding in an eruption of gore and red mist. Knowing that Sam's killers had suffered a similarly gruesome fate didn't bring her back.

Just as she was drifting off, loud pop music echoed from the courtyard, accompanied by raucous laughter and the sounds of splashing water. This was the fifth night in a row this bullshit had been going on. A bunch of asshole students from nearby Glendale Community College.

She'd moved in only a week ago. It hadn't occurred to her that getting an apartment so close to the campus would mean listening to a bunch of idiots make noise into the wee hours. It didn't help that by nature, she tended to be an early bird.

According to the rules posted on the fence surrounding the pool, all music and loud noises were supposed to stop at nine o'clock. And the pool itself was supposed to close at ten. It was now nearly midnight. Didn't these assholes have classes to study for? Since it was late May, surely finals were coming up. Or maybe they were already over. Avery wasn't sure. She'd never gone to high school, much less college.

The first night it'd happened, she had asked them politely to keep it down. They'd laughed and ignored her. When she complained the next morning to the property manager, a guy with the physique and intellectual capacity of a loaf of bread, he'd claimed there was nothing he could do.

"Most of our residents are students. They party," he'd said with a shrug.

Here it was a few nights later, and she'd reached her limit. She tried listening to Panic Priest's *Second Seduction* album using noise-canceling earbuds, but she could still hear the bass beat coming from the pool.

At one thirty, when the music, shouting, laughter, and splashing showed no signs of abating, she slipped out of her apartment and crept toward the rental office. The complex's breaker panel was secured with a padlock, of course, but she had expected that.

After checking for security cameras, she retrieved a leather pouch from her pocket and pulled out a half-diamond pick and an L-shaped tensioner. In minutes, she had popped the padlock, opened the breaker panel, and was studying the switches. Two were labeled POOL.

"Party's over, asshats." She flipped the switches.

The lights around the pool area went dark. Shouts of anger replaced the pop music and laughter. Savoring the quiet, Avery relocked the breaker panel, slipped back to her apartment, and fell asleep in minutes. Avery the Avenger was back.

CHAPTER 7

HARDASS

Avery woke the next morning to the ominous notes of Bauhaus' "Bela Lugosi's Dead," her default ring tone.

She grabbed it, her mind still cluttered with the cobwebs of sleep. "Yeah?"

"Ms. Byrne, this is Detective Hardin. I got your email. How can I help you?"

She sat up and rubbed her face, remembering why she'd reached out to the man. "I need to speak with you."

"I'm listening."

"Not over the phone. We need to meet in person." She had decided the night before that it would be too easy for him to dismiss her concerns over the phone. But he might take her seriously if she was sitting in front of him.

"Is this about your girlfriend's murder? Or about Lieutenant Ross?"

"In person," she insisted.

"Very well. I'll be in my office until ten this morning. Ask the desk sergeant at police headquarters to page me when you arrive."

"I'll be there." She hung up before he could say anything else.

After a quick shower, she opted for more of a pinup style than trad goth style, hoping it would make her seem more credible. She selected a knee-length polka-dot dress that exposed enough cleavage to get a man's attention. After giving her makeup a last look and quickly combing her grown-out bangs, she grabbed her bag and drove downtown.

Squeezing the Gothmobile into the downtown parking garage's narrow spaces took precision maneuvering and an advanced understanding of geometry. Neither of which she had. So she drove to the top floor and took up two spaces, hoping nobody got pissy and keyed her door.

Temperatures were already in the London broil range when she strolled down Washington Street. Fortunately, it was a short walk from the garage to the Phoenix police headquarters building.

A few minutes after she'd informed the desk sergeant of the purpose of her visit, Detective Hardin appeared wearing a lightweight brown suit. He was a Black man in his late fifties, and the years showed in the deep lines on his face. His short-cropped hair was mostly gray.

He extended a hand when he saw her. "Ms. Byrne, a pleasure to see you."

Despite his being a cop, she had come to trust him. At least so far.

"Can we talk someplace private?"

"Certainly." He provided her with a visitor's badge and escorted her to the Violent Crimes Bureau on the third floor and into a small conference room. She had half expected to be put into one of those claustrophobia-inducing interrogation rooms Hardin's lieutenant had stuck her in before.

"Would you care for some coffee?" Hardin asked as he stood by his chair.

"No thanks."

He sat. "Then how can I help you this morning? Did you remember something we need to know regarding your girlfriend's murder?"

"No. I'm here about Hatchet and Boze."

"Who?"

She realized she didn't know Boze's real name. "Dwayne Hatchet. He and his friend Boze were members of the Sonoran Crows. Both were murdered recently. But you people chalked their deaths up to an accidental overdose. I'm here to correct that."

"Of course. I do remember that case. Detective Valentine was handling that one, as I recall."

"I thought you two were partners."

"Sometimes, although we work a lot of cases solo. The Dwayne Hatchet and Leonard Bozeman cases were Detective Valentine's. I'm not involved."

"Fine. Inform him it wasn't an accidental overdose. Someone murdered Hatchet and Boze. That is what you people do here, isn't it? Investigate murders?"

"As I said, I'm not involved in the case. If Valentine closed it as an accidental overdose, then that's probably what it was. Unless you have evidence to the contrary. In which case, you should speak with him directly."

"He here?"

"I can certainly check. Wait here a moment."

While Hardin was gone, she wondered if coming was a mistake. After all, why would they listen to a goth chick who was connected to the murder of their own former boss?

Five minutes later, Hardin returned. She could read the bad news on his face.

He handed her a business card. "Detective Valentine is in court this morning. You can call and leave a message. Let him know it's about the Hatchet and Bozeman cases."

"Will he reopen the case?"

"If you have compelling evidence suggesting their deaths were homicides, I'm sure he'll consider it."

"Whatever."

"How are you doing otherwise?"

"How do you think I'm doing? After you and Valentine chased me all the way to New Mexico. Then you set me up to get kidnapped and nearly murdered by your boss."

"I'm truly sorry for Lieutenant Ross's part in all of that mess. Had I known he was dirty, I never would have asked him to pick you up from the train station that evening. Have you looked into trauma counseling?"

"Why do you care?" She pulled her parking stub from her purse. "You people validate?"

"I'm afraid not."

She tossed Valentine's card into her purse and walked out.

As she got into the Gothmobile, the clock on the dash read nine thirty. She would have to rush to make it to the tattoo studio in time for her ten-o'clock appointment. She left a quick voicemail message for Valentine before leaving the parking garage.

"Detective Valentine, this is Avery Byrne. I need to speak with you as soon as possible about the murders of Dwayne Hatchet and Leonard Bozeman." She left her phone number and hung up.

CHAPTER 8

NOT-SO-FUNNY VALENTINE

Avery's first client was already waiting when she arrived at ten after. She was a white woman with short bleach-blond curls, a body that was sliding into a midlife spread, and a face that looked like she'd been sucking on uncoated aspirin. Avery didn't judge as long as the woman's money was good.

"Sorry I'm late." Avery said.

"I've been waiting here for twenty minutes. Don't you know anything about customer service?"

Avery wanted to tell the woman to kiss her ass, but she remembered the lessons Bobby J. had taught her about de-escalating. "Why don't we get started so we don't lose any more time? My station's right over here, if you'll follow me."

It seemed to work, because the woman's only response was "Fine."

Once the woman sat in the revamped barber's chair, Avery struggled to remember her name. "So, Tina, what are you looking for, tattoo-wise? And where on your body do you want it?"

The woman pulled a folded piece of paper out of her purse and handed it to Avery. "I want this. On my arm."

Avery unfolded it. The image was a skull in front of two crossed flags—the United States flag and the Confederate battle flag. Underneath, the words *We Won't Be Replaced* were printed in a gothic font.

"Nope." Avery handed the paper back to the woman. "Won't do it."

"I have a right to have whatever I want on my body. It's freedom of speech. This is America."

"I have the right to refuse any design I find objectionable, which that is."

"You one of them commie socialists or something?"

Avery resisted the urge to launch into a rant about white-trash fascism. "I don't do Confederate flags or any other racist designs or language."

"The Confederate flag ain't racist. It's history."

"Won't do it."

"I want to talk to the manager." Red splotches blossomed on Tina's face.

"I'm my own manager. I'm an independent artist that leases space in this shop. And I say no to that design. You'll have to find someone else. I won't do it, and neither will any other artist here."

"I demand to speak with the manager of the shop."

Avery turned to where Bobby J. was working on a client behind a folding privacy screen. His tattoo machine was buzzing away happily.

"Bobby?"

"Yes, Avery?"

"Lady here isn't happy that I'm refusing to tattoo a Confederate flag and a racist slogan."

"Huh" was all he said.

"Sir, I demand you tell this woman that I have a right to whatever tattoo I want." Tina stood up with her hands on her hips.

"You do have that right, ma'am." Bobby's machine went quiet. "Freedom of expression is a beautiful thing."

"See?" Tina sneered at Avery.

Bobby stepped out from behind the screen. "But no one here is required to ink it."

Tina's face grew blotchier and twisted into a snarl. "Figures, a Chinaman."

"Korean American, actually." He offered a beatific smile despite her racism. "I'm sorry, but we can't help you here.

Perhaps you can get what you're looking for somewhere else."

"I've tried three other shops. No one will do it. Typical woke cancel culture."

"Try prison," Avery said with a chuckle, unable to stop herself.

"How dare you!"

"You're going to need to leave," Avery said more seriously. "No one here wants your business."

"Figures. You illiterates name your shop Seoul Fire but don't even know how to spell it. It's S-O-L-E. Maybe if you read your Bible, Jesus could save your souls. Or do they not have Bibles in China?"

"Time to go, lady." Avery stepped into her space and pointed toward the door.

"And if I refuse?"

"You really want me to answer that?"

"Are you threatening me? This creepy bitch just threatened me. I'm calling the cops!"

Bobby gently pulled Avery away from the woman. "Ma'am, what my daughter was trying to say is that if you do not leave, we will have no choice but to have the police escort you from the premises and charge you with trespassing. But if you prefer to call them yourself, I have no objection."

"This bitch is your daughter? Figures. What kinda mongrel family are you people?"

"The kind that doesn't tolerate ignorant white trash like you," Avery said firmly.

"You people are pathetic." She turned on her heels and marched out.

Frisco, the other woman working in the shop, burst out laughing as she worked on the back piece of a male client straddling a chair. "Well, she was sure charming."

Butcher, a tall and mostly silent man, looked over from where he was prepping his own workstation. "Glad she's gone. Giving me a headache." That was more words than Avery had heard him speak in weeks.

"You okay, kiddo?" Bobby asked, placing a hand on her shoulder.

"Fine."

She wasn't. And she didn't need to explain. Bobby knew. The entitled bigoted bitch was just icing on the trauma cake.

Since Avery's next client wasn't due for another few hours, she pulled out her computer tablet and began drawing.

An hour later, her phone rang.

"Ms. Byrne, this is Detective Valentine returning your phone call. Your message said you had information regarding the deaths of Mr. Hatchet and Mr. Bozeman?"

"Yeah, they were murdered." Avery stepped into the back room to avoid disturbing any of the customers.

"And what leads you to believe that?"

"Because they weren't junkies. Somebody must've drugged them."

"Hold on a moment."

She waited for a few minutes until Valentine returned to the line. "I've got the file here. Dwayne Hatchet, white male, thirty-seven years old. And Leonard Bozeman, African American male, age fifty-two. Single-vehicle crash into a utility pole at the intersection of Seventh Street and Montebello Avenue. The medical examiner's report and tox screen confirm that the cause of death in both cases was respiratory failure due to high levels of fentanyl in their systems. Vehicle was traveling at approximately seventy miles an hour when it struck the pole. Your friends got high and went for a high-speed joyride that cost them their lives. I'm sorry. Cased closed."

"But they wouldn't have knowingly taken that shit. That's what I'm trying to tell you. Boze was a drug rehab counselor who'd been clean for ten years. Hatchet might take a drink now and then, but he'd never touch that serious shit.

Not after what his mother put him through. Somebody slipped the drugs into a drink or something."

"And how did you know the decedents?"

"They were friends of mine."

"Well, I'm truly sorry for your loss, Ms. Byrne, but I have no evidence of foul play. I spent several years in narcotics. Sometimes the first time someone uses is also the last time. Especially with a drug as potent as fentanyl. Mr. Bozeman had a history of drug use. And while he may have been clean for some time, addicts relapse all the time. Hardly surprising, considering his medical recent history."

"What medical history?" Avery remembered Boze had fallen from a ladder a few months ago and injured his back. *Is that what Valentine is referring to?*

"I'm sorry, but I'm not at liberty to discuss that with anyone but immediate family. My guess is that Mr. Bozeman had a slip, and Mr. Hatchet joined in for the ride. Unfortunately, it cost both of them their lives."

"This is bullshit." Avery replied, but she wasn't entirely sure at this point.

"I know this is hard, Ms. Byrne. No one likes to think of their loved ones as drug users. It's an ugly disease, especially when opiates are involved. And fentanyl overdoses are on the rise."

"At least reopen the case and look into the possibility."

"I will not do that. There are simply too many cases right now. Homicides are up forty percent over last year in Phoenix alone. I'd like to help you, especially considering what you went through recently. But this department simply doesn't have the time or resources to devote to a wild-goose chase."

"It's not a wild-goose chase. It's murder. I bet if the victims were rich white guys with powerful cops and politicians in their pockets—say someone like Theodore Bramwell, you'd reopen the case in a heartbeat. You and your buddy Hardin chased me all the way to New Mexico, convinced I'd murdered my girlfriend because Bramwell was trying to pin it on me. But surprise! Your own lieutenant was involved, and I was innocent. That was a fucking wild-goose chase."

"I'm truly sorry, Ms. Byrne. I can't change what happened. We were following the evidence. We'd found a gun with your fingerprints at the crime scene. That made you our prime suspect. If you have evidence that shows someone intentionally drugged Mr. Hatchet and Mr. Bozeman without their knowledge, I would consider reopening the case. But just a wild theory from a grieving friend is not sufficient, I'm afraid. Is there anything else I can do for you today, Ms. Byrne?"

"Yeah, you can go fuck yourself."

Avery hung up, shaking with rage. She was pissed at the world for being such a fucked-up place and angry at herself for losing her cool on the phone. But more than anything, her heart ached for all the people she'd lost.

CHAPTER 9

IN MEMORIAM

Her next client was a regular, which should have put her at ease. But she kept thinking about Valentine's refusal to consider Hatchet and Boze's deaths as anything other than an accidental overdose. So what if the homicide unit was overworked and understaffed? Why should justice depend on Phoenix PD's staffing issues?

If the victims had been VIPs, Phoenix PD would've spared no expense. Every detective on the squad would have left no stone unturned. They had chased her all the way to New Mexico when they suspected she had murdered Sam, an employee of one of the Valley's wealthiest, albeit corrupt, businessmen.

Avery caught herself making mistakes as she inked the rainforest scene onto her client's back. She was only outlining this session, but the crouching jaguar looked more like a dog. The feet of the poison dart tree frog were way too big. And the beak of the toucan resembled that of a flamingo.

Photorealism wasn't her specialty, but she scolded herself for letting her wandering mind distract her from her work. She tried to reassure herself that she could fix it in the shading and coloring stages, but she knew even then, it wouldn't be her best work.

While she was sterilizing her station after the client had left, Bobby J. approached her. "You still going to Hatchet's memorial tonight?"

"Yeah."

"You want company?"

She could tell from his expression he was only offering to be supportive. He didn't know any of the Sonoran Crows or the other people who showed up at their events.

"You don't have to come. I probably won't stay long anyway."

"You sure?"

"Go have fun with Dana." It came out more dismissively than she'd intended.

"You're still my number-one gal," Bobby said with a wink. "Me dating Dana doesn't change that. If you need some support at this memorial, I'm there for you."

"I know. I appreciate it. Like I said, I probably won't stay long."

"I'd say 'Have fun,' but it's a memorial, so…" He stammered in a dad sort of way that was endearing. "Be safe. Call me if you feel you've had too much to drink. Or if you just want to talk. Okay?"

"I will, Appa. I promise."

He hugged her, and she left after she finished cleaning.

Despite having lost so many people in her life, the only funeral or memorial Avery had attended had been for her foster mom, Melissa Jeong. She hadn't held a memorial for Sam. At the time of her death, she didn't have any friends outside of work or family she was still speaking to. And Avery had been too busy escaping the Desert Mafia and the cops to worry about such things.

But if there was one thing a goth girl like her was equipped for, it was a memorial. She had black dresses for all occasions. Granted, many were decorated with skulls, bats, or other whimsically macabre images, but she had some outfits that were suitable for the situation.

She picked a plain black dress, touched up her makeup, and drove to Tailfins. The parking lot was packed. Many of the vehicles were classic cars like her own.

She sat for a moment, feeling nervous before she got out. *Is my makeup too goth? Will people make fun of me?*

She'd hung out at Tailfins many times to hear a rockabilly band she liked. Dressing goth for that or at one of the Sonoran Crows street races or car-show events was one thing. But this was different. It was a memorial. One of those weird social situations where she didn't know the rules. She might have to make small talk, which was as terrifying as driving the Gothmobile blindfolded.

She should've accepted Bobby's offer to come with her as a sort of wingman. He was loquacious enough for both of them and seemed at home in any situation.

Finally, she mustered up her courage and followed the driving beat of Eddie Cochran's "C'mon Everybody" into the building.

On the stage where the bands usually played, large portraits of Hatchet and Boze mounted on easels stood on either side of a podium, surrounded by a cascade of flowers. The air was redolent with alcohol and cheap cologne.

It took a moment for Avery to recognize the people who had gathered. Gone were the grease-smeared faces and raggedy T-shirts and jeans. The guys were all spit and polish in suits and ties. The women wore nice dresses, their hair no longer in their usual ponytails.

They stood chatting in clusters or sat in groups around tables. The conversations seemed hushed by the somber mood of the occasion, unlike the raucous noise that usually accompanied the tunes on the jukebox by the door.

Despite the familiar faces and surroundings, she felt like an intruder this evening. She'd never raced the Gothmobile against any of the other hot rods, though there were a couple of women who did race. Avery preferred to be a spectator. She felt the same way about this memorial.

"Hey, girl. I see you made it."

She turned to see a bald white guy in his forties drinking a glass of whiskey. He was tall and brawny, with a goatee that reminded her of Heisenberg from *Breaking Bad*.

"Rocket Man, hey," she whispered. "What're you drinking?"

"Single-malt Scotch. My poison of choice. How about you?"

"Nothing for now. Sorry about Hatchet and Boze."

"Thanks. They'll be missed."

"Your wife here?" Avery asked, trying to think of a way to keep the conversation going.

"Tiffany? Nah, she's staying with her sister."

"You two have a fight?" Avery teased.

Rocket and Tiffany had always seemed like the perfect couple. Two of the best-looking people in this odd bunch of gearheads and old ladies. Always smiling and laughing. Avery had attended a few Sonoran Crow barbecues at their house.

"Fight? Naw, we're good. She's taking care of her sister, who just had a medical procedure. Female stuff."

"Good that Tiffany could be there for her, I guess."

"Yeah." Rocket Man didn't look too happy about it. "Did you hear the Velocity Network is looking to feature the Crows in a spinoff of their *Speed Demons* series?"

"No, I hadn't. That's exciting."

"I hope they don't change their minds in the wake of Hatchet and Boze's deaths."

"I'm sure it'll be fine."

The music went silent in the middle of Imelda May's rockabilly cover of "Tainted Love." Someone tapped a microphone. Mic in hand, Walrus stood in front of the podium.

"Ladies and gentlemen, if you could all find a seat. I was waiting until Mendez arrived, since he's the club president. But seeing as how he's still not here, why don't we get started?"

Avery took a seat alone next to Rocket at a table in the back. A woman Avery recognized as Hatchet's girlfriend stepped up to the podium. Her tan face looked pale and was streaked with mascara. In her hand, she clutched a crumpled tissue.

"Thank you all for coming," she said in a frail voice. "Most've y'all know me. But for those who don't, I'm Emily

Yazzie, Hatchet's girlfriend. Hatchet was… well, he was my world. He mighta never gone to college, but he was smarter than most people with fancy degrees. He knew just about everything there was to know about cars, old and new.

"But more importantly, he was dedicated. To me, to his friends, and to his business, which he built from the ground up. We were supposed to go out the night he died, but he canceled because he was trying to finish up a repair on a car that a customer desperately needed for work the next day."

Her hand trembled, and her face flushed with emotion. "I still don't understand what happened that night. The Hatch I knew would never take drugs. His mother struggled with addiction all her life. He saw what it did to her and their family. All I do know is that he will be missed by me and…"

Her hand wrapped around her belly, which showed the slightest hint of a baby bump. "And our baby and of course, by all of y'all. I'm so grateful to have the Crows as my family. Hatchet once told me if something ever happened, y'all would take care of me. And he was right. Ever since that horrible night, y'all have been there for me. Especially Grace Bozeman and Tiffany Floyd. Holding my hand. Telling me funny stories about him. And giving me more food than I could possibly eat in a year." She managed to laugh and wipe a tear. "So thank you all for being here and for being such good family. Thank you."

Emily sat down, and a Black woman in her thirties with a freckled face and no makeup took her place at the podium. She wore a tailored pantsuit and an expression of sad acceptance.

"My name's Grace Bozeman. A lot of y'all don't know me. Street racing and classic cars aren't really my jam. But Leonard Bozeman was my dad.

"Honestly, I didn't expect him to live as long as he did. He was pretty messed up when I was a child. Snorting or smoking or shooting up whatever he could get his hands on.

In and out of jail. Even hocked the gold pendant he'd given me for my thirteenth birthday so he could get a fix."

She took a deep breath, and as she released it, a faint smile spread across her face. "But then he got clean. I was in college at the time. And I finally got to know the man rather than the addict. And the man turned out to be a pretty spectacular dad. The real Boze was kind, generous, and helped countless people get clean. He put his life back together, and I was proud to be his daughter."

The sadness returned to her expression. "Unfortunately, addiction is a ruthless disease. And it claimed him in the end. I'm incredibly sad that he's gone but equally grateful for the time that I got to spend with him while he was clean. Thank you."

Walrus returned to the podium. "Thank you, Emily and Grace. We're sure as hell gonna miss those guys. If anyone else here would like to get up, share their thoughts, a funny story, or even to propose a toast, you're welcome to do so."

After Grace took her seat, others stood up to share memories of Boze and Hatchet, eliciting a mixture of laughter and tears and no end of toasts to their names. But no one else mentioned the drugs in their anecdotes.

Avery considered Grace's words. If Boze's own daughter believed he'd relapsed, maybe he had. Maybe Valentine was right not to investigate it.

At the same time, Emily and Walrus were convinced Hatchet wouldn't have been using. Not in a million years. Would Boze have slipped some fentanyl to Hatchet? That didn't feel right. Her gut was telling her that someone had gotten away with murdering two decent people. What worried her was that the killer might not stop.

When nearly everyone but Avery had gotten up to speak, Walrus returned to the podium. He held a bottle of Red Dragon ginger beer glistening with condensation.

"Again, I want to thank all y'all for coming to pay your respects to Hatchet and Boze. Hatchet used to drink this Red

Dragon ginger beer." He held up the bottle. "Seems fitting I pour one out in their honor. Ride in power, my brothers."

Walrus poured out a little ginger beer onto the floor then took a swig himself. "Whoo! Spicy!" He raised the bottle, and the others in the room did the same with their drinks. "To Hatchet and Boze."

The crowd echoed his words.

The jukebox cranked up again, starting with Hot Boogie Chillun's "Black Cat's Bone." Avery watched as people swarmed around Emily and Grace, offering their condolences. She considered doing the same, but she didn't know what to say. Any words that came to mind seemed pointless and trite.

She was about to leave when a voice asked, "You're not drinking?"

CHAPTER 10

RUFFLING CROW FEATHERS

Avery looked up to see Walrus standing nearby. A glass of what she assumed was whiskey had replaced the bottle of ginger beer. The new tattoo she'd created peeked out from beneath his short-sleeve shirt, as vivid as it would ever be.

She shrugged. "I might drink later. How was the ginger beer?"

"I don't know why Hatchet loved that shit. It's awful."

"Is it like ginger ale?"

"A little. But stronger. And spicier." He nodded to the empty chair next to her. "You mind?"

"Help yourself."

He sat. "So, what do you think?"

"About?"

"How they died."

"I think you're right. Someone killed them. But who would want to?"

"Far as I know, they didn't have any enemies. There's the rivalry between the Old Schoolers and the Innovators. Has been for a few years. But that was all trash talk and posturing. Nothing any of the guys would kill over."

Walrus was referring to the two factions in the Sonoran Crows. The Old Schoolers felt the hot rods they raced should be limited to vehicles and parts from the 1970s and before. The Innovators, on the other hand, enhanced their vintage vehicles with the latest tech under the hood, including ECU, fuel injection, and modern turbochargers—classic looks but modern engineering.

Boze and Hatchet had both been Old Schoolers who took issue with Innovators.

"You think one of the Innovators did this?" Avery asked.

"Well, Hatchet and Mendez almost came to blows a couple of months ago. Got heated. Don't think they've spoken since."

"What were they fighting about?"

"The new engine in Mendez's '68 Satellite. Engine didn't sound right, almost like it was a recording played over speakers rather than an actual engine revving. Hatchet was convinced it was one of these state-of-the-art all-electric deals. Mendez refused to raise the hood and let anyone see it. Hatchet and a few others voted to have it banned."

"Why? Because it's modern?"

"Not just that. Lithium-ion batteries are a safety hazard. Damned things catch fire, even explode. That, and when the two of them raced a couple weeks ago, Mendez's Satellite left Hatchet's Mustang in the dust, costing Hatch five grand on the race. Naturally, Hatchet said things he shouldn't have that Mendez interpreted as racist. Took five of us to keep them from beating the shit outta each other."

"Sounds like a motive."

"Maybe. Hey, you want something to drink?"

"Bottle of Guinness would be good." Maybe if she took the edge off, she could talk to some more people.

"Coming up."

Avery pulled a ten out of her purse and offered it to him.

He waved it away. "My treat. Love the new tat, by the way. It's better than I imagined it."

"Thanks."

No sooner had Walrus walked off toward the bar than Emily strolled by. Avery pushed herself out of her comfort zone. "Hey, Emily."

Emily turned and managed a somber smile. "It's Avery, right? The tattoo artist? I've seen you at race nights and at Classic Auto a few times with your Caddy. What do you call it?"

"The Gothmobile," Avery replied, a little embarrassed. "So sorry about Hatchet."

"Thanks. He really liked the tattoo you did in honor of his sister. It meant a lot to him."

"I'm glad." Avery gathered her courage to ask the question that had been plaguing her. "You don't think he knowingly took the fentanyl, do you?"

"No." The grief on the woman's face deepened. "He always hated drugs after growing up with his mom. It's why he and Boze got along so well. They both were very antidrug. Unlike some members of the club."

"Who?"

She shook her head. "Not important."

"You don't think Boze…"

"Relapsed? It's possible. Grace fears he might have. But even so, I don't see Boze convincing Hatchet to try it, or worse, drugging him without his consent. Honestly, I'll probably never know what happened. The detective on the case believes they both took it knowingly and intentionally."

"I know. I talked to him."

"You what? Why?"

Suddenly, Avery felt embarrassed, like she'd been prying into Emily's business without permission. In a sense, she had. *Why the hell did I say that?*

"When Walrus mentioned it the other day, I thought it was worth asking Detective Valentine to take a second look into the case."

"And will he?"

"No. Says they're too short-staffed. Personally, I think he's just a lazy idiot. When my girlfriend was murdered last month, Valentine and his partner were absolutely convinced I'd done it."

Emily's expression changed from one of grief to one of empathy. "Your girlfriend was killed? They catch who did it?"

"More or less."

"I'm so sorry." Emily hugged her.

Avery stiffened. She was not a hugger, except with family and close friends like Kimi.

Emily released her. "What is this world coming to?"

Avery didn't have an answer. "If Boze didn't slip and Hatchet wouldn't take them, who would have done this to them?"

Emily's gaze narrowed. "You're really interested in this, aren't you?"

"Don't like people killing my friends."

"Honestly, I don't know. I can't think of anyone who hated him that much. I know he and Mendez had their issues, but that was just a silly Innovator–Old Schooler rivalry. Nothing worth killing over. Maybe Boze did relapse. Ever since he fell from that ladder back in February, he'd been struggling with back pain."

Avery remembered Boze walking with a cane at recent race nights. He'd been dropped from the list because he couldn't race to defend his spot.

"A fall like that can be brutal," I admitted.

"Grace had been nursing him back to health and taking him to doctor appointments. They were talking back surgery, but Boze wasn't keen on it. Maybe the pain got to be too much to manage. But I don't get how the drugs got into Hatchet's system. Maybe the police lab got the results mixed up."

"Maybe." The more Avery thought about it, the more she wanted to know the answer. Mysteries like this ate at her, especially when her friends had been hurt.

Walrus returned with her beer. "Hey, Em. We're sure gonna miss that son of a bitch."

"Thanks. Well, I was on the way to the ladies' room," Emily said. "It was nice talking with you, Avery. Thank you for coming. And again, I'm sorry for your loss, as well."

"Thanks."

"You lost someone, too, huh?" Walrus asked.

"My girlfriend, a month ago." She hadn't mentioned it to any of her clients. The ones whose appointments she'd postponed while out of town had been told it was for a family matter.

"What the fuck's this world coming to? So full of violence and hate. It's why I miss the good old days. Wish we could go back to the fifties."

"You mean when women had no access to birth control or a bank account of their own?" she replied sarcastically. "Back when Black people had no civil rights and were lynched for nothing more than smiling at a white woman? When cops brutalized queer people in our own bars? Yeah, those sure were the good old days." *Maybe I'm getting a handle on this small talk thing.*

"You know what I mean."

"Obviously, I don't. What do you mean, Walrus?"

He emptied his glass, staring at the floor. "Fuck if I know."

Okay, maybe small talk still isn't in my skill set.

He then asked, "You gonna be at the car show up in Prescott on Saturday?"

She hadn't originally planned on going because of clients scheduled later that day. "I'll be there."

"Guess I'll see ya then." Walrus wandered off.

She took a long pull on her bottle of stout. The bitter taste matched her mood. She considered just leaving. She'd paid her respects and even talked to Emily. She should probably say hi to Grace.

Avery scanned the room and saw the young woman sitting by herself, the lone Black face in a sea of white. Empathy punched Avery in the gut. She knew what it was like to be ignored for being different. She wanted to tell herself it was because people didn't really know Grace the way they knew Emily. But there was probably also a little racism that had the street racers keeping their distance.

Avery approached her. “Hey, Grace. I’m Avery Byrne. I’m really sorry about your dad.”

Grace offered her a weak smile. “Thanks.”

“Mind if I sit?” Avery pointed to a chair.

“No one else is.”

“I lost someone recently too. My girlfriend was murdered.” Goth, she sounded like an idiot looking for sympathy.

Grace’s gaze softened. “I’m sorry to hear that.”

“I didn’t know Boze real well. But he was always nice to me at race nights. I know he fell from a ladder a few months ago. Didn’t realize he was so badly hurt.”

“He was no spring chicken. Between his age, the fall, and half a lifetime spent using, it all caught up to him. Had trouble sleeping at night, the pain was so bad. But he refused to take anything for it because of his history. Nothing but aspirin. And he was getting better. He swore he was going to race again despite my begging him not to.”

“You think he relapsed in the end?”

“That’s what people are saying. Not sure if I buy it. Between you, me, and the fence post, I wouldn’t put it past one of these guys to use his situation to take him out, make it look like he slipped.”

“Why would they do that?”

“He’d been rising to the top of the list before his accident. Maybe they got tired of an old Black man kicking their asses on the asphalt. Or maybe someone wanted Hatchet dead and used my dad’s addiction to cover it up. Take your pick.”

“It’s hard either way, I imagine.”

“It is. I’m just glad he’s out of pain.”

Fisch, one of the Old Schoolers, walked up to their table. He was a short, nerdy-looking guy who had worked with Hatchet at Classic Auto Repair. He looked odder than usual without his ever-present bandana covering his head. Avery had never imagined him with hair, much less the mess of tight dark curls he had. But what really struck her were the yellowing bruises on his face.

"Can I talk to you?" Fisch glared at Avery, his words as sharp as glass shards.

Avery had no idea what his deal was, but she said, "Go ahead. Talk."

"Privately."

"Fine."

"Good to talk with you," Grace said when Avery stood.

"You too."

Fisch grabbed her arm and led her over to the back hallway near the restrooms. "What the hell are you doing?"

"Excuse me?"

"Emily's all upset about you asking questions and insinuating that someone murdered Hatchet and Boze."

"She's upset because her boyfriend's dead. Not because I asked questions."

"You need to stop."

"Stop what?"

"Police closed the case as an accident. You need to leave it alone."

"Why?"

Something in his expression told her he was wrestling with what to say. She could feel his energy like a coiled snake ready to strike.

"We don't need you playing amateur detective and stirring up a lot of shit. People feel bad enough about what happened. Just let Hatchet and Boze rest in peace."

"What aren't you telling me? Does this have to do with what happened to your face?" She couldn't figure out how they would be related, but her gut told her there was some sort of connection.

"Nothing. Just drop it, or I swear, I'll…"

"Hey!" Rocket Man appeared and stepped between them. "What's going on? This is a memorial for Hatchet and Boze.

You two are acting like a couple of squabbling kids. Have some respect for the dead and the bereaved."

"Keep your nose out of this." Fisch jabbed a finger at Avery and walked away.

"And if I don't?" Avery called after him. She stared as he disappeared into the crowd. If she had been ambivalent about the cause of death before, Fisch's little tantrum had tipped the scales. She was definitely looking deeper into this.

"What was all that about?" Rocket looked at her sternly.

"Hatchet and Boze didn't die from an accidental overdose."

"What?"

"I think someone murdered them."

Rocket Man looked surprised. "Don't be ridiculous! Who would do something like that? Everybody loved those guys."

"Fisch."

"You're kidding, right? Fisch would never hurt Hatchet. Him, Hatch, and Boze were thick as thieves."

"Well, he sure got pissy over me asking questions."

Rocket Man put an arm around her in an almost-fatherly way.

Avery pushed it away. "Hey, don't like to be touched."

"Sorry. I'm a bit of an overhugger, I guess." He held up his hands in apology. "Thing is, Fisch getting riled up over nothing? That's just Fisch being Fisch. This whole thing has him all torn up. It ain't about you. When he gets upset, he lashes out. Don't take it personal."

"I'm not. But it makes him look awful guilty."

"Fisch may be a lot of things, but a murderer, he ain't. Their deaths have been hard on all of us. We'll miss the hell out of them. Boze was like the group's therapist. Always talking that twelve-step, touchy-feely stuff. And it hurts my soul to think he relapsed. But darling, that's the nature of the disease. And he would've been the first to say it.

"And Hatch… shit. All his trash talking and bravado, his goofy antics. Yeah, we're gonna miss him too. But that's life.

We're Crows. We live fast. We push limits. We do a lot of stupid shit, like racing these old cars. And sometimes it catches up to us sooner than we'd like."

"Yeah" was all Avery could think to say.

"Do me a favor, kid. Don't go digging into this mess. Cops already ruled it accidental. You asking questions is just going to upset people already struggling with their grief. And God forbid, someone actually is responsible…"

"Like Fisch."

"Like anybody. You going around playing Nancy Drew could make them come after you too. I sure as hell don't want nothing to happen to you. You're a sweet kid. And I like your unique fashion sense."

"But if someone really did kill them…"

"Look, let me do a little nosing around. I'm a Crow and know these guys a lot better than you. I know how to ask the right questions that won't ruffle too many feathers. And if I find anything out, I'll let you know. Deal?"

Avery studied him for a bit. Rocket always had this fun-uncle vibe about him. And he was right. He knew the group dynamics a lot better than she did.

"All right. Deal."

"You gonna be there in Prescott on Saturday?"

"I'll be there."

If Rocket hadn't learned anything by then, she would resume poking around herself.

CHAPTER 11

INTRUDER ALERT

Avery spent the rest of the memorial trying and failing to be sociable while keeping a wary eye out for Fisch. But she didn't learn anything new and grew increasingly uncomfortable watching other people have conversations.

She'd only drunk half her Guinness, which had gone warm on her and begun to taste like asphalt. Eventually, she slipped out without another word to anyone.

On the drive home, she cranked up the Cocteau Twins on her stereo. Anything to kill the dreaded silence and stave off the miserable memories in her brain.

When she got to her apartment complex, the college kids were back at it. She considered cutting the power again, but sooner or later, someone would complain to management, even though the assholes were clearly the ones in the wrong. Management would somehow figure out it was her, and she'd be evicted.

Even if, in the end, she found a better apartment that actually enforced their own noise rules, she didn't have the energy pennies to deal with another move now. She had to come up with a better solution that would put an end to their after-hours carousing.

From her window, she had a clear view of the party below. The music came from a set of Bluetooth speakers controlled by the phone of one of the guys she'd nicknamed Chad. He looked like a fucking Chad. White and handsome by conventional standards, ripped like a romance novel cover model and with a cocky attitude as if he were God's gift to women. Probably a jock.

A glance at her living room clock told her it was going on eleven thirty. She felt restless like a caged tiger. Her body was fatigued, but her friends' suspicious deaths nagged at her. And the noise from outside was pissing her off. No way she could sleep.

I could call Kimi. Maybe Bobby. See if I can crash at their place.

But she couldn't bring herself to call either of them. Kimi and Chupa were probably getting it on. And Bobby… she didn't want to think about what Bobby and Dana were doing. Besides, she didn't feel like going back out anyway.

With nothing better to do, she took her meds, resenting the need for pharmaceutical help just to sleep, and cranked up her own music. Eventually, she drifted off to Elizabeth Fraser's ethereal vocals on the Cocteau Twins' *Blue Bell Knoll* album.

As hard as she tried to hold them back, the tears flowed. For Sam and for Melissa. For the Lost Kids. And for Boze and Hatchet.

At the studio on Friday, she had a full schedule—three clients and one walk-in. Despite her PTSD simmering below the surface, she managed to immerse herself enough into her art that she barely thought about Hatchet and Boze.

"Hey, kiddo. You doing okay?" Bobby asked as she was coloring a goth-styled faerie sitting on a crescent moon on the forearm of her last client of the day. It was the latest of the multiple faerie tats Avery had created on the woman's ivory skin.

"Yeah."

"You've been awfully quiet today. More so than usual. Butcher's been a chatterbox by comparison, and you know how laconic he is."

"Just tired."

"You getting enough sleep?"

She shrugged.

"Taking the meds your doctor prescribed?"

"Appa, I'm working here."

"Sorry." He paused a moment. "You're still coming to dinner tonight, aren't you?"

She glanced at her watch, having lost all track of time. It was a quarter to six. “At seven, right?”

“Don’t be late.” He kissed her forehead.

“I won’t.”

She didn’t want to admit she had completely forgotten about the dinner. And as much as she enjoyed spending time with her dad, playing third wheel to him and his new girlfriend sounded about as enjoyable as being eviscerated with a dull knife.

Until now, Avery had always had an excuse for not joining them for dinner. Plans with friends. Evening clients. Too tired.

Avery didn’t have anything specific against meeting this woman. Nothing as inane as resenting her for replacing Melissa, the only mother who had ever really loved Avery. That was such Psych 101 bullshit.

Everything Bobby had told her about Dana was good. She made Bobby laugh. She didn’t make fun of his obsession with *Star Wars*. She thought his action figure collection was adorable. And she was smart and a decent cook.

Maybe the fact that the woman was an accountant at a financial firm made Avery wary. Of the three of them, Dana was the only one who’d gone to college, though Bobby often encouraged Avery to go. If her obnoxious neighbors were any indication, college kids were a bunch of rich, arrogant assholes.

Why would I want to spend more time with people like that?

When Avery finished with her client, she said her goodbyes to Frisco and Butcher, who were working until nine.

She rushed home and debated what to wear. She considered going as hardcore goth as possible. Something to chase away this woman. But that would hurt Bobby, which was the last thing Avery wanted to do.

She settled on a black lace top and a knee-length skirt, leggings, and Victorian-style ankle boots. Blood-red lipstick instead of her preferred black and toned-down eye makeup. Tiny Celtic knot heart earrings dangled from her earlobes, paired with a matching pendant.

It was still her, just not as over-the-top as she might have liked. Of course, as soon as she smiled, her vampire aesthetic shone through. She'd been born without upper lateral incisors. Their absence made her canine teeth look fang-like by contrast, giving her a distinctly vampiric smile. That was one birth defect she'd never had any interest in correcting.

She walked through Bobby's front door at seven on the dot. Some ancient Phil Collins song was playing on Bobby's stereo. Typical. On the other hand, the aromas of sweet bulgogi sauce and cooked beef made her mouth water.

"That you, kiddo?" he called.

Avery stepped into the kitchen. "It's me."

Bobby and Dana stood intimately close in front of the stove, dishing up dinner. Dana stood six inches taller than Bobby. She was wiry where he was adorably chunky.

"Dana Kim, I'd like you to meet my daughter, Avery Byrne. Avery, this is Dana."

Dana smiled in a way that Avery assumed was meant to be charming. "Such a pleasure to finally meet you."

"Yeah. You too." But she didn't feel it.

The table had been set for three for the first time since Melissa's death. A small bowl of kimchi sat at each place setting. A lump formed in Avery's throat, along with a growing resentment toward this woman invading their little family.

"Avery, why don't you put the beef bulgogi on the table." Bobby held out a dish covered in the savory meat. His earnest expression told her to be nice.

She placed it on the table without a word and found her usual seat. Bobby carried over a large bowl of rice and sat next to her. Dana took the chair opposite her, setting down a plate of baby bok choy. As delicious as it all looked and smelled, Avery didn't feel very hungry.

"Shall we say grace?" Dana asked, her hands folded for prayer.

"I'm not a Christian," Avery replied.

With another pleading glance, Bobby folded his hands. "I think it would be nice to say grace for once."

Dana bowed her head. "Heavenly Father, bless these gifts which we are about to receive from your bounty through Christ our Lord. Amen."

"Praise Mother Goddess," Avery added defiantly.

"Who's hungry?" Bobby served himself some beef then offered the bowl to Avery. "Here, kiddo. And try the bok choy! They're amazing."

Avery could see the hurt in his eyes. "Mi-an ham-ni-da, Appa," she whispered as she took the bowl. *I'm sorry, Father.*

"You speak Korean?" Dana asked after filling her plate.

"A little. Melissa taught me." It wasn't meant as a dig. Just the truth.

"She sounds like a wonderful woman. I'm sure you miss her a lot."

"I do. A lot." Avery took a bite of her beef. The flavors differed slightly from what she was used to. "This tastes weird. I think the beef went bad."

"No, it's Dana's family recipe," Bobby announced proudly. "I like it."

"I marinate the beef in pear and pineapple purée. It helps to tenderize the beef and gives it a more complex flavor profile."

Avery was tempted to say she preferred Melissa's recipe, but she stopped herself. She was trying not to ruin this for Bobby. The beef was good, and the bok choy doenjang was better. The kimchi tasted like it was from a can, but she kept that to herself.

"I understand you work for your dad," Dana said.

"I work for myself."

"She's not an employee," Bobby explained. "She rents space at the shop, just like our other two artists do."

"So you're an entrepreneur. How bold! Takes a lot of skills to wear the many hats of a business owner. Marketing, management, and of course, production. Who does your accounting?"

"I handle it myself, thank you very much. Math isn't that hard."

"Even so, you really should consider hiring a professional. Tax law is always changing and□—"

"I said I can handle it myself!" Avery set down her chopsticks and stared daggers at Dana.

"I'm sure you can, but beyond the basics, there are so many considerations. It's one thing to be able to file your taxes, unless, of course, you get audited. It also takes training to understand how to grow a business, how to optimize ROI, capitalizing fixed assets, investing for future growth. What was your major in college?"

Avery stood up and kicked her chair back. "I didn't come here to be lectured about my lack of education. So what if I didn't go to high school or college? Didn't need no fucking diploma to teach me how to be an artist. And I know how to run my own business. Bobby taught me. And he's doing all right. I'm doing all right. We don't need any help from the likes of you."

Avery threw her napkin on the table, grabbed her purse, and stormed out, slamming the door behind her. Angry tears dripped onto her chest as she marched out into the stifling night. She revved the engine of the Gothmobile as loud as she could before peeling off down the street, triggering a few car alarms in the neighborhood.

She knew she was overreacting, but all of the trauma and emotions of the past few weeks were all just too much. She had struggled after losing Melissa, at times resorting to cutting and other forms of self-injury just to feel something other than the unbearable weight of grief.

At Bobby's insistence, she'd gotten therapy, what little good it did. But over time, she and Bobby had formed a special father-daughter bond. She loved and trusted him in a way she'd never thought she could after living on the streets.

But now this bitch was wheedling her way into their tidy little family, tossing out unsolicited business advice. *Like she's got any idea how to run a tattoo artist business.*

Avery was a few blocks from home when she called Kimi. "Hey! Wanna grab a drink?"

"Sure. The Alien Devils are playing at the Zombie Room, starting at eight. Wanna meet there?"

"Sounds perfect. Just the two of us?"

"Absolutely. Chupa's out with Torch and McCobb doing their guy thing."

CHAPTER 12

ZOMBIE ROOM

The Zombie Room was one of the last remaining clubs in the Valley dedicated to the goth community. A few other clubs hosted a goth night once or twice a month, but the Zombie Room, small as it was, was all goth, all the time. It played everything from classic '80s postpunk, trad goth, and shoegaze to industrial, dark wave, and psychobilly

Before getting out of the Gothmobile, she wiped off her red lipstick with a tissue and replaced it with Nyx Alien black then doubled the thickness of her eyeliner.

The Zombie Room's interior was dark with purple accent lighting. The Birthday Massacre's "Cold Lights" was playing on the sound system when she paid the cover charge. Avery didn't see Kimi anywhere, so she grabbed a stool and a Guinness at the bar while she waited.

She had taken Sam here once and had offered to give her a goth makeover so that she wouldn't stand out so much. But Sam had declined, not being one to wear makeup of any type.

"Hey, girl! How you holding up?" Kimi claimed the stool next to her and ordered a blood orange martini.

Avery shrugged. "Just had a disaster of a dinner at Bobby J.'s."

"Shit. What happened? You two get along better than I do with my folks."

"He invited his new girlfriend. Dana," she said derisively. "Wanted us to meet."

"Uh oh. Is she hideous? Judgmental? Transphobic?"

"Not hideous. Skinny. Tall. But nosy as all hell. Oh, and a Jesus freak."

"And not Melissa, huh?"

Avery winced. Kimi always had a knack for reading her. She had suspected Avery was queer long before she'd come out to anyone but herself.

"That too. Melissa was… everything I wanted in a mom. I never even felt as close to my birth mother as I did with Melissa. She never shamed me for being trans or goth or anything. She just loved and accepted me as I was, just like Bobby."

"She was something special."

"And now this bitch…"

Kimi grasped Avery's hand. "I'm sure it's hard when a parent starts dating someone new. And on the heels of losing Sam and your friends in the Crows. You got a lot of shit going on, girl. Lotta trauma. Speaking of which, you go to that memorial for your friends?"

"Last night."

"How was that?"

"I'm ninety-five percent sure they were murdered. Okay, maybe seventy percent."

"Why?" Kimi sipped her martini.

"I was on the fence until this one guy, Fisch, told me to stop asking questions."

Rolling her eyes, Kimi grinned. "He obviously doesn't know you that well. Telling you to back off is like dumping blood in the water and not expecting sharks. You think he did the deed?"

"Hard to tell. But he was all up in my grill about it."

"Maybe he didn't want to believe someone would kill his friends."

"No, it was more than that. He's involved somehow. I can feel it. Just not sure how."

"And you intend to find out, huh? Avery the Avenger back from the dead?"

Avery picked at the label on her beer bottle. "I'm not saying that."

"You're not *not* saying it either." Kimi sucked on the blood orange slice from her martini glass.

"If I had proof who the killer was, maybe the cops would reopen the case."

"And if they didn't reopen it?"

"Shouldn't murderers be punished?" Avery asked.

"Of course they should. But… I don't know, girl. After what happened with the Desert Mafia, maybe it's better you just let this one go."

"What if the killer hurts more people?"

"Then the cops will catch them. Eventually."

"Or not."

"Okay, complete honesty now." Kimi locked eyes with Avery. "Say you had definitive proof who the murderer was and the cops refused to open the case, what would you do about it? I know you, Avery. You're a good person. You're not a murderer."

"Except for, you know, that one time I was."

"Vinnie D, the abusive pimp. Yes, I remember you told me about him. But he was already shooting up dope. It was only a matter of time before he OD'd or someone else killed him over his pimping or drug dealing. You definitely did the world a favor."

"And thanks in part to me, the people who killed Sam and shot Chupa are dead too."

Kimi didn't respond right away, instead staring at her reflection at the bar. When she did speak, her eyes were watering. "I was so scared when that psycho shot Chup. I thought I was going to lose him, Ave."

"I know. I was too."

"And I hate to admit it, but I was glad when you told me the asshole who shot him was dead."

"Exactly. Hatchet and Boze had family too. Hatch had a girlfriend; Boze's daughter was helping him recover from a recent back injury. Not to mention all the Crows. These people are grieving. And the person responsible is still out there. But are the cops looking for the killer? Of course not. The detective on the case wrote off their deaths as an accidental overdose. The same idiot that was so convinced I killed Sam that he and his partner chased me all the way to New Mexico."

"Detective Valentine. I remember. He sure seemed to have a hard-on for you regarding Sam's murder."

"They'll move heaven and earth to protect a corrupt businessman but won't lift a finger for a couple of street racers."

"I don't know what the answer is, Ave. But the thought of you getting involved in this mess scares the shit out of me. I don't want to lose you."

"You're not going to lose me. I'll be fine."

"But this Fisch guy was threatening you…"

"Not threatening exactly. He's just a skinny punk. He doesn't scare me."

"But if he killed Hatchet and Boze…"

"I survived three years on the streets as a homeless teenager. I survived when the Desert Mafia came after me. I even escaped that dirty police lieutenant. I can handle one little rat rodder."

"I hope so."

They didn't speak for a few minutes. Avery let the thoughts percolate in her brain as the driving beats of Joy Division's "She's Lost Control" played over the sound system.

"Maybe Roz can help you," Kimi said at last.

"Who the hell's Roz?" Then Avery remembered. "The woman you were with at Johnny Heretics."

"Exactly. She owns the Spy Gal shop. Sells all kinds of surveillance equipment. Might come in handy."

"Tell me the truth. That was totally a setup, wasn't it?"

"No. Well, not consciously. But you gotta admit she's kinda hot. And she's single. And she runs a spy shop. So maybe she can assist you in your hunt for the killer."

"She may be single, but I'm still…" She struggled for the right word. "Grieving."

"I know you are."

"But if I need any surveillance equipment, maybe I'll stop by her store."

The sound of an electronic hum followed by a pop caught Avery's attention. The evening's scheduled band, Alien Devils, was taking the stage.

"Showtime!" Kimi said with glee.

CHAPTER 13

COOL TEMPS, HOT TEMPERS

After the Alien Devils wrapped up their concert, Avery wished Kimi a good night and drove home feeling better than when she had left Bobby's, though guilt still nagged her. She had behaved like a brat and planned to call Bobby in the morning to apologize.

When she reached her apartment, she was relieved that the college kids weren't partying at the pool for once—surprising, considering it was a Friday night. Maybe they were out hitting the bars.

Still, she slept fitfully, haunted by nightmares of being pursued by some unseen menace. But somewhere in the night, the dream changed. She managed to flip the script, and suddenly, she was the pursuer. Whoever or whatever she was chasing after, she wasn't sure. But each time she got close, it eluded her.

Early the next morning, she filled up the Gothmobile's gas tank and drove north on the I-17 to the Prescott Valley Classic Car Show. She'd picked out a low-cut dress with bare shoulders and a black bodice. Below the cinched waist, the black broke up into a flurry of bat shapes against a salmon-pink background.

During the ninety-minute drive through the desert and mountain passes, she replayed her conversation with Kimi. Was she willing to kill again to avenge Hatchet and Boze? Helping Vinnie D overdose on his own heroin was one thing. For months, he'd been physically abusing Jessie and Lindsey, two of the Lost Kids who turned tricks for him. They were her family. And going to the cops hadn't been an option.

As for bringing down the Desert Mafia, it was only a matter of time before the Mexican cartel discovered for themselves that Bramwell was double-crossing them. She had only tipped them off sooner. Since Bramwell's guys had murdered Sam and shot Chupa, she didn't lose any sleep over her part in their deaths.

Hatchet had been a friend and Boze an acquaintance, but she didn't consider either of them family per se. Was she willing to risk her freedom and possibly her life to avenge them? She only had to remember the grief on Emily's and Grace's faces to know the answer was a solid yes. Someone had to. Detective Valentine had had his chance to do the right thing, but he'd dropped the ball.

Avery needed to find out who was responsible. And when she did, then she would decide how best to punish them. Maybe there was a way to avenge Boze and Hatchet that didn't involve murder, like the way she busted Pastor Paul at Samariteen.

When she pulled into the Prescott Gateway Mall parking lot, she remembered she needed to apologize to Bobby. She pulled into a space near the car show's cordoned-off area and dialed his number.

"Bobby J.'s phone. This is Dana. Oh, Avery, I see your name on the caller ID. How are you this morning?"

Avery hung up. *What the fuck! Why the hell is she answering his phone?* But she knew the answer. *Because she's sleeping with him. Ugh, gross!*

She winced, desperate to get the image of the two of them out of her mind.

Focus, girl! You're here to have fun. Maybe drum up some new tattoo clients. And to find out who killed Boze and Hatchet. Avery the Avenger is back.

It was refreshingly cool when she stepped out of the Gothmobile. Prescott's mile-high elevation kept it ten to twenty degrees cooler than Phoenix's sun-scorched low desert.

The driving beats of a Chuck Berry tune filled the air, no doubt intended to attract mall shoppers. It must have been working, because the car show had already drawn a decent crowd. Most were men, but Avery saw a few women and children too.

She strolled through the three dozen cars parked with their hoods up. She recognized some from the Sonoran Crows street races. Most were fully restored vintage cars from the previous century. There were also bizarre rat rods that looked like creations from a Mad Max movie. Semirecognizable rust-patina bodies welded onto extended chassis with oversized engines. Mid-century hearses cut into gothic-inspired convertibles. Some vehicles were so bizarre, she wondered if they were even roadworthy.

Avery wasn't sure what it was about these classic and reimagined vehicles that drew her interest. She wasn't mechanically inclined. She never raced the Gothmobile at Crow race nights. But something about these relics of a lost era called to her like ghosts in a haunted Victorian mansion.

The sound of angry voices caught her attention. She turned to see a short bald man arguing with a big, beefy guy with a mullet. The little guy was Carlos Mendez, the Sonoran Crows' current president. The same man Walrus said had gotten into a fistfight with Hatchet a couple months earlier. The one who hadn't bothered to show up to the memorial.

Mendez was shouting at "Big Eddie" Myles, one of his crew members. She didn't recall seeing him at the memorial, either.

They were arguing next to Mendez's 1968 Plymouth Sport Satellite, one of the only vehicles at the car show without its hood open. Avery couldn't make out what they were saying, but Mendez's face was so red, he looked like a blood blister about to pop.

"You're a fucking idiot!" Mendez shouted. "No one tells me what to do."

Big Eddie replied in a low voice Avery still couldn't make out.

"Don't threaten me, pinche puto. I'll fucking end you."

Big Eddie stalked away and disappeared into the crowd.

Avery approached Mendez tentatively. It seemed unlikely that this argument had anything to do with Hatchet's death, but it was time to start digging.

"Hey, Mendez," she said.

He looked over at her. "What the hell you want?"

"Wow, bite my head off, why don't you?"

"Sorry. Just not having a good morning."

"What was that about between you and Big Eddie?"

"Nothing. Just team stuff."

"Missed you at the memorial."

"Yeah, well, I had other shit to do that night. Besides, I was at their funerals. Not that I owe you or anyone else an explanation for my whereabouts." He stared down at his phone, scrolling on the screen.

"I hear you and Hatchet got into it not too long ago and hadn't spoken since. What was that about?"

Mendez looked up at her, menace smoldering behind his eyes. "It was Sonoran Crow business, and none of yours."

"Must be hard, that being the last encounter you had with him. The two of you used to be friends."

"Who says that was our last encounter? And yeah, we used to be. Emphasis on *used* to be. The asshole never shoulda stuck his nose into my business. If he weren't already dead, he'd be facing jail time."

"Jail time? For what"

"What the fuck is this? Twenty questions? You suddenly a detective now, freak?"

"No, I□—"

"Then get the fuck outta my face. Go play amateur sleuth somewhere else."

His threatening countenance was enough to send Avery on her way. He clearly knew something. Maybe he was even the killer. But she clearly wasn't going to get anywhere by asking him questions.

She walked away, strolling past the row of hot rods, wondering what Hatchet could have done to make Mendez so pissed at him. She'd never heard anyone accuse Hatchet of doing anything criminal.

Farther on, she spotted Big Eddie studying the engine of a '40s-era Chevy pickup truck.

The man turned as she approached. "She's a real beaut, eh?" he said in a thick Texas drawl. "Built in 1948 and still looks like it just rolled off the factory floor."

"Pretty," she replied, not knowing what else to say. "What's going on between you and Mendez?"

"What're you talking about?"

"The two of you were arguing about something."

"Oh, that. Nothing. Just a technical issue about his car. No big deal."

She gave him her most convincing "that's bullshit" look. "Looked pretty heated. Enough for him to call you an idiot and threaten you."

Big Eddie sighed. "Shouldn't be telling you this, but it's bound to get around anyhow. Mendez got out of rehab recently. He's still a little on edge."

"Rehab? For what?"

"Got himself hooked on pain pills. Been clean almost two months now, so that's something. But it's hard, ya know?"

"Pain pills? You mean like fentanyl?" Avery asked.

"Don't know the details. But especially with Boze and Hatchet dying in a DUI crash, shit's got him shook. Like it coulda been him instead. Doesn't help that he and Hatchet parted on bad terms. So every little thing is setting him off right now. Best to give him a wide berth for the time being."

Avery thought about it. "He said Hatch was poking his nose into his business. That he might've faced jail time for something. Any idea what he's talking about?"

"Hatchet and a few of the others tried to get a look under the hood of Mendez's car. Typical Old Schooler bullshit. Any excuse for why they keep losing to us Innovators. Best just leave it alone and give the guy some space. He's dealing with a lot of shit right now."

"Good to know. I'll see you around, Eddie."

"You too."

She wondered if she had enough to get Detective Valentine to reopen the case. Mendez believed Hatchet had done something criminal, though she didn't know all the details. Would this be enough to establish motive? Since he knew how to get his hands on pain pills, he clearly had the means. And if he was out of rehab when the guys were killed, he had opportunity.

"Looking good, goth girl." Rocket Man strode toward her, a big grin on his face. "How're you doing?"

She shrugged. "I'm okay. How's your sister-in-law?"

"My sister-in-law?" He looked confused.

"You said Tiffany was taking care of her after a medical procedure."

"Oh, yeah. She's recovering. Glad to have Tiff there to help her out, I'm sure."

"That's good. You find out anything?"

"About?" There was a little wariness to his voice.

"Hatchet and Boze's deaths. I'm still convinced they weren't an accident."

"I've asked around. Didn't learn anything."

"You talk to Fisch?"

"I did. He was in the hospital at the time of the crash."

Avery remembered Fisch's bruised, swollen face. "What happened?"

"Fisch was filling up at a gas station and overheard some redneck twice his size spewing a lot of antisemitic shit. And Fisch, being Fisch, got in the man's face. Angry words were exchanged, which turned into a fight. Fisch ended up with a busted face and a concussion. He was still in a lot of pain at the memorial, so no wonder he was in a foul mood."

"Guess that makes sense."

"Yep. Your theory that Hatchet and Boze were murdered doesn't, I'm afraid. Just a tragedy. Nothing more."

She shrugged. "Just seems odd. Boze having a slip? Maybe. But Hatchet hated that shit."

"Look, I don't know how or why Hatchet and Boze did what they did. Both were good guys, and they'll be missed."

"But not by everyone."

"Meaning?"

"Carlos Mendez."

"Mendez? He's your current prime suspect? I thought Fisch was supposed to be the one."

"Walrus said Mendez and Hatch got into a big fight a while back and quit speaking. Then Mendez goes into rehab for, of all things, addiction to pain pills. And right after he gets out, Hatch and Boze overdose on fentanyl. And Mendez didn't attend the memorial. That doesn't strike you as strange?"

"Mendez has had some issues of late. And yeah, he and Hatchet got into it a while back. But that don't make him a murderer."

"What were they fighting about? He says Hatch should've been in jail."

Rocket shook his head. "Don't know nothing about anyone going to jail. Hatchet had been bitching that Mendez had installed an all-electric engine in his Satellite, which, until recently, was a violation of the bylaws. At least until Mendez made the top of the list and got the rule changed. Just typical Old Schoolers-versus-Innovators shit. But nothing worth killing a guy over."

"I'm not so convinced."

Rocket Man didn't say anything for a few minutes, staring at the cracked pavement and looking like he was considering what Avery had told him. "Honestly, I don't know. I know you mean well, but it's probably best you not get involved in Crow business. Whatever happened between Hatch and Mendez, that's between them. Let it go, kid."

"And if I don't? If someone murdered him and Boze, they should be held accountable."

"Not saying they shouldn't, but a sweet girl like you shouldn't get involved. Don't want you getting hurt. And honestly, as much as I hate to admit it, my gut says that Hatch and Boze got high and decided to go for a joyride. Stupid, but hey, we're Sonoran Crows. We do stupid shit. If we were in our right minds, we wouldn't be street racing. Am I right? If Mendez or someone else hurt those guys, it will come to light, and the Crows will handle it internally. Understand?"

She could imagine what "handling things internally" meant. And he wasn't the only one telling her to leave the matter alone, as much as it pained her to do so.

"Yeah, maybe you're right."

CHAPTER 14
SURPRISE VISIT

Avery strolled around the show, looking at the cars, many of which she'd seen race at Sonoran Crow events. A few passers-by complimented her outfit and tats. She even handed out some business cards to people who asked.

She spoke with a few more members of the Sonoran Crows and their significant others, but she didn't learn anything new. She remained convinced someone had murdered Hatchet and Boze. And that someone was most likely Mendez, Fisch, or both.

After a few hours, she headed back to the Valley, since she had a client scheduled for one o'clock. She turned on Buzz Kull's *Chroma* album, skipping the short instrumental intro song "Christina" in favor of the driving beat of "We Were Lovers." She cranked it up so she could hear it over the wind rushing through her open windows.

She had just turned onto I-17 South when her phone rang. Frantically, she rolled up her window and killed the music before answering the call.

"Avery Byrne," she said while keeping her eyes on the road.

"Kiddo, we need to talk." Bobby sounded pissed.

"I suppose we do."

"Where are you?"

"Coming back from Prescott. I should be at the shop a little before one. I have a client."

"Then we can talk when you get here."

"Okay. I'm sorry, Appa."

"Like I said, we'll talk when you get here. I love you, kiddo."

"Love you too."

A mountain of guilt hung on her chest as she raced through the high desert toward the Valley. Of all the people in her life, Bobby was the one person who had treated her with nothing but compassion and respect. And she had acted like a spoiled brat at dinner.

Not that Dana didn't deserve a little of what she got after all that unsolicited tax and business advice. She wasn't right for Bobby. He could do so much better. But that was his decision not Avery's. She shouldn't have interfered like that.

Avery arrived at Seoul Fire Tattoo at half past noon and was shocked to find Rosalind Fein in the waiting area, flipping through a photo album of Avery's work. Her face brightened when she looked up, and their eyes met.

Rosalind was wearing a black T-shirt with the words "In Goth We Trust" in a font Avery recognized as Cloister Black. The outline of a skull decorated each of her western-style boots. Strong notes of jasmine in her perfume evoked a feminine sweetness combined with a masculine wildness.

A flurry of excitement and attraction mixed with guilt and nervousness hit Avery all at once, as if a colony of bats were swarming through her. What was it about this woman's goth-cowgirl-tomboy style that set Avery's body on fire? And why was she here?

"Rosalind. Hey." It was the best that her stunned brain could come up with.

"It's just Roz." The woman's warm smile could melt steel. "Good to see you again."

Avery struggled not to hyperventilate. Her grip on her purse tightened to keep her hand from trembling. "Yeah, uh, you too."

"The creativity of your tattoos impressed me when we met the other night at Johnny Heretics. So I checked out your website. So amazing."

"You looked me up online?"

"I did. And I wanted to see about getting inked myself."

Avery took a deep breath to clear her mind and checked her watch, instantly feeling a sharp pang of regret. "Unfortunately, I've got a client scheduled in about twenty minutes, but we can discuss what you're looking for until she gets here and schedule an appointment. My station's over here."

"That'd be perfect. I have to head out soon anyway to take the afternoon shift at the Spy Gal shop."

Although Bobby and Butcher were working on their own clients, she caught curious glances from each of them when she escorted Roz to her station. Frisco gave Avery a congratulatory wink. Avery's face warmed with embarrassment.

"You're Jewish, right?" Avery asked when her brain and mouth started working again. "Aren't tattoos forbidden in Judaism?"

"I am Jewish, but my family was never all that religious. My dad had a couple of tats. I figured it was time I got one for myself."

"What kind of design were you looking for?"

Roz's face flushed ever so slightly, which only made her look sexier. "I looked online but couldn't really find what I was looking for. I'd like a mermaid on my upper arm." She raised her T-shirt sleeve to expose more of her bicep.

"Nothing like Ariel from *The Little Mermaid*," she explained. "Something darker, grittier, more dangerous and intimidating. Like a goth mermaid. And having seen more of your work online and in the photo album, I'm convinced you're the right artist to do it."

"You like mermaids, huh?"

"Always have. When I was a kid, growing up on the Oregon coast, I dreamed of seeing mermaids playing in the surf. Always imagined that the sea lions were secretly mermaids in disguise. My mother thought I was meshuga."

"I can probably come up with some ideas, and if you like any of them, we can go forward from there."

The idea of designing a goth mermaid intrigued Avery. She had always liked them too.

At the same time, spending more time with Roz was stirring up a lot of emotions. Avery wasn't ready for a new relationship so soon after losing Sam. The thought of opening up her heart and being vulnerable again terrified her.

And yet this woman's golden-brown eyes, endearing smile, and unique sense of style were nothing short of mesmerizing, as if she herself were a mermaid, luring Avery into unknown depths.

What am I thinking? she admonished herself. *Just because I find this woman attractive doesn't mean she feels the same way about me.*

"How soon do you think you'd have something to show me?"

Avery shrugged, staring down at the floor. Looking into this woman's eyes was giving her heart palpitations. "A few days, maybe."

Roz clasped her hand around Avery's. It was warm, gentle, and soft. Her fingers were delicate yet strong. Avery felt her soul go into free fall. She was seriously crushing on this woman.

"I look forward to seeing what you create."

"I do too." *What the fuck does that mean?* "Er, I mean, I look forward to seeing you again."

"Me too." Roz pulled a business card from her wallet and scribbled on the back. "This is my card for the store, and that's my cell number. Call me when you've got something to show me. Or if you just want to grab a drink somewhere."

"I'll do that."

Without warning, Roz hugged her and gave her a peck on the cheek. "Good seeing you again, Avery. I'm glad Kimi introduced us."

After Roz walked out of the shop, Avery stood staring out at the parking lot.

"Someone's got a crush," Frisco said in a singsong voice.

Avery snapped out of the stupor and replied sharply, "Do not."

"Tell that to your face."

Avery caught her reflection in the large mirror on the wall. She was smiling. Not a subtle Mona Lisa smile. A big goofy-ass, lovesick-teenager toothy grin. What the fuck was that about? It vanished into her usual deadeye resting-goth face.

"Shut the fuck up, Frisco!"

"Avery!" Bobby said as his client was leaving. "Follow me."

"Yes, Appa."

She followed him into the backroom where they kept supplies, seasonal decorations, and other assorted items.

"I'm sorry for storming out last night," Avery said.

Bobby stood in front of her, arms crossed, a rare scowl on his face. "What's going on with you?"

"I don't know. Dana was just too…"

"Too what?"

"I don't know. Like she was getting into my business, trying to tell me what to do."

"No one is trying to tell you what to do, kiddo. Least of all Dana. She was just trying to get to know you. And be helpful."

"With unsolicited business advice?"

"Maybe she went a little too far with that. But that doesn't excuse your rudeness."

"Does she know I'm trans?"

"I've never brought it up. It's not my place to share your history with her. That will always be your call. Perhaps you could tell her yourself. If you choose."

"She hates me."

"No, she doesn't hate you. She…" Bobby sighed. "Your rude behavior hurt her feelings. She understands you've been through a difficult time recently, though I've been vague on the details. She knows Sam was killed and that you were wanted by the police for a time because she saw it on the news. I've assured her you weren't involved, that you were a victim. She wants to get to know you, Avery."

"She's not right for you, Appa."

"Why not?"

"Too straitlaced. I mean, really? An accountant?"

"Oh, I see. I wasn't aware there were restrictions on the occupations of the women I can date."

Avery didn't reply. She knew she was still being stupid.

"You're dealing with a lot of trauma right now, kiddo. I get it. On top of everything you've dealt with in the past. I haven't brought it up in a while, but I still think it'd be a good idea if you talked with a therapist again. Dr. Ballou knows your history, and he helped you stop cutting after Melissa died."

Avery closed her eyes, pushing down hard on the terror that threatened to erupt. "I don't think I can do it again, nothing against Dr. Ballou. Talking to someone about Sam. It just… It'd just be too much."

"It's already too much. And it's poisoning you."

She knew he was right, but the thought of unpacking all the shit around Sam's death terrified her.

"I can't force you to go. You're an adult now. But untreated trauma is like a cancer, kiddo. I don't want you to start hurting yourself again. Or worse."

"I'll think about it."

"You know I love you. And I've been on this planet more than twice as long as you. I do know some things. You have a lot of anger inside of you. Anger leads to hate. Hate leads to□—"

"Appa, please. No *Star Wars* quotes."

"Sorry. Old habit. But still true."

"Yeah, okay. Maybe I'll give him a call."

"You still have his number?"

"Yeah."

"Someone else I want you to call."

"Who? Another therapist?"

"Dana."

"Appa, no. I can't."

"You were rude to her. Not only last night but when you hung up on her this morning."

"You knew about that?"

"Like I said, your old man knows things. So call her. I'll text you her number."

"Okay, I will. But right now, I have a client waiting." She tapped her watch.

"Later, then. Oh, and who was that cute gal who was waiting for you earlier?"

Avery shrugged as nonchalantly as she could. "Just a friend of Kimi's."

"Oh, not a friend of yours?"

"Don't really know her."

He gave her a disbelieving glance. "Okay, go take care of your client. Then call Dana and apologize to her."

"Okay." She hugged him. "I love you."

"Love you too."

CHAPTER 15

TOO BUSY

Avery spent the next several hours working on clients. It helped to get her mind off everything else going on in her life. That was what she most loved about her work. Creating art was the closest thing to magic. Better than therapy.

When it was just her and the needles and the ink and her client's bare skin as a canvas, something transformative and healing happened inside of her. Bobby called it the spiritual alchemy of creativity, whatever the hell that meant.

By the time nine o'clock rolled around and her last client was gone, she was exhausted physically, creatively, and emotionally. But in a good way.

"Okay, kiddo. Let's call it a night," Bobby said when she was sanitizing her station. The two of them were the only ones left in the shop.

"Yeah, okay." She had started thinking about Hatchet, Boze, and Mendez again as she cleaned, trying to determine her next step in discovering what really happened.

"Have you apologized to Dana?"

"Not yet. I had back-to-back clients. I'll call her in the morning."

"Be sure you do." He beckoned her with her hand. "Come on. Grab your purse, and let's go home."

For an instant, she considered following him back to his house, where she had stayed shortly after Sam's death. But Dana would probably be there, and Avery didn't have the energy to do the apology thing.

At the same time, the thought of rattling around her empty apartment again felt depressing.

"Maybe we could grab a drink somewhere," she suggested.

Bobby laughed. “Raincheck, kiddo. Dana’s waiting for me at home.”

Of course she is, Avery thought. “She moving in?”

“No, just sleeping over a couple of nights.”

“Okay, ’cause I wouldn’t want you to rush into anything.”

After he set the studio’s security alarm, he put an arm over her shoulder and walked with her into the back parking lot. “At my age, I’m taking advantage of every opportunity I can.”

“Whatever you say. Good night, Appa.”

He kissed her on her forehead. “Good night, kiddo. Love you.”

“Love you too.”

On the drive home, she thought more about Hatchet and Boze. She felt out of her depth, having never solved a murder before. She’d committed murder and been accused of a murder she didn’t commit. But she’d never solved one.

As the day’s events replayed in her mind, she remembered Bobby encouraging her to make an appointment with Dr. Ballou. Avery had only agreed to see him after Melissa’s death because she already knew his daughter, Jinx Ballou. Like her, Jinx was transgender, so Avery didn’t have to worry about dealing with a therapist who was uneducated on the subject. Or worse, transphobic.

Jinx was also a professional bounty hunter whose job was to track down people who didn’t want to be found. She also occasionally did private investigation work. Would she be willing to help Avery identify Boze and Hatchet’s killer?

She dialed Jinx’s number, hoping her friend was still up this late on a Saturday night.

“Ballou Fugitive Recovery. Jinx speaking.”

“Jinx, it’s Avery.”

“Well hey, girl! What’s up?”

“I didn’t wake you, did I?”

“No, I’m staking out a fugitive’s girlfriend’s house. Happy for the distraction. What’s going on? Ink anyone interesting lately?”

“No. I’m calling because someone killed a couple of my friends.”

“Wow, that’s horrible. I’m sorry for your loss. And so soon after losing Sam.”

“I need your help finding out who did it. The cops aren’t doing shit. Wrote their deaths off as an accidental drug overdose, but neither of them would have touched that shit. I tried talking to Hardin and Valentine, but they’re too busy with other cases to worry about a couple of murdered hot-rodders.”

“I think I heard about that case. Weren’t they members of that street-racing club?”

"The Sonoran Crows, yes.”

“I’m really sorry for your loss. Unfortunately, if you’re looking to hire me to do some PI work, my docket’s a little full now. I’ve got four fugitives to apprehend. And if I don’t get one of them in custody by Monday, the judge will force the bail bond agent to cough up the full two and a half million dollars in bail. So I’m under a bit of a time crunch.”

“So what do I do? I’ve never had to find a murderer before. I don’t even know where to start.”

“You’re considering finding the killer yourself?”

“They were my friends, Jinx. They deserve justice.”

“I hear you. But if they really were murdered, you could be putting yourself at risk by getting involved.”

“I lived on the street for three years when I was a teenager. I can handle myself.”

“Well, when I’m investigating a murder, I start by creating a timeline of events, beginning with the time of death and working backward. Where did your friends die?”

“On Seventh Street. They crashed into a utility pole.”

“Where were they driving from?”

"According to Hatchet's girlfriend, they'd been at his auto repair shop."

"What happened at the repair shop before they left? Was anyone else with them at the shop? If so, did they take anything or drink anything that might have contained the drugs? I had someone put something in one of my drinks once. Happens a lot to women at bars, but it could happen to guys too, I suppose."

"That's what I've been thinking."

"Do you have any suspects?"

"A couple."

"Find out where they were at that time. Talk to anyone and everyone who might know something. Spouses, lovers, family members, neighbors, coworkers, whoever."

"What about background checks?"

"Yes, when I'm working on a case, I'll run fugitives and suspects through a background database like SkipTrakkr. They provide criminal history, credit report, bank statements, phone logs, that kind of stuff. But it's only accessible to licensed professionals. There are background services available to the general public, but their information isn't reliable or worth the money."

"But you could run background checks on the people I'm investigating?"

Jinx didn't answer right away. "SkipTrakkr only allows me to run checks for cases I'm actively working. But I might make an exception. Who do you want me to run a background check on?"

"Carlos Mendez. He's a member of the Sonoran Crows."

"Hold on. Let me write this down," Jinx said. "Do you have a middle name for Mendez?"

"No."

"Home address?"

"No."

"Place of employment?"

"Um, no."

"No date of birth or social either, I suppose."

"Definitely not."

"Well, this is Arizona. Probably hundreds, if not thousands, of Carlos Mendezes in the Valley alone. It would take me a while just to narrow it down. And as much as I'd like to help you out, I'm totally slammed right now."

"I understand."

"Let me ask you—if you find out who drugged your friends, what do you plan to do with that information?"

"Give it to Detective Valentine, I suppose. Get him to reopen the damn case."

"Okay, just wanted to make sure you're not planning on taking matters into your own hands and putting yourself at risk. I'd hate to see you in prison or, worse, dead."

"I want justice for my friends. And I don't want whoever killed them to hurt anyone else."

"I understand. Well, right now, I don't have a lot of spare time to look into it, and you haven't given me much to go on. Once I get some of these fugitives back into lockup, maybe I can do some real digging."

"Yeah, okay. Thanks."

"Sorry I couldn't be more help. How are you doing otherwise?"

"Managing. Sucks not having Sam here."

"I understand. When I lost Conor, I went into a tailspin. It was bad. You seeing a therapist?"

"Bobby keeps bugging me to make an appointment with your dad again."

"Not a bad idea, whether it's with my dad or some other therapist. When I was struggling with my trauma, I kept telling myself I could handle it, that I didn't need anyone else's help. Nearly cost me everything."

"I got it handled."

"I'm serious, Avery. I was about to eat my gun. And if I had, I would have missed out on Conor coming back."

"Sam's not coming back. She's dead."

"I know. But you'll meet someone else one day. I think about all the people I would have hurt if I'd killed myself. My folks, my brother, my friends, my dog. You are an amazing person, Avery. And you have a dad that loves you. And you have me and the people in Phoenix Gender Alliance. You're not alone. And as soon as I get some time, I'll look into this Sonoran Crow business for you."

"Thanks for being there for me, Jinx."

"Hey, us trans women have to stick together, right? We're family."

"Yeah, we are. I'll talk to you later."

Avery wasn't tired when she got home. To make matters worse, the college assholes were back at it, as loud and annoying as ever.

She considered calling Kimi, but Damaged Souls was playing a gig at a bar in Gilbert. She didn't have the energy to drive out to the East Valley despite how much fun their shows were.

Instead, she grabbed her sketch pad and colored pencils and began drawing mermaids for Roz. Some monochromatic. Others in vivid color. Some mermaids dripped with sexuality. Others threatened a gruesome death in the murky depths. She did her best work when she really knew the person she was designing for, but she'd only met Roz twice and then only briefly. Yet, on some level, she felt she did know this woman.

Eventually, she fell asleep on the couch and dreamed she was manning the helm of an old wooden sailing ship on storm-tossed seas. Out of nowhere, an enormous wave crashed over the deck and washed her overboard.

She sputtered and struggled as wave after wave crashed over her. She cried out for help, but all she could see was the ship vanishing into the distance without her. Exhausted, she sank beneath the surface, unable to rise no matter how hard she kicked or flailed.

Avery's lungs burned for for air until a mermaid appeared, with short raven-black hair and eyes a metallic gold that shone with the brilliance of the sun.

The mermaid kissed her deeply. All at once, air filled Avery's lungs. She woke with a gasp, pulse racing.

CHAPTER 16

WAKE-UP CALL

It was still dark out when Avery woke the next morning at five. She tried to get back to sleep, but after tossing and turning for ten minutes, she resigned herself to getting up. It was one of the hazards of being a dyed-in-the-wool early bird.

She pulled on some clothes and walked outside onto the second-floor balcony that ran the length of the building. With sunrise still thirty minutes away, the sky was pale and filled with a frantic swarm of dark creatures. At first, she mistook them for a murmuration of starlings but quickly realized they were something else. Something wonderful.

She raced down the stairs and circled the building until she found what she was looking for—a ladder leading to the roof. The only problem was that the bottom of the ladder was a good ten feet above the ground. No doubt to keep unauthorized people off the roof. Not that it would stop her.

She gripped a conveniently placed drainpipe next to the ladder and found it solidly mounted to the wall. Fueled by adrenaline and a fondness for mischief, she shimmied up the drainpipe until she reached the ladder. Carefully, she gripped a rung, swung over, then ascended to the roof.

The top of the building was flat and covered with gravel. All around her, hundreds of bats swarmed past while they hunted for their morning meal of mosquitoes and other insects.

She had experienced something like this only once before, when Bobby and Melissa took her on a guided bat tour to a cave outside of Sedona. The guide hadn't allowed them inside the cave, which disappointed her. Instead, they'd sat quietly outside the entrance until the sun dipped below the horizon.

Just as her impatience was reaching critical levels, a sharp chirping sound caught her attention. First one bat then several more streamed out to the delight of the onlookers. Soon, the cave's entire bat population swarmed above their heads for an evening meal.

Despite the guide's reassurance that these bats were strictly insectivores or pollen feeders, Melissa had been terrified. Avery, on the other hand, was enthralled by the aerobatic ballet of these misunderstood mammals, amazed by how they whizzed past with such precision, never colliding with each other.

Now, as Avery stood on the roof of her apartment building, the same exhilaration filled her. The bats flew within inches of her face. But she felt no fear. No threat. Only a sense of oneness with these agile creatures of the night.

Eventually, the bats had their fill and vanished into a nearly invisible opening in the roof, just under the gutter. She wondered if property management knew about the colony. She hoped not for fear they might try to exterminate the bats.

When the last of the bats had vanished inside for the day, she returned to the ladder. Climbing down was going to be trickier. With each rung, her pulse quickened. When she reached the bottom of the ladder, she was still ten feet above the ground.

She considered dropping. She'd studied gymnastics in middle school. But there were no pads below her to soften her fall, only hard, sunbaked earth. Twisting an ankle would be easy.

The drainpipe she'd used to get to the ladder was easy enough to reach, but gripping it tightly enough to support her weight was another matter entirely. She tried to come up with another solution, but nothing came to mind. Panic set her heart racing. *Why am I so stupid?*

She remembered the meditation lessons Bobby and Melissa had taught her to deal with the panic attacks she'd had when she was younger.

Breathe in peace. Breathe out fear. She repeated the mantra a second and third time, letting go of the fear with each exhalation. The panic attack gradually subsided.

She turned back to the drainpipe. *I can do this. One, two, three!*

She leapt.

It took all her strength to grip the pipe tightly enough to slow her descent. Friction blistered her hands. With another deep breath, she carefully lowered herself to the ground.

On the way back to her apartment, a red plastic cup bobbed in the pool. A remnant of the college kids' previous night's festivities. As her resentment rose, an idea came to her that might teach them a lesson.

Chad, or whatever his actual name was, lived a couple of doors down from her. She stopped outside his apartment. All was quiet inside. No doubt, still asleep after a late night of partying.

She pulled out her phone, opened the Bluetooth settings, and found an open Bluetooth connection named Jaden's Speakers.

So, that's your name. Jaden the fucking jock. Get ready to party, Jaden.

With the press of a button, her phone connected to the Bluetooth speakers. She opened her music app and pulled up the most extreme death metal playlist she could find. She hit play then cranked the volume to the max.

A wall of sound composed of wailing guitars and screeching metal vocals shook Jaden's apartment.

"What the fuck is that?" screamed a panicked male voice barely audible above the music.

"Turn it off!" a second replied.

Avery chuckled and sat next to her front door, enjoying the chaos. The sound was so intense, she could feel the vibrations through the concrete walkway. The shouts inside the apartment grew increasingly frantic as Jaden and his roommate tried to stop the music.

By the time the silence came, Avery was struggling to contain a belly laugh. Giving these fuckers a taste of their own medicine felt good.

Lucas, the man who lived in the apartment between hers and Jaden's, stepped out his door and looked down at her. He was in his thirties and worked as an electrician. She'd seen him in his work shirt with his name stitched in blue. They'd spoken a couple of times in passing.

"What the hell was that?" he asked. "And why are you laughing?"

Avery shrugged and gave him her most innocent look.

"I was just sitting here enjoying the sunrise. Noise came from over there." Avery pointed.

The shouting between Jaden and his roomie continued and had turned into a heated argument.

Lucas gave her a look of disgust. "Fucking college kids."

"Fucking A, man," Avery replied.

He disappeared back into his apartment, and she returned to hers. The blisters on the palms of her hands looked nasty and ready to burst. She rubbed some ointment on them and covered them with gauze.

At nine o'clock, she pulled out Roz's business card. According to the card, the Spy Gal shop was closed on Sundays. Maybe Roz would be interested in looking at her mermaid sketches from the night before.

"Hello?" Roz asked, when Avery called her cell.

"It's Avery Byrne from Seoul Fire Tattoo."

"Good morning, Avery Byrne from Seoul Fire Tattoo. How's it going?"

"Same old. Listen, I've been working on some tattoo designs for you."

"Wow, that was fast. Thought I wouldn't hear from you for a few days."

"Had trouble sleeping last night, so I did a little sketching."

"Couldn't stop thinking about me, huh?"

Avery swallowed hard, glad Roz wasn't there to see her face turn bright red. "Uh…"

"Just messing with you. I can't wait to see what you've come up with."

"I can take photos of the sketches and send them to you. Let me know which one you prefer or if you want to make some changes."

"You sketched them on paper?"

"In my sketch pad with colored pencils."

"Kicking it old-school, huh? Figured you for the computer-tablet type."

"I do that too, but sometimes, I prefer a more tactile approach."

"If they're on your sketch pad, I'd love to see them in person. Why don't we get together for brunch if you're free?"

Nervousness snaked up her spine. Afraid these feelings of attraction would lead her to do something stupid, she wanted to say no. But she had nothing else going on and couldn't bring herself to lie to this woman. "Yeah, I'm free."

"There's a French café that serves a great Sunday brunch. And they have the best macarons outside of Paris. All kinds of amazing flavors."

"Macarons? You're talking about Essence Bakery?"

"You've been there?"

A wave of sadness hit her. The last time she'd eaten there was with Sam, shortly before she was killed. "A time or two."

"How about we meet at eleven? And don't forget the sketchbook."

This almost sounded like a date. *Is it a date?* "Yeah, okay."

"See ya there, Avery Byrne of Seoul Fire Tattoo."

CHAPTER 17

SUNDAY BRUNCH DATE

Avery hung up, her pulse racing. What had she gotten herself into? Sam had only been dead a month. And here she was going on a date?

No! It's not a date. I'm simply meeting with a client to discuss designs for a tattoo... at a café where Sam and I used to go for brunch. So why does it feel like a date? Goth help me!

She walked into Essence Bakery at ten minutes after eleven, having spent too much time deciding what to wear. Ultimately, she'd settled on a black sundress decorated with red roses that matched her femme-fatale-red lipstick. It was a return to her previous pinup goth style, but she liked the way the sweetheart neckline showed off her cleavage and the tats on her chest. She had also removed the gauze from her hands. Her palms were still red, but the blisters didn't look as nasty as they had.

Roz sat at a table by the plate-glass window and shot her a smile when Avery sat down.

"I was worrying you wouldn't show."

"Sorry, I was..." She was tempted to blame traffic or the ever-present construction, but she didn't want to lie to this woman. "I was running late."

After a server appeared and took their orders, Avery pulled her sketchbook out of her computer bag. "It's okay if you don't like any of the designs," she said as she opened to the first of the mermaid drawings. "I can always try something else."

"I'm sure they're all fabulous." Roz took the book, and her eyes widened in delight. "Wow! These are amazing."

Avery's heart fluttered with nervousness while Roz took her time examining each drawing. She normally wasn't this anxious when a client studied her work. If they liked her sketches, great. If not, no biggie. *So why am I nervous now?*

"They're all so… beautiful and enthralling. Each so different from the one before. But I think I like this mermaid best."

Roz pointed to a mermaid with black, violet, and emerald-green scales. Her orange hair flowed freely in the current. She was bare-breasted, no cheesy scallop-shell bra. One hand beckoned temptingly; the other held a trident.

"This drawing is exactly what I imagined. The colors, the sensuality, the strength. But what really sells it is the eyes. One look in her eyes, and you know this creature is no mere mermaid. She's a fucking goddess of the sea. Even Poseidon would say, 'Don't fuck with this bitch!' This is what I want."

A long-absent feeling of pride flowed through Avery. "You really like it?"

"Hell yeah! I wouldn't say so if I didn't mean it. I could tell when we met that you were the right woman for the job."

Her eyes narrowed. "What happened to your hands?"

Avery quickly tucked them into her lap, embarrassed about her climbing to the apartment building roof earlier. "Nothing. Burned 'em a little opening the door of the Gothmobile."

"What's the Gothmobile?"

"Just a stupid name I call my car. It's a black '57 Cadillac. Gets hot in the summer heat."

"Stupid? Not hardly! Cool name for a classic ride. But sorry about your hand."

"It's nothing."

The server brought their breakfast.

Avery was glad for the distraction. She wasn't usually this self-conscious around other people. In fact, normally, she didn't give two shits about what other people thought about her. So why now?

Roz had ordered a bagel loaded with lox and tomato and sprinkled with capers. Avery had strawberry crêpes with a side of bacon. Each of them had ordered a trio of macarons in different flavors.

Avery put the sketchbook into her bag and began eating. She was biting into a piece of bacon when she stopped and looked up at Roz. "Do you keep kosher?"

"I don't eat pork or shrimp, but I'll have a cheeseburger, minus the bacon, now and then." She whispered conspiratorially, "Just don't tell my mom."

"I guess I shouldn't have ordered the bacon. Sorry."

Roz laughed so hard, she nearly choked. "Don't be silly. You're free to eat whatever you like. I don't get offended by someone else, particularly a Gentile who eats treif. I simply choose not to eat it."

Avery's face warmed with embarrassment, and she changed the subject. "How did you end up running a spy shop?"

"Ah, that is a story. My dad was a private investigator up until the early '90s, when he figured out he could make more money selling nanny cams and other surveillance and security devices. Not only that, he could keep regular hours. No more all-night stakeouts snooping on cheating spouses. I started working there as a teenager. When he died a little over a year ago, I took over. Originally, the store was called Spy Guy, but I changed it to Spy Gal."

"Your dad died? How?"

"Stroke. It was sudden."

"I'm so sorry. I lost my mom a few years ago. Technically, she was my foster mom, but I thought of her as my mom."

"I'm sorry for you too. It's tough losing a parent."

"It sucks."

They ate in silence for a while.

"You like running Spy Gal?" Avery asked when the silence grew uncomfortable.

"I do. We get a lot of interesting people coming in."

"Do you also do PI work like your dad?"

"I've considered it. Could be fun if I were working on criminal cases, like for a lawyer or something. None of that domestic cheating-spouse mishegas. But to get a license, you have to schlep around as an apprentice to a professional for a few years. I don't have time to do that and run the shop."

"Damn, I was hoping you were."

"Why?"

Avery poked at the remnants of her breakfast. "I'm sort of working on a case."

"A case? Color me intrigued. What kind of case?"

"It's stupid."

"I'm sure it's not. You don't strike me as a person who would be interested in something stupid."

Avery took a deep breath and let it out. "Couple weeks ago, some friends of mine were killed in a car crash. But the cops say what really killed them was the high levels of fentanyl in their system."

"Oy! I'm so sorry."

"Thing is, I knew them well enough to know that that was bullshit. Hatchet's mother had been a junkie. He hated drugs. And the other guy, Boze, had been clean for a decade. I'm telling you, someone slipped them something."

"Wow. The cops got any suspects?"

"That's just it. The detective on the case wrote it off as an accidental overdose. Too busy to do any real police work, apparently. The guys, they were members of the Sonoran Crows hot-rodders. Cops don't give two shits about them."

"That fucking sucks."

"That's why I'm looking into it."

Roz's eyes glistened with excitement. "Is this what Chupa meant the other night about Avery the Avenger."

Avery shrugged. "My friends deserve justice. And whoever did this to them deserves to be punished. If the cops won't help…"

"So, what are you doing about it? You have any suspects?"

"A couple. There's a member of the Crows who just got out of rehab. Had a major grudge against Hatchet. Another member has been threatening me to mind my own business. I think he's involved somehow."

"Sounds suspicious," Roz agreed.

"I asked a friend of mine, who's a bounty hunter, if she could run some background checks on SkipTrakkr, but she's super busy right now."

"I think my dad had a subscription to SkipTrakkr, but it's probably lapsed."

"Too bad you don't have a PI license. Apparently, you need one to get a subscription."

"I still have a copy of my dad's old PI license. Maybe it would still work to renew his SkipTrakkr subscription."

A glimmer of hope sparked to life inside of Avery. "Would you be willing to try?"

"Sure. When I get home, I'll dig up the license and see what happens."

"Wow, that would be great."

"No problem. But tell me, if you find out who killed your friends, what do you plan to do about it?"

It always came down to that. "Inform the detective who had the case. Assuming he'll listen."

"And if he won't?"

She'd been pondering this ever since Bobby and Kimi asked her the same question. She looked Roz square in the eye. "What would I do to stop a murderer? To make sure he never kills another innocent person again? Whatever it takes."

"I see."

Avery wondered if she'd overplayed her hand, revealed too much.

"I've been dealing with bullies and abusers most of my life," Avery continued, feeling the need to explain herself. "If they get away with hurting someone once, then they think they can get away with it again. So they keep hurting people and hurting people and hurting people. Until someone stops them."

"I get it. So how do you plan to stop them? Murder them back?"

Avery wasn't sure what to say. What would Roz think of how she wiped out the Desert Mafia?

She took a deep breath and let it out. "Dig deep enough into these people's backgrounds, you sometimes find something you can use to make them stop. Maybe something you can blackmail them with, or maybe they screwed someone else over who'd have no problem retaliating if they knew. And if that fails, well, you just do what you gotta do to protect innocent people."

Neither of them spoke for several minutes. The server came by and refilled their coffee cups.

Now Avery was sure she had said too much. Roz seemed like a decent person. Not a vigilante, like her. But then again, Roz hadn't had to survive on the streets and deal with greedy slumlords, abusive pimps, dirty cops, or pedophile shelter directors. Her survival instincts hadn't been sharpened like a katana.

"I agree," Roz said.

Avery looked up in surprise. "You do?"

"Yeah. Most people are decent folks. But there are some real schmucks out there who get their kicks hurting innocent people. And if the cops won't stop them, who will?"

"So you don't think I'm some psycho?"

"Honestly, I don't know you that well. Maybe you are a psychopath. Or a sociopath. I can never remember which is worse."

A knot formed in Avery's stomach.

A smile spread across Roz's face. "I'm kidding. Kimi's known you since what? High school?"

"Junior high, actually."

"I don't see Kimi being your friend if you were some crazy axe murderer."

"No," Avery said.

"As a Jew, I know what can happen when evil, violent assholes are not held accountable for their actions. Want to know one of my family secrets? One of my great-grandfathers was a Nazi hunter after World War II."

"Seriously?"

"Seriously. A lot of those Nazis ended up in Argentina or here in the States, many with the help of the US government, no less. All the shit they did, all our soldiers who died fighting them, and our own fucking government was protecting these putzes. But Zadie Moshe and his friends refused to let them go unpunished. Don't know how many he killed, but I gathered it was a lot."

"Shit."

"And these days, half the states are passing laws against queer people for no other reason than to be cruel. We can't count on the system to protect innocent people. When the system is run by schmucks like that, who is left to do the right thing?"

"Exactly." Avery felt a weight slide off her shoulders. Roz got it.

"Tell ya what. When I get home, I'll dig up my dad's license and reactivate his SkipTrakkr subscription. I want to help you get justice for your friends."

Avery's heart swelled. She couldn't have been more blown away than if Roz had shown up with a dozen red roses.

"I can pay you for whatever it costs. And as for your tat, it's on the house. Hell, any other tats you want. Free of charge."

A smile spread across Roz's face. "I accept. So, when can we get started on my tattoo?"

Avery checked her schedule on her phone. "I've got an opening on June twentieth. Pretty booked until then."

"Damn. I have to wait three weeks?"

The disappointment in Roz's eyes touched her. It looked like the same disappointment Avery had felt when Jinx told her she couldn't help her run background checks on Mendez and Fisch.

"Tell you what—I probably shouldn't do this, but what the hell? You doing anything this afternoon?"

Roz chuckled. "Nope. I must confess, I lead a pretty boring life."

"I have the keys to the shop. It'll just be the two of us."

"And just like that, my life just got interesting."

CHAPTER 18

BRING THE PAIN

Avery cranked up Damaged Souls on the Seoul Fire stereo, and once Roz was prepped, she transferred the mermaid sketch onto Roz's arm with the tail encircling her bicep.

"That look about right?"

Roz studied her arm then her reflection in the nearby mirror. "Looks good."

"This is your first tattoo, right?" Avery laid out her ink and set up the machine.

"Yep. Is it gonna hurt a lot?" Roz actually looked nervous, which Avery found endearing.

"On the arm? Not really. Might get a little uncomfortable when I start coloring and shading. But you look like you can take it. And any time you need to take a break, let me know."

"How long will it take?"

"A large, elaborate design like this? We'll break it into three sessions of about three hours each, especially since this is your first tattoo. I'll do the outlining today. Then we can start the coloring and shading in a few weeks."

"A few weeks? Can't we shorten it to one week?"

Avery sighed. "I prefer to give it a little time to heal and make sure there aren't any issues. But since we're just outlining this session, why don't we see how you do with the pain. If you're doing okay, we can see about scheduling the next session in about a week."

"Okay, then. Bring on the pain."

Avery began outlining the mermaid. After a few minutes, she paused. "How's that feel?"

"Hardly felt it at all. I would've figured getting jabbed with a needle a gazillion times a second would hurt a lot more."

"Good. Then I'll continue."

Avery settled into her work. The blisters from her slide down the drainpipe stung, but she ignored them.

For a long while, neither of them spoke, which helped Avery focus on the art. It felt a little awkward, being so close to this beautiful woman and not speaking. But it helped not to have too many distractions.

After about an hour, Avery sat up. "Need a break?"

"I could use a pee break, if you don't mind. All that coffee from brunch went right through me."

"Restrooms over there past the last station on the left. Don't touch your arm. Don't want to risk getting infected."

While Roz used the facilities, Avery tossed her gloves and drank a bottle of water. A lot about this woman reminded her of Sam. The tomboyish looks, the sly grin. But there was a lot that was different. Unlike Sam, Roz was goth and a lot less impulsive. And Roz didn't secretly work for a mobster.

Still, Avery missed Sam terribly. Her absence felt like a hole carved into Avery's chest with a chainsaw. But the more time she spent with Roz, the less it hurt. Not that she planned to date this woman. But the prospect of it seemed a little less scary than it had when the two of them met at Johnny Heretics.

"Wow, I can't believe how amazing it looks. And it's just the outlines," Roz said when she emerged from the restroom. "I can't stop staring at it."

She was fixated on the mirror by Avery's station, mouth agape.

"It'll look better once I put in the color and shading."

Roz turned to her. "I just… I can't believe I waited this long. It's just so…"

Without warning, Roz kissed her. Hard. Avery didn't know what else to do, so she went with it, ignoring the red flags screaming in the back of her mind.

When Roz pulled away, Avery's heart was beating faster than the pistons in one of the Sonoran Crows' hot rods. She felt dizzy and drunk and euphoric and terrified.

"I don't know why I did that," Roz sputtered. "I'm sorry. I just... I felt the need to kiss you. But I probably should have asked permission. You probably think I'm some sex-crazed□—"

"No, I don't. I... I liked it. It's just..."

"I know. We barely know each other."

"Yeah, but it's fine. As I said, I liked it."

Avery felt the urge to tell Roz she was transgender, to get it out of the way so that there was no misunderstanding or hurt feelings later. And yet she couldn't bring herself to speak the words.

Bobby had once told her that while being trans had shaped her experience, it didn't define her. That it was little more than a part of her medical history and none of anyone else's business. Certainly nothing to be ashamed of.

And yet, she knew that if things got more intimate, she would have to tell Roz eventually. And the longer she waited, the harder it would be. And the more things might go horribly, possibly violently wrong when she did.

"What's wrong, Avery? You look sad."

"What? Oh, nothing."

"Didn't look like nothing. You okay?"

"I'm on the rebound," she managed to say. It wasn't coming out, but it was true, at least. She'd always heard that rebound relationships never worked out. "My last girlfriend was killed a month ago."

"But that's like seven months in lesbian years."

When Avery didn't laugh, Roz continued, "Sorry, that was rude of me. I've got a bad habit of using humor to deflect difficult feelings. Seriously, though, I'm truly sorry about your loss. Was her death connected to your two friends getting killed?"

"No, she was murdered by someone else."

"Oy, that's awful. And here I kissed you while you're still grieving. Damn, I'm a total putz."

"No, you're not. And the kiss was nice. I liked it. I just thought you should know."

"Of course. And whatever you need, I'm here for you." Roz looked pensive for a moment. "On a different subject, could I ask you a rather personal question?"

Oh, shit! She clocked me. She knows I'm trans. "Uh, sure. I guess."

"Your teeth kind of look like vampire fangs. Is that some sort of body mod?"

It took a moment for Avery to realize she hadn't been clocked after all. "My teeth? Oh, no, I was born without lateral incisors. My dentist calls it anodontia. My birth parents were too cheap to get it fixed, but I've always kind of liked it."

"I like it too. Fits your style. Very goth."

"Thanks." Avery tried to refocus. "Shall we continue the outlining?"

Roz settled back into the chair. "Bring on the pain, vampire girl."

CHAPTER 19

PERSON OF INTEREST

When Avery had finished the outline, she cleaned away the excess ink and the blood, massaged in some antibiotic ointment, wrapped it, and gave Roz the aftercare instructions, along with a tube of antiseptic cream and a small bottle of liquid soap.

"The instructions are also on the Seoul Fire website, in case you forget anything. And if you see any redness or other signs of infection, call a doctor immediately. You should be fine, but it happens in rare cases. Usually when clients pick at the scabs or don't follow my instructions."

"Thanks, doctor," Roz replied with a twinkle in her eye. "I'll look for my dad's PI license and try to restore his account on SkipTrakkr."

"Thanks, I appreciate it."

Roz hugged her, and it didn't make Avery feel uncomfortable this time. She had to admit this woman was cool, and she was a little sad when they parted ways.

When Avery got back to her apartment, she remembered her promise to Bobby and called Dana's phone.

"Hello?"

Avery felt like the Gothmobile was sitting on her chest. "Hey, Dana. It's Avery, Bobby's daughter."

She knows who you are, you idiot, she scolded herself.

"Hi, Avery. How are you this afternoon?"

"I'm… I'm okay. Look, I want to apologize for my behavior the other night. I was very rude. I…" She wasn't sure what to say. "I'm just sorry."

"Thank you, Avery. Apology accepted. I heard about your girlfriend's death. Bobby hasn't shared with me all the details, only that it was very traumatizing. I can't imagine what you've been through."

No, you can't, Avery wanted to say. But she reminded herself she was calling to make amends, not to stir up more shit.

"Thank you for understanding."

"I'm not trying to replace Melissa. I know the two of you were very close."

Grief hit Avery like a punch to the throat. She blinked back tears. "Yeah, we were."

"I only want to make Bobby as happy as he makes me. That's all. I think we both can agree he deserves to be happy."

"Yes."

"And I'd like to get to know you. Bobby hasn't told me much about how you came to live with him or what happened in your life before. And I don't want to pry. But maybe in time, you can trust me enough to share what feels comfortable to you."

"Well, for starters, I'm transgender." The words popped out before she knew she would say them. She wasn't even sure why she said it. She hadn't even told Roz. "Is that a problem? Is it against your Christian beliefs?"

"I… well, wow. So you're changing, or you already got the change?"

Not the reaction she was expecting.

"I transitioned when I was a teenager. Before Bobby took me in."

"I see. Well, no. It's not a problem. I'm a Unitarian Universalist. We're very 'live and let live' and value diversity."

Whatever, Avery thought, but she kept it to herself.

"Besides, I have a niece who's a lesbian. Or pansexual. I'm not sure exactly. And I know that's not the same thing as being transgendered, but I get it. And I am honored to know you."

"The word is transgender. No -ed on the end. It's an adjective, not a verb or a noun."

"My apologies. Thank you for correcting me. And it's not a problem. You are who you are. A beautiful woman. It takes a lot of courage to do that sort of thing."

"Not courage. Just necessity," Avery corrected again, perhaps a little too sharply.

"Of course. I'm glad you knew yourself well enough to do what you needed to do. And I'm happy to be your friend."

We're friends now? Not quite. "Okay. So we're good?"

"Yes, thank you so much for calling and sharing with me. Perhaps the three of us can try for dinner again. Say next Friday?"

"Yeah, I'd like that." And she meant it.

After Avery hung up, she decided to do a little sleuthing on her own.

She needed to find out more about Mendez and Fisch. She started by running an online search for "Carlos Mendez mechanic Phoenix." The results were a mishmash of social media profiles, auto repair shop websites, obituary notices, and websites offering background checks. None of the social media profiles looked like the man she was searching for. And she could safely ignore the obituary notices.

She remembered Jinx Ballou's advice that most online background-check websites wouldn't provide much useful information, even on the paid services. So that left her with checking out the websites for the auto repair shops.

She drilled down on the sites with photos of owners and staff, even looking at their social media pages when links were provided.

As her eyes were crossing from staring at the screen for what felt like hours, she landed on a website for Valley View Auto Repair. The owner was listed as Carlos Ybarra-Mendez.

It took a minute to recognize him because he was smiling in his profile photo and had hair. The Mendez she knew was bald. She'd never seen him smile. At the Sonoran Crow events, he was always pissed off about something, usually a mechanical issue with his car, especially if he'd lost a race.

His short bio mentioned he loved classic hot rods. It was definitely him.

She scoured the website for every tidbit of information about him, but there wasn't much more than that he'd been a licensed mechanic since 2002.

Reviews of the shop were mixed. Some praised him as if he were the second coming. Others gave scathing one-star reviews, accusing the shop of overcharging customers or suggesting unnecessary repairs. A few accused the shop of deliberately sabotaging cars in order to get more work. Not that any of that was definitive or relevant.

She followed links to the shop's social media pages and found photos of Mendez at Sonoran Crow race nights and related events. This led her to Mendez's page.

She scrolled through slowly, looking for anything that might point to his guilt, especially where he was on the night Hatchet and Boze died.

A week-old post featured a photo of him with Hatchet and Boze, saying they would be missed. Had they reconciled before the end? Or was this post nothing more than performative grief so that he didn't look like a jerk? What better way to look innocent if he was the one who'd doctored their drinks with fentanyl?

On the day before Hatchet and Boze died, Mendez had posted a photo of himself holding what looked like a plastic coin with the words "30 Days CLEAN AND SERENE" printed on it.

Above the photo, he had written:

Can't believe it's been 30 days. Hardest fucking month of my life, facing my demons w/o drugs.

So grateful to my wife and kid, to Serenity River Recovery Center, and to my Higher Power. U saved my life.

Still got a lotta work 2 do. Done a lotta bad shit. Some I can't undo. Hurt a lotta good people. Asking my Higher Power 4 forgiveness. Making amends where I can. Cleaning up my messes. ODAAT.

Avery stared at the post for a long time. Mendez admitted to doing bad shit he couldn't undo. *Did that include murder? Was this a confession?*

What was he so angry at Hatchet about? What did Hatchet do that was criminal? Was any of it enough to drive a newly clean Mendez to murder?

She found a month-long gap in his timeline with no posts. No doubt when he was in rehab. Before that, Mendez had made a lot of vague posts spewing venom at unnamed people who had broken into his garage. *Hatchet perhaps? And Boze too? How does Fisch factor into all of this?*

Earlier posts were mostly bragging about how his 1969 Plymouth Satellite was rising fast on the Sonoran Crows' list. He threw shade at other Crows, including Hatchet and Walrus. These people posted comments in kind. Avery couldn't tell how much was good-natured kidding around and what was more serious.

She found links to other members of the Sonoran Crows, including Hatchet, Big Eddie Myles, Jude "Fisch" Fischman, and Stephen "Rocket Man" Floyd. On these other pages, she found nothing of interest. Just a lot of pics, many of them from race nights.

Hatchet's page was filled with condolences from friends sharing memories and photos. On his pre-mortem posts, he complained the Innovators were violating Sonoran Crow bylaws and putting lives in danger.

Half the comments agreed with his views. Others called him and the other Old Schoolers arrogant snobs and Luddites. She continued to search his feed, but nothing else pointed to his killer.

She found no account for Boze. Maybe he wasn't on social media.

She moved on to Fisch. To her surprise, Jude Fischman worked at Hatchet's garage, though she'd never noticed him there when Hatch was restoring the Gothmobile. Fisch was also in the Old Schoolers' camp and did his fair share of shitposting about using modern tech. So maybe he and Mendez weren't in cahoots, though she couldn't be sure of much at this point.

Considering how pissed Fisch was about Avery looking into Hatchet's death, she wondered if there might have been some conflict between the two men. Maybe an employer–employee beef. But she didn't see any evidence of it on either of their social media feeds. So why had he been so angry at her? Was he afraid she would learn something that would paint Hatchet in a bad light?

Were Mendez's claims about Hatchet deserving to be in jail legit? Maybe Hatchet stole something. Possibly in an attempt to get his former friend clean? Or something related to cars? And why hadn't Mendez reported this so-called crime to the police?

The bigger question was why Detective Valentine hadn't even bothered to look into any of this. Why was he so eager to write their deaths off as an accidental overdose?

CHAPTER 20

SPY GAL

On Monday morning, Avery longed to climb onto the roof again and commune with the bats. But she wasn't up to playing Spider-Man on the drainpipe and further blistering her hand.

So she'd contented herself with enjoying the show from the second-floor balcony. After the last bat had turned in for the morning, Avery returned to her apartment.

Her phone rang while she was eating breakfast and listening to Emilie Autumn's "Fight Like A Girl."

"Hello?"

"Sorry. Did I call too early?"

It took Avery a moment to recognize the husky, energetic voice on the other end. "Roz? What's up?"

"Good news. I found my dad's PI license and reactivated his SkipTrakkr account. We can run background checks on the people you suspect killed your friends."

"That's great. I did some searching online last night. I'm convinced more than ever that Mendez is the killer. And Fisch is involved, but I'm not sure how. Also, I have their full names."

"Great. Do you know where the Spy Gal shop is?"

"Indian School Road and Thirty-Second Street?" Avery replied, remembering what Kimi had said when they met at Johnny Heretics.

"Exactly. On the south side of the Indian School, just east of Thirty-Second. In the shopping center with the Arby's out front."

"Yeah, I know where that is. You want me to come there?"

"Oh, that's right. You have clients scheduled."

"My first client's not until eleven today, so I have a little time."

"Cool. Get here quick as you can. I look forward to seeing you. And I promise not to kiss you this time."

Roz hung up before Avery could say anything else.

Where was this thing with Roz going? Was it strictly professional? Just friends? More than that? Did she want it to be more than that?

Honestly, she did want more. She was horribly lonely, which was probably the worst reason to get into a relationship. She was needy, wounded, and broken. What kind of girlfriend would she be? And what would Roz do when she found out Avery was trans? Sam hadn't cared one bit, but there were some, even in the lesbian community, who were severely transphobic.

She picked up a couple of black coffees with packets of cream, sugar, and artificial sweetener at a Dutch Bros shortly before she got to Spy Gal. Just seemed like the thing to do since Roz was helping her out like this. If Roz wasn't a coffee drinker, she could toss it.

"Oh my goth! You shouldn't have." Roz opened the door before Avery had to figure out how to do so while balancing the tray of coffees with her purse.

"Thanks. I was going to get lattes but wasn't sure if you preferred real milk or an alternative, so I just got black coffee."

"It's fine. I'm rather fond of vanilla lattes, but black coffee with cream is fine. Thank you."

A woman with a nose ring and a pierced eyebrow stood behind one of the glass cases arranged in an L-shape. She had a sleeve of ink on each arm.

"Avery, this is Polly, my assistant manager. Polly, this is my friend Avery, who's been working on my mermaid tattoo."

Polly cocked her head. "Avery Byrne?"

“Yes,” she replied warily, hoping the woman didn’t recognize her from her photo being plastered on the news as a person of interest wanted by the cops for Sam’s murder.

“I thought I recognized your style in Roz’s new ink. You did a vampire queen on the back of a friend of mine. It was badass. You got a card?”

Avery breathed a sigh of relief and handed Polly a business card. “Sorry I didn’t bring another coffee for you. But you’re welcome to mine. I haven’t sipped it yet.”

“No thanks! I hate coffee. Tea’s more my, well, cup of tea.”

Avery looked around the shop. One glass case featured a collection of nanny cams, surveillance and digital cameras, lenses, and similar equipment. The other case displayed personal security devices such as stun guns, pepper spray, and key-fob alarms. Signs advertising security systems and monitoring lined the walls. The place had a no-nonsense, industrial vibe that jived with the store’s purpose.

“Nice shop,” Avery said, not knowing what else to say.

“Thanks.” Roz sipped her coffee. “I keep thinking of changing the decor to make it feel less cold and masculine. A lot of my customers are women. Any suggestions?”

“I don’t know shit about decorating. Bobby J.’s in charge of Seoul Fire. Most of what’s on the walls are photos of our art, with some *Star Wars* posters and traditional Korean art thrown in.”

“Well, I suppose that fits for a tattoo parlor. By the way, I love how my tattoo feels. I know it’s just the outline, but I like feeling the raised lines like that. Although, should my tattoo be this scabby?”

Avery studied Roz’s arm. The skin around the tattoo was light pink, as expected, but didn’t appear infected. “It’s going to scab and flake a bit. Just don’t pick at it, and keep using the lotion and the soap I gave you. It will be fine. And the raised lines will flatten over time.”

"Bummer, I kind of liked the texture. Can't wait to see it in color."

Avery smiled, glad Roz appreciated her work.

"Shall we run some background checks on your suspected murderers?"

"Yes, please."

"Follow me."

Roz led her into the back, where there was a large desk with three computer screens surrounding a keyboard. "Welcome to Spy Gal Central Command."

"Wow, what's with all the screens?"

"I also offer security-video-feed-hosting services for homes and businesses. It's not the same as hiring a security alarm service, where they call the police. But it's good for catching porch pirates, and if there is a break-in, the burglar can't destroy the feed because it's not stored on the premises."

"What if they break in here?"

"Well, they'd have a helluva time doing that. My dad had inch-thick polycarbonate windows installed and hellacious security locks. I'm pretty good at picking locks—strictly as a hobby, mind you—and these locks are insane. Also, I store the security feeds in the cloud. So even if they somehow got in and stole my computer setup, which would still suck, I'd still have the security feed."

"Smart."

"But you're not here for that. Pull up a chair."

They sat down at the desk, and Roz woke up the computer. Immediately, multiple camera feeds appeared on the screen, including one of Polly assisting a customer up front and another of the two of them sitting down at the computer. It made Avery a little uncomfortable seeing herself from that angle. She glanced up and saw a tiny camera with a red glowing light.

With a few keystrokes and mouse clicks, Roz closed the video feeds and opened a web browser. She pulled up the

SkipTrakkr website and logged in. "Let's find ourselves some bad guys."

CHAPTER 21

SUSPICIOUS BEHAVIOR

"So who are we looking up first?" Roz asked when she had the SkipTrakkr site up.

"Carlos Ybarra-Mendez. I don't know his middle name, but he's the owner of Valley View Automotive Repair on Cave Creek Road. And a member of the Sonoran Crows."

"Do you know his home address?"

"No."

"Tricky. Okay, let's see what we can find."

Roz fed the information into the search bar. Nine results came up as a match for the name.

"There." Avery pointed to the screen. "That's him."

Roz clicked on the entry. "What do you want to know? Criminal history? Bank records? Telephone call logs?"

"Wow, I can get all that? Legally?"

"Well, we are using my late father's PI license, so…"

"Does it bother you that we're technically breaking the law?"

"I don't know about the law, but it's definitely a violation of SkipTrakkr's terms of service. But only if they find out, and I don't intend to tell them." Roz grinned. "And if it helps us find who killed your friends, hell no, I don't care! I see it as my father still doing good, even after his death."

"I like your perspective. Let's start with Mendez's criminal history."

"Okay. Here goes."

The information that appeared on the screen didn't surprise her. "Multiple arrests for reckless driving and speeding. Figures for a member of the Crows. And a few months ago, he was charged with possession of a controlled substance. Looks like he got probation and mandatory drug treatment. You sure he's your murderer if he was in rehab?"

"He got out two days before Hatchet and Boze were killed. He's got no alibi. What kind of drugs did they arrest him for?"

Roz clicked on one of the scanned court documents. "Methamphetamine."

"Not fentanyl?"

"Doesn't mention it. Though sometimes, meth can be cut with fentanyl. Or maybe he bought fentanyl from whoever used to sell him crank. Why do you suspect he killed your friends?"

"Mendez said Hatchet deserved to be locked up, that he was poking his nose into Mendez's personal business. Wouldn't give any specifics, but I suspect it had to do with Mendez's car and rumors it used an all-electric engine. The two of them had been good friends for years, but lately, this rivalry between the Old Schoolers and the Innovators had gotten intense."

"The what?"

Avery explained about the different attitudes about allowing modern technology into the classic cars and how it was affecting the races. "The Innovators are now dominating the list, with Mendez on top, so the rivalries are intensifying. And word is that Mendez has been using an all-electric engine, which wasn't allowed until he topped the list, became club president, and changed the bylaws."

A look of disgust played on Roz's face. "Gah, such typical guy shit. Everyone wants to be top dog. Like, who cares? Why not just race and have fun?"

"Apparently, there's a lot of betting and trash talk going on. I go to their race nights a couple of times a month. It can be exciting to watch these old cars race. But like you said, they can be real idiots about it sometimes."

"You said Mendez accused Hatch of doing something illegal. Something to do with the engine in Mendez's car. Right?"

"Yeah. Why?"

"What if Hatch broke into Valley View and saw something he shouldn't have? Maybe it had to do with the car. Or he got Mendez busted, who then found out and retaliated."

"That's what I'm thinking. But how do we prove it?" Avery asked. "We need something solid if I'm going to convince the cops to reopen the case."

"Well, we can pull Mendez's phone and text logs. And we can run his bank records for the past couple of months."

"Let's do it."

"Your wish is my command."

Roz started with the phone logs. A list of phone numbers scrolled down the screen along with dates, times, length of calls, and the other party on the call if known. From late April through early May, there were only a few calls, and all but one were incoming.

Avery pointed at the screen. "This must be when he was in rehab. Only one outgoing call during that time. Blanca Mendez, his wife."

"Makes sense."

"Then a lot of calls the day Hatchet and Boze died, including three to Hatchet himself. First two were less than a minute long, then one for five minutes." Avery studied it. "Any way of knowing what they talked about?"

Roz shook her head. "Nope. Calls are logged but not recorded. At least not by the carrier."

"Some of his outgoing calls are to phone numbers with no name. What's up with that?"

"Most likely prepaid phones."

"Burners, huh? Like something a drug dealer would use." Avery studied the list closer. "Pull up Mendez's text history."

Roz clicked on the button that read SMS Log, and a list of text conversations appeared. Roz clicked on one with Hatchet the day before Mendez got arrested.

Hatchet:

Dude, get off the crank. It's destroying your life.
Mendez:
F U. Mind ur own biznez.
Hatchet:
Think of Felicia & Gabi. Your addiction's ruining their lives. You're racing while high. And with a stolen engine. You even see yourself? Wanna end up in prison?
Mendez:
U fuckers broke in my shop. Got it on video. I could have u arrested for B&E. Keep ur mouth shut about the engine or Ill shut it for u. Permanently.
Hatchet:
Don't threaten me, you fucking junkie. You don't give a shit whose lives you ruin. Matter of time before you get busted. I'm calling an officers meeting, getting you voted out as president. You don't deserve it.
Mendez:
Try it & see what happens. Ill fucking end u.

"Wow, that sounds like a threat," Avery said.

"Enough to take it to Detective Valentine?"

"Maybe. It confirms Hatchet broke into Mendez's shop, presumably to get a look at this engine Hatch claimed was stolen. Pull up this one he sent the day Hatch and Boze died. Posted at five thirty p.m."

Mendez:
Meet me at ur shop @ 7. We need to talk.

"No reply," Roz noted.

"This proves he was there that night."

"Well, it proves he said he was *going* there."

"Any way of tracking where his phone was?" Avery asked.

"A geolocation? No. SkipTrakkr doesn't provide that. But we can run his bank records. If he used his card that evening, it might tell us where he went, which could further incriminate him, or it could exonerate him. Or it might not provide anything useful at all."

"Do it."

Roz ran the search. SkipTrakkr displayed a list of bank transactions, including dates, times, amounts, and vendors.

Avery pointed to a transaction. "He spent twelve bucks at a Dawson and Sons Convenience Store around six thirty that night. Where is that?"

Roz smiled but didn't bother to search. "On the corner of Seventh Street and Maryland. Avenue."

"Wow! How do you know that?"

Roz gave her a conspiratorial wink. "I'm the Spy Gal. I know many things."

"You've been there."

"A few times."

"Seventh Street, huh? Hatchet's shop's on Seventh Street and Ocotillo, just a few streets north of Maryland. Will SkipTrakkr tell us what he bought there?"

"SkipTrakkr won't. But I might provide an answer." Roz opened a different website called Spy Gal Security Service.

"This is your security-feed side of the business," Avery observed.

"Yup. I don't monitor them, but for clients that want that, I subcontract out to another company. Most just want recordings because it's less expensive and still meets their insurance requirements."

A window appeared showing video of four security feeds, all different views inside and outside of a convenience store.

"Dawson and Sons is one of your clients. That's how you knew where they're located."

"Give the lady a cookie. Now, what's the timestamp for Mendez's purchase?"

"Friday, May 20, 6:32 p.m."

“Okay, 6:32 p.m.” Roz fast-forwarded through the feed then hit Play at 18:28.

Avery pointed to a familiar figure on the screen. “That’s him. He’s buying beer? He just got out of rehab, for goth’s sake.”

“Looks like a four-pack of Red Dragon ginger beer. He’s got taste, at least. It’s good stuff. Makes a helluva Moscow Mule.”

“Is Classic Auto Repair one of your clients, by chance?” Avery asked. “I’d really like to see what happened the night Hatchet and Boze died, especially once Mendez got there.”

Roz made a face. “Sorry, no.”

“But we know Mendez was pissed at Hatchet for threatening him over his drug usage and a stolen electric engine. I wonder if Hatchet got him busted.” Avery recalled the memorial. “Walrus said Hatch liked Red Dragon ginger beer. Mendez probably knew that.”

“Maybe this was Mendez’s idea of a peace offering.”

“Maybe. Or the murder weapon. Put the drugs in an open bottle and give it to him.”

“Or even a closed one,” Roz explained. “Red Dragon uses twist-off caps. He could have removed the bottle caps, poured in the drugs, and resealed them.”

“And Boze was just collateral damage. Unless…”

“Unless what?” Roz asked, a quizzical look on her face.

“Unless Mendez wanted to kill Boze as well.” Avery reread the text conversation from before Mendez went into rehab. “He said ‘you fuckers broke into my shop.’ Plural. So maybe Boze was with Hatch when he broke into the shop.”

“It’s possible.”

“We’ve established that Mendez is a junkie who had access to illicit drugs. He was furious at Hatchet, possibly Boze, and threatened to kill them. He brought Hatchet his favorite ginger beer and met him at the shop the night he and Boze died and could have put the drugs in the bottles with no one the wiser.”

"Sounds like motive, means, and opportunity. Enough evidence to take to this detective and for him to take a second look at the case."

"I hope so."

CHAPTER 22

THEORIES ARE NOT EVIDENCE

After putting everything they'd found onto a thumb drive, Avery called Valentine.

"How can I help you, Ms. Byrne?" Valentine asked in a tired, condescending tone.

"I need to meet with you." She glanced at her watch. It was almost ten o'clock. She would be hard-pressed to meet with him downtown and still get to the shop on time to meet with her first client of the day. But seeing a murderer punished was more important.

"Oh? And why is that?"

"I've uncovered new evidence in the murders of Dwayne Hatchet and Leonard Bozeman."

"Really?" He sounded skeptical. To her relief, he added, "I'm just getting out of court. I can meet you at the police headquarters building in fifteen. You remember where it is?"

"I remember."

Avery hung up and hugged Roz. "He agreed to meet. Thanks so much for your help."

"It's kind of fun. I don't know why my father gave up being a PI for running a shop. Maybe if he'd had a partner like you, he wouldn't have."

Partners? Is that what we are? Avery wondered. "It has been fun. I better run, or I'll be late."

"Give 'em hell, girl!"

Valentine met Avery in the lobby of the police headquarters building. "So you have new evidence on the Hatchet and Bozeman deaths?"

The sardonic tone in his voice told her he wasn't taking her seriously. "Is there someplace we can talk?"

He studied her for a moment. “Sure, follow me.”

On the third floor, they sat in an interview room lined with soundproofing tiles. Valentine’s asshole of boss had put her in this very room when he tried to shake her down for the money Sam had stolen from her mobster boss. The letters “ACAB”—short for “all cops are bastards”—had been scratched into one of the tiles.

“Carlos Ybarra-Mendez. He’s your murderer. Or rather, their murderer. He had a stolen engine in his car. Hatchet and Boze found out about it. Mendez killed them before they snitched.” She deliberately left out the part about them breaking into Mendez’s shop. “Also, Mendez, who just got out of rehab, was at Hatchet’s auto repair shop not long before they were killed. He put dope into bottles of ginger beer and gave it to them. They drank it, probably started feeling sick, and tried to drive to the hospital. Only they died from the overdose before they could get there.”

“Interesting. This is your theory? Because you promised me evidence. Theories are not evidence.”

She took the thumb drive out of her purse and set it on the table between them. “It’s what happened. The evidence is here. Bank transactions, text messages, phone logs, and even security footage. You’ve got motive, means, and opportunity.”

Valentine leaned back in his chair, arms folded. “Wow! That’s some damn fine detective work, Ms. Byrne.”

Avery felt a flush of pride then wariness as she wondered if he was patronizing her. “I think so.”

“And how did you come by all of this information?”

Avery hesitated before she pushed the thumb drive across to him. “A private investigator.”

“You went to the trouble of hiring a PI? Who did you hire?”

“Her name’s not important. What is important is that you arrest Mendez and send him to prison for murdering Hatch and Boze. That is what you do, right?”

Valentine picked up the thumb drive and studied it. "Tell ya what. I will look through this so-called evidence. If it warrants a second look into the case, I will do so."

"That's all I ask." She wanted to say, *Do your fucking job*. But she restrained herself. She remembered she had a job to get to herself. "I gotta go. Thank you for looking into it."

"My pleasure."

On the drive to Seoul Fire, the traffic on Grand Avenue came to a standstill a half mile south of Camelback Road. A solid line of cars stood between her and the nearest turnoff. She had no choice but to sit and stare. She bumped the A/C up a notch. It was almost June, and the high temperature was projected to reach 107 degrees.

The needle on the Gothmobile's temperature gauge was also creeping up. Not quite into the red zone, but she had an unsettling feeling that if she didn't get moving soon, it would.

When was the last time I flushed the radiator?

When her phone rang, she half expected it to be Valentine, saying he'd looked at her evidence and was reopening the case with Mendez as his prime suspect. Or at least a person of interest.

But no, it was Bobby.

"Hey, kiddo! You've got a rather impatient client sitting in the waiting area."

"Shit. I'm sorry, Appa. I'm stuck in traffic on Grand Avenue."

"Grand? Don't you usually come down Fifty-Ninth?"

"I had to meet someone downtown. I figured out who killed Hatchet and Boze."

"Ave, I thought we agreed you weren't getting involved."

"I'm not. I turned over what I found to the police. Nothing more."

"Glad to hear it. Get here when you can. I'll entertain your client until you arrive."

"Thanks, Appa."

"Also, thank you for apologizing to Dana. That meant a lot to her."

"Yeah. I'll see you shortly."

She stared out again at the sea of cars that were inching forward finally. Her temperature gauge was just below the red line, and her stress level was rising along with it. If her radiator blew, who knew how long she'd be stuck in this heat? And despite Bobby's advice to always have a gallon of potable water with her for drinking, she didn't. "Fuck!"

She was in the right lane and was tempted to pull onto the sidewalk until she reached a side street to turn onto. According to the GPS app, Thirty-Ninth Avenue was just a little ways ahead. She leaned her head to the right and spotted a turnout lane ahead. Unfortunately, there was also a utility pole between the curb and the sidewalk. So even if she pulled onto the sidewalk, she couldn't reach the turnoff.

Just as the needle on the temp gauge reached the red line, the car in front of her started moving. Slowly at first but without immediately braking again. Avery reached the turnout lane just as wisps of steam escaped from under the Gothmobile's hood.

She roared the engine and drove well above the speed limit onto Thirty-Ninth. The needle on the gauge dipped below the red, and Avery breathed a sigh of relief. She considered pulling into the gas station on the corner of Camelback, but even if she bought coolant, she would have to wait for the engine to cool down before adding it. Getting burned by boiling antifreeze would not be helpful.

By the time she reached the shop, acrid steam was spewing from the radiator, matching her mood. She rushed into the shop and apologized to her client for being late.

During a brief break between clients at two in the afternoon, Avery called Roz. She had been daydreaming about Roz ever since leaving Spy Gal to talk with Valentine. Despite still grieving for Sam, Avery couldn't dismiss the childish crush she'd been developing toward this new woman in her life.

But Roz was way out of Avery's league. The woman absolutely radiated charm and coolness—without even trying. And when Roz found out Avery was trans, any chance of the two of them dating would be out the window. Avery was sure of it.

Not that Roz had said or done anything to suggest she was transphobic. But that would be consistent with the ongoing shitshow that was Avery's life.

Still, she hadn't been able to get the woman off her mind when she'd been inking her previous. Roz's husky alto voice, her intoxicating fragrance, her comforting smile. If any woman were a drug, it would be Roz.

Considering Bobby was always telling her to trust her feelings, she allowed herself to make the call.

"Hey, girl," Roz said when she answered. "How'd it go at police HQ?"

"Valentine took the thumb drive and promised to look into it."

"Awesome! You got the ball rolling for justice."

"I couldn't have done it without you."

"Pfft! Lucky for us, the old man's credentials still worked. And honestly, it was a lot of fun. You're a lot of fun."

Embarrassment hit Avery hotter than if she'd stepped outside into the summer sun's fury.

"I enjoy spending time with you." Avery struggled for what to say next. "Well, I got my next client coming in. Just wanted to say thanks for your help."

"You're most welcome. See you 'round, Avery Byrne from Seoul Fire Tattoo."

CHAPTER 23

JOB OFFER

After work, Avery asked Bobby if he had any coolant. He didn't, but Frisco had a jug in the back of her pickup truck. Avery filled her radiator, which was, unsurprisingly, low. She ran the engine for about ten minutes, and it didn't overheat. On the drive home, she checked the gauge obsessively every thirty seconds.

When she arrived at the apartment complex, the assholes were back at it again. She entertained the idea of stepping inside the fenced-in pool area and smashing the speakers on the deck. But she wasn't in the mood to be arrested for destruction of private property.

She put on a pair of noise-canceling headphones and tried to drown out the sound so she could get to sleep.

The next morning, she again woke before dawn. This time, she had a plan to commune with the bats. She picked the lock on the complex's maintenance shed and found a stepladder. With that in place, she raced up to the mounted ladder and onto the roof in no time.

Being surrounded by these amazing creatures, flying frenetically around her, energized her in a way that few experiences did. Her need to avenge Boze and Hatchet, her reservations about Dana Kim, and her conflicted feelings about Roz faded into the Zen of communing with nature. *Breathe in peace. Breathe out love.* Even with her eyes closed, she felt at one with the bats swarming and swooping around her.

When the bats had their fill and began squeezing their way back into the building's roof, Avery climbed down, carried the stepladder back to the maintenance shed, and returned to her apartment.

Once inside, she opened her phone and tried to connect to Jaden's stereo again. She found it in the list of open Bluetooth devices, but it wouldn't connect. She stepped outside onto the balcony and closer to Jaden's apartment.

The device connected. In her music app, she selected an old classic from the feminist punk band the Pink Trinkets. The name of the song was "Sad Tromboehner." The song title's odd spelling was a reference to a right-wing politician who used to cry a lot of crocodile tears. She hit Play.

"He walks the halls of power, with a smile on his face!" screamed Wicked, the band's lead singer.

Avery's body thrummed to the blaring rhythms.

"But deep down, he's a fraud, in a state of disgrace!" Avery sang along as she disappeared back into her apartment. The Bluetooth connection held, and the roar of the music continued through two sets of walls.

Shouts started coming from outside, followed by pounding on doors. Avery sang along as the joy of revenge filled her heart.

She got to the chorus and belted out, "Crybaby, crybaby, hypocrite in a suit! Crybaby, crybaby, you'll get what's coming to you!"

She imagined Mendez as she said the words, "You'll get what's coming to you!"

The song stopped abruptly in the middle of the second verse, much to Avery's disappointment. She was really getting into it. The fun was over, but the mission had been accomplished.

Avery was coming out of the shower when she heard knocking on her own door. She threw on a black Jack Skellington robe and peeked through the peephole. Two uniformed officers. *Shit!*

"Who is it?" she shouted as she hustled to her bedroom.

"Glendale Police. We need to ask you some questions."

"I'm not dressed. Hold on!"

She pulled on a black tie-dye summer dress and answered the door. "Can I help you officers?"

"We were wondering if you knew anything about the disturbance that occurred thirty minutes ago."

"You mean that loud music?" Avery shrugged. "Sounded like it was coming from Jaden's place."

"Is Jaden a friend of yours?"

Avery shook her head. "Definitely not. I only moved in a few weeks ago. He and his friends are really fond of loud music. They're always at the pool after hours, despite the rules. And lately, he's been getting up early and playing loud music then too. Guess school must be out, and they're partying around the clock. Honestly, I wish they would stop. A girl's gotta get some sleep sometime."

"Have you spoken to him about it?"

"I asked him to turn down the music about a week ago when he and his friends were at the pool after hours. They ignored me. I reported it to the management, and they didn't seem interested in doing anything about it. So I'm just trying to ignore them. Live and let live."

She wondered if they could tell she wasn't being completely honest, but they seemed to buy it.

"Anything else?" one cop asked.

"Nope. I hope you talk to them about it."

"Okay, thank you for your time."

They left, and she let out a long breath and smiled. "Fucking assholes. Teach you to mess with Avery the Avenger."

She checked her emails while eating her breakfast. Spam from tattoo supply companies. A notification about an upcoming convention in Tucson she was planning to attend with Bobby, Frisco, and Butcher. And an email from Roz. She opened it.

Hey, girl.

I enjoyed playing amateur sleuth with you. I hope that detective reopens the case.

BTW, I'm looking for a girlfriend. You interested in the job?

Hope to talk to ya soon.

Roz

A billion thoughts and emotions stormed inside of her. More than anything, she wanted to say yes.

But Sam had been murdered just a month earlier. The horror of finding her brutalized body and the terror of running from her killers had left her raw and broken. Was she was even capable of having a healthy relationship anymore?

And then there was the issue of her being transgender. Maybe Roz would be cool with it. Maybe she wouldn't. Some people were okay with friends who were trans but had a different standard for lovers.

And then there was her curse. So many people, especially women she'd loved, had been murdered. The Lost Kids, Melissa, and Sam. Maybe it was irrational, but she felt like the universe or God or karma was punishing her. Maybe for being transgender. Maybe for killing Vinnie D. Maybe both.

Avery didn't want to see Roz fall victim to the same horrible fate.

She debated whether to respond by email or to call her. Before she knew what she was doing, her finger clicked on Roz's phone number.

"Hey, sexy!" Roz said in a playful voice.

"Hey. I got your email. I haven't heard from Valentine. I'm taking that as a good sign."

"Fingers crossed."

"About your other question." Avery took a deep breath. "Why would you want to date me? I'm a wreck. I'm on the rebound. My last girlfriend was murdered. And… well, there's a lot you don't know about me."

"I know that you've been close friends with Kimi since you two were kids. She talks about you like you're the coolest person on the planet. In fact, she said, and I quote, 'If I were into chicks, I would totally date her.'"

"She did not say that."

"I swear to goth! So if she thinks you're so awesome, whatever it is I don't know about can't be that bad."

Avery wasn't sure what to say to that. Kimi knew all of her darkest secrets. Not that she would share them with anyone else without Avery's permission.

"Kimi likes everyone."

"Oh, no she doesn't. You know her. Is she best friends with just anyone?"

"I come with a lot of baggage."

"Who the hell doesn't these days?"

"Not like this. Roz, you're sexy as hell. And you're sweet and funny. Probably the coolest person I know."

"Well, thank you. I like you. You like me. So what's the problem?"

Avery considered coming out to Roz, but doing it over the phone didn't feel right. The thought of doing it in person was scary as hell. "Maybe we can meet over drinks after work. I get off today at six."

"Drinks sound great, but I'm working at Spy Gal until eight most of the week and helping my mom out afterward. She's having her carpets replaced and needs my help moving furniture. How about dinner on Friday night? What do you like? Seafood? Mexican? Burgers? Chinese? Pizza?"

"There's an upscale pizza joint called La Dolce Vita at the Esplanade on Camelback." Avery was thinking about the tall booths with lots of privacy. "Would that be okay?"

"Nice place. You've got good taste. What time? Seven?"

What are getting yourself into, girl? "Yeah. That works."

"It's a date. Or not. Just two friends trying to figure things out."

"Okay. I'll see you then."

CHAPTER 24

DOUBLE-BOOKED

She spent the next few days obsessing over her upcoming date with Roz. How would she explain she was trans without Roz freaking out?

Maybe I should just call and tell her over the phone. Rip off the fucking bandage. At least then, I won't have to see the horrible disappointment on her gorgeous face. No, don't be a coward, girl. This is something better done in person.

She debated asking Bobby for his advice. But already, she knew what he would say: "Just be yourself. If she doesn't like you, she's not the one."

He wasn't necessarily wrong, but he'd never had to come out to anyone.

She also considered talking to Kimi since she knew both Avery and Roz. But she didn't want to put Kimi in the awkward situation of choosing between friends if things went badly. But maybe it would happen anyway.

Or maybe Roz had already guessed she was trans. Avery always worried that her voice was too deep, her tits too small, or her hips too narrow. Being able to pass as well as she did was not a privilege all trans people had, but it was also a mindfuck. It made her paranoid.

On the plus side, she had slept rather well at night because her rowdy neighbors had been remarkably quiet since her little stunt had brought the police on a noise complaint. No more late-night pool parties.

Early Friday morning, her phone pinged with an email message.

Ms. Byrne,

I reviewed the contents of the USB drive you provided me. I can understand how you think this information implicates Mr. Mendez in the deaths of your friends. But after further research, I determined it doesn't warrant reopening the case.

Your friends died from an accidental overdose, tragic though it may be. I realize this isn't the outcome you wanted, but I must follow where the evidence leads.

I wish you the best.

Detective Lorenzo Valentine

Phoenix Police Department

Homicide Unit

"Fucking coward!" She called his phone number.

"Phoenix Homicide Unit, Detective Valentine speaking."

"You lazy son of a bitch!"

"Excuse me?"

"You and Hardin chased me all the way to New Mexico for a murder I didn't commit. But you won't get off your ass to investigate these two murders."

"Good morning, Ms. Byrne."

"Don't 'good morning' me, you asshole. Do your fucking job!"

"I did my job, ma'am. Even went down to Classic Auto Repair and found a bottle of ginger beer that Mendez bought in the shop fridge. I tested their contents for opioids, fentanyl, meth, and cannabis. All came back negative. So unless he put the fentanyl only in the ones your friends drank or he delivered the drugs some other way, there is no evidence of foul play."

"Did you talk to Mendez?"

"I did. He said he went to the shop to make amends to Mr. Hatchet for a disagreement they'd had prior to his going into treatment. Part of his addiction recovery, apparently. Also, the engine in his Plymouth was not stolen. He had documentation proving that. His only crime was DUI and possession. He has been meeting the sentencing requirements handed down by the drug court. I've got nothing to arrest him for."

"That's bullshit. He didn't even show up at their memorial."

"That's not a crime."

"He did it, Valentine. He's a murderer, and you're letting him get away with it."

"I'm sorry you feel that way, but I have to follow the evidence. Right now, the evidence still points to my original conclusion. Your friends died from an accidental overdose. It's tragic, but no crime has been committed. You have a good day, Ms. Byrne." He hung up.

She wanted to drive downtown and shake him until he actually got off his ass and did some real investigating. But she knew it wouldn't do any good. He was too busy, too lazy, or too stupid to pursue the case properly.

If Hatchet and Boze were to get justice, it was up to her to provide it. Would she have to kill someone again? She didn't own a gun, but Sam had taught her how to shoot.

She remembered slipping into Vinnie D's home. He'd been beating her friends who worked for him, but they refused to report Vinnie's abuse to the cops for fear of getting locked up themselves or facing retaliation from him.

So one night, when he and his buddies were shooting up, Avery snuck into his apartment and gave him an extra dose of heroin with a nice fat air bubble for insurance. She'd stood over him and watched as his breathing stopped.

A chill had come over her the moment she realized he was gone. She was a murderer. She had snuffed out a life. The life of an abusive asshole, but a life nevertheless.

She had considered doing the same to Vinnie D's two buddies who were passed out next to him. But they hadn't hurt her friends, as far as she knew.

In retrospect, maybe she should have. Not long after she sent Vinnie D into the afterlife, someone had murdered every one of the Lost Kids. It must have been one of the two of them.

All that was in the past. What the hell was she going to do now about Mendez? What if she took out her vengeance on Mendez, only to learn that he wasn't responsible? Avery wasn't willing to take that risk. She had to know for sure.

She had previously suspected Fisch of being the killer. Maybe her first instincts were right. He worked with Hatchet at Classic Auto Repair. It would have been easier for him to poison Hatch and Boze. But what would be his motive? A disgruntled employee? She'd never seen Fisch argue with either of them.

Avery needed to know for sure who the murderer was before she did anything to avenge her friends.

She called Roz.

"You're not cancelling our date for tonight, are you?" Roz asked, worry evident in her voice.

"What? Uh, no. I just wanted to tell you I just spoke with Valentine. The son of a bitch refused to reopen the case. "

"Oy vey! That's disappointing. Did he say why?"

"Too lazy to do his job if you ask me."

"What do you plan to do?"

"I don't know. Valentine claims Mendez showed up at Hatchet's garage to make amends. Some sort of Twelve Step recovery thing."

"So maybe Mendez isn't the killer."

"Or maybe he's good at covering his tracks."

"Could be. Look, I hate to cut you off, but a customer just came in. I'll see you tonight, okay?"

Avery shivered, again replaying her trying to come out to Roz. "Yes, definitely."

On the way to work, she was a few miles from Seoul Fire on Glendale Avenue when the Gothmobile's temperature gauge once again rose into the red.

"No, no, no!" She tapped the gauge, hoping that would make it go down. It didn't.

A Lincoln Town Car with Minnesota plates slogged along in front of her at five miles under the speed limit.

There was no one in front of the Lincoln for at least a quarter mile. A lazy pickup truck was cruising along beside it—two idiots who weren't in a hurry to go anywhere. And she was stuck behind the slow parade.

"Go, go, go!" she shouted at the Lincoln in front of her. "Fucking snowbirds!"

By the time she pulled into the Seoul Fire Tattoo parking lot, steam was once again spewing from under her hood. "Fuck!"

She grabbed her stuff and went inside. It would need to be towed. That was when an idea occurred to her. Of course! She would have it towed to Classic Auto Repair. After all, Hatchet was the one who'd restored the car for her. That would give her an excuse to ask more questions and maybe poke around the place a bit.

"Morning, kiddo," Bobby said when she walked in. "I'm looking forward to our dinner tonight. "

"Dinner?" And then Avery remembered she had agreed to go to dinner with him and Dana.

"We're planning on going to the Poké Bar on Bell Road. I think Dana will enjoy it." He gave Avery a look. "Assuming there's no unnecessary drama."

"No drama, Appa," she replied regretfully. "However…"

"However?"

"I kinda sorta double-booked myself."

"Double-booked yourself? Do you have another foster father that I don't know about?"

"Don't be silly." She explained about her date with Roz. "I'm really sorry. I do want to make up for ruining dinner last time, but…"

Bobby nodded. "I see. Well, why not bring her along? It can be a double date."

"It's not even really a date. I mean, it's only been a month since Sam died. I don't think I'm ready to be in another relationship. And it'd be super weird to bring my dad along."

"I wouldn't be there to chaperone. It'd be a double date. Or not really a date. Whatever you want to call it."

She glared at him as if he were being extraordinarily dense.

He held up his hands in surrender. "Okay, you don't want this girl to meet your adorable old dad—the man who rescued you from a life on the streets." He winked at her.

"That's not it, and you know it. I'm going to come out to her."

"I think she already knows you're gay."

"Appa…"

"Just kidding. You're going to tell her you're transgender. Sure you don't want me along for moral support?"

Frisco walked in, and they exchanged hellos.

"Might feel like we're ganging up on her," Avery said, watching Frisco prep her station.

"Ganging up? No one's ganging up on anyone."

"I know. It's just… I don't know. Just feels like something I should tell her on my own."

"Any idea how she might react?"

"No."

"Well, if you change your mind, I'm there for you."

"Thanks, Appa. As if that wasn't enough to deal with, I have to get the Gothmobile fixed. It's overheating. Any chance you can take my first client this morning?"

Disappointment spread across Bobby's face. "You and I need to have a talk about customer service. You've been late and missing appointments again."

"It's not my fault. Something's wrong with the radiator. I filled it with coolant the other day. And now it's like Old Faithful out there. It's not my fault."

He sighed. "Perhaps not this. But that's why it's important to be on time when you can help it. No more playing Harriet the Spy. You are not a cop. You are not a private eye. You are a tattoo artist. And a damn talented one.

But when word gets around that you're routinely late or missing appointments, you're going to be an unemployed tattoo artist. I built this shop not only on my skills as an artist but on my dedication to my clients. They know when they book an appointment with me, I will be there, on time, and I will deliver. You understand me?"

"Yes, Appa." She hated that he was right.

"That reminds me." Bobby turned to Frisco. "Mrs. Abbott left a message, said she needed to cancel. Her kid caught a summer cold."

Frisco looked up and made a sad face. "Poor thing. I'll call her and see about rescheduling."

"Since you've got an opening, you mind filling in for Avery's ten o'clock? She's got to take the Gothmobile to the shop."

"Sure. Happy to help. New client?"

"Existing," Avery replied. "But a new tat. I can send you the sketches she approved. And thanks."

"Any time." Frisco flashed her a smile.

"Okay, let me see about a tow truck. And a rental."

"Call your client first," Bobby instructed Avery. "Let her know you have to take your car to the shop and that Frisco will cover for you. Make sure she's okay with it."

Avery didn't see why that was necessary, but she figured Bobby was right, as usual.

CHAPTER 25

NEXT OF KIN

Avery's client wasn't thrilled about switching artists, but she understood. Avery then arranged for a tow truck and called for a rental car.

An hour later, Avery was driving what felt like a tin can on wheels that would easily fit into the Gothmobile's trunk. It was better than ending up stranded on the side of the road, but not by much.

At Classic Auto Repair, Emily Yazzie was manning the customer service counter. She wore little makeup but was gorgeous without it.

"It's Avery, right?" Emily asked. "Nice to see you again. How can I help you today?"

"I had my '57 Caddy towed in."

"Arrived ten minutes ago. What's going on with it?"

"It keeps overheating, even though it's got plenty of coolant."

"How frustrating! We'll take a look. Could be a bad thermostat or a blockage somewhere. When was the last time you had it flushed?"

"A while."

"Okay, we'll check it out. You're already in our system. We'll call you when we know something."

"Thanks. How are you holding up?" Avery asked.

Emily managed a stoic expression, but Avery could see the pain in her eyes.

"As best as can be expected. Cops were here again the other day, asking more questions. I thought for a moment they might actually reopen the case since Hatch would never have taken drugs. But no, still calling it an accidental overdose."

She wiped a tear and glanced up at Avery. "I'm sorry. You just asked how I was doing, and I go on a rant."

"Nothing to apologize for. I've been there."

"That's right. You mentioned your girlfriend died recently. My condolences."

"Thanks. That same asshole detective chased me all the way to New Mexico, thinking I killed her. Turns out his lieutenant was working for the people who did."

"Shit, are you serious? You think Valentine's dirty?"

"I don't know."

"I thought about hiring a private investigator. But this shop's barely breaking even, and Hatch had put so much of our personal savings into his racing. I didn't mind at the time. But now, with him gone, I could sure use it to find out what really happened."

"Maybe I can find out what happened."

Fisch walked in from the service bay. "What the hell's she doing here?"

"She brought her Caddy in for service," Emily snapped. "You got a problem with that?"

"No. We just don't need her nosing around, asking questions, and getting you all upset."

Suddenly, Avery worried about leaving the Gothmobile here. Would he sabotage it?

"I'm already upset, Fisch. Hatch is dead, remember? And I'm left trying to keep this place afloat, which you're not helping by chasing off our paying customers."

Fisch's gaze dropped to the floor. "Sorry. Just came to tell you the Nelson repair is complete."

"Great. Thanks! Now you can get to work on her Caddy. It's overheating."

He looked at Avery. "Forget to put coolant in it?"

She glared back at him. "No, it's got plenty of coolant. Still overheating."

"Whatever. I'll check it out." He shuffled back into the service bay.

"Sorry about him," Emily said. "He's been a little overprotective since Hatch died."

"I understand," Avery replied, though she suspected he had a different motive for telling her off. "As I said, I'm happy to look into what happened. But only if you want."

"I'd like that. Thank you."

"Figured I owe it to him. He gave me such a good price for restoring the Gothmobile in the first place."

"He was a great guy. Let me know if you find out anything. And thank you."

"You're welcome." Avery hesitated. "Maybe I could look at the security feed, if you still have it from that night."

A cloud passed over Emily's face. "The system only stores a week at a time."

"Yeah, I guess that makes sense. Video takes up a lot of memory, I imagine."

"We only have cameras on the outside. And no audio. I watched it. Didn't really show anything."

"Nothing?"

"The only person who showed up before Hatch and Boze drove off was Mendez. He stopped by to patch things up after their big fight before he went into rehab."

"So Mendez was here. Did he drop off a four-pack of ginger beer?"

"Yeah, Red Dragon. It was Hatch's favorite. How'd you know?"

"I've…" Avery hesitated, ashamed to admit she'd already been looking into the matter. "I think Mendez put the drugs into the ginger beer."

"I wondered about that. But there was one bottle left in the shop fridge when Detective Valentine came back by a few days ago. He tested it and said it was clean. No drugs. Besides, Fisch told me that Mendez came by to make amends. Some Twelve Step recovery thing. I don't think it was him."

"Fisch was here that night too?"

"He and Hatch were working late on a car for a client. Boze showed up to lend a hand too."

"And what did Fisch say happened that night?"

"Boze arrived around the time we closed at six. Mendez showed up an hour later and apologized for how he'd treated Hatch before going into rehab. Said his addiction had turned his whole life to crap, and he had no one to blame but himself."

"Did he sound sincere?"

"Fisch thought so. Then after Mendez left, Boze started not feeling well. He fell and hit his head, so Hatch drove him to the hospital."

"And Fisch didn't go with them?"

"He was finishing up the repair job Hatch had been working on. Also, they were expecting Big Eddie Myles to drop off a part."

"Big Eddie? What was he dropping off?"

"I don't know specifically. Just some part Hatch needed that was on back order through our regular suppliers. Big Eddie had a spare he was bringing over."

"And did Big Eddie show?"

"A couple of hours after Hatch and Boze left."

"And you believe Fisch?"

"About what?"

"About everything he claimed happened that night."

"No reason not to." Emily shrugged. "I know this rivalry between the Old Schoolers and the Innovators has been heated lately. But I don't see Mendez wanting to kill Hatch. Especially just after getting out of rehab."

Avery didn't bring up the text conversation where Mendez threatened to kill Hatchet, but another thought occurred to her. "The bottle was still in the shop fridge more than a week after Hatch died?"

"No one else drinks it around here. And I'd forgotten about it until Valentine came to test them. Why?"

"Maybe someone switched out the bottles."

"Who would do that?" Emotion crept into Emily's voice. "Fisch?"

"You can't be serious. No way! Fisch, Hatch, and Boze were like the Three Musketeers. Practically brothers."

Brothers fight, Avery thought. *Some even kill each other.* "At the memorial, Fisch looked like he'd been beaten up. He say what happened?"

"On the way home from the shop that night, some asshole at a gas station called him a 'Jew boy'. They got into fist fight, which Fisch lost. Why?"

Avery shrugged. "I don't know. Just seems odd. He gets beaten up the same night that Hatch and Boze get killed. Doesn't Big Eddie work on Mendez's crew?"

"Sure, but like I said, Mendez came by to patch things up. Eddie just dropped off a part and left."

"Maybe you're right. I just can't think of how else someone could have drugged them. Or why. But I'll keep looking into it for you."

"I appreciate that. I'll call you when we know what's going on with the Gothmobile."

"Thanks."

CHAPTER 26

CLOSER TO FEIN

Avery arrived at La Dolce Vita at exactly seven. She'd had time to change into her favorite low-cut midnight-blue dress, which showed off her cleavage. She toned down the goth makeup, but just a smidge.

"Will someone be joining the lady this evening?" asked a heavyset maître d' with a thin mustache and even thinner hair.

"Yes, my… uh, a friend of mine." She'd almost said *girlfriend.*

Jumping the gun, aren't you? she thought.

The door behind her jingled. Avery turned to see Roz, again dressed in a white button-down shirt, a bolo tie, and a black silk jacket that looked stunning on her.

"You made it." Roz's smile sent shivers of excitement down Avery's spine.

"I did."

"I didn't see the Batmobile out there."

"Gothmobile," Avery corrected. "It's at the shop. Engine's been overheating."

"Bummer." Roz turned to the maître d'. "Two for dinner. Reservation's under Fein."

The man checked the calendar. "Ah, yes. Your table awaits. Right this way, ladies."

After their server had taken their drinks order, Roz again flashed that million-dollar smile. "So, what's the big secret that you couldn't tell me over the phone?"

Avery drew in a big breath. "Roz, when I was thirteen, my birth father kicked me out of the house."

Roz's eyes widened. "What a putz! Was it because you're lesbian?"

Avery wanted more than anything to say it was because she was trans. But again, her courage failed her. "Something like that."

"How horrible! What did you do?"

"Lived on the streets for a while. Then me and some other homeless teens squatted in an empty house for a few years until Bobby and his wife, Melissa, took me in."

"Wow, I can't imagine. That must've been so scary. What did you do for money?"

Avery stared down at her drink. "Whatever I had to."

"Yeah, you don't have to give me the gory details." Roz put her warm, gentle hand on Avery's. "I'm just glad you survived. And now here we are, having a nice dinner together."

"What was it like when you came out?" Avery asked, desperate to change the subject.

A chuckle escaped Roz. "Well, it was a week before my bat mitzvah. I was going into an emotional tailspin. Finally, my folks sat me down to ask me what was wrong. They were afraid I'd been raped or bullied. When I finally told them, my dad laughed and said he already knew. Being a PI, he didn't miss much. Mom insisted that my being a lesbian didn't mean I didn't have to practice safe sex. My brothers didn't care. I'd grown up playing football with them. They already considered me a tomboy. "

"I'm glad it went so well. We should all be so lucky."

"I agree."

"So this job offer… it's still… valid?"

"In all fifty states. Avery, I can only imagine the horrible things you've been through. But let me assure you, I would never judge you for any of it. You are sexy and weird—in a good way—and funny and wickedly talented and have awesome taste in music, and I like your mind. And I'd like to be your girlfriend. Again, if you're interested in the job."

A tidal wave of emotion flooded Avery's mind. It took everything inside her not to cry. "Thank you."

"Is that a yes to my offer."

"Yes, yes, for goth's sake, yes!" Avery clasped Roz's hand.

She caught the eye of a middle-aged couple a few tables over, eyeing them suspiciously. Avery didn't care.

Their server approached. "So do you ladies know what you'd like to order?"

"How are your fish tacos?" Roz asked with a wink.

The absurdity and innuendo in the question caused Avery to do a spit take as she sipped her drink.

"On second thought, we'll have a medium-sized Margherita pizza."

"Excellent choice."

While they waited for their order, Avery filled Roz in on what she'd learned from Emily that morning.

"I'm still not convinced it wasn't murder. This other guy, Fisch—real name Jude Fischman—works there at the garage. He, Hatchet, and Boze were all really close. But on the same night Hatch and Boze died from an unexplainable drug overdose, Fisch got beaten up."

"Did he say by whom?"

"Claims he got jumped by a guy making antisemitic remarks. But I don't buy it. Emily says Fisch was still at the garage when Hatch and Boze took off for the hospital. And a little while later, a guy on Mendez's crew showed up at the garage, supposedly to drop off a part needed for a car repair."

"You think Fisch is lying?"

"My gut's telling me Big Eddie beat up Fisch."

"Who's Big Eddie?"

"Big Eddie Myles. About six foot something, mullet haircut, built like a side of beef. Could lift an engine block with his bare hands."

"So, pretty much a wimp," Roz replied with a wry smile.

"Totally."

"Why would Big Eddie beat up Fisch if Mendez was trying to patch things up?"

"I don't know. But I don't like coincidences. When I was asking questions at the memorial, Fisch got in my face, telling me to mind my own business. Like he was afraid I might learn something."

"You want me to do a background check on him?"

"You mind?"

"Hell no. I paid for SkipTrakkr for the whole month. Might as well get my money's worth, right? Besides, it's fun."

"You had to pay for it? How much? I'll repay you."

"Forget about it. I got it covered. You're my girlfriend, after all." Roz winked.

A warm feeling spread through Avery. "Thanks."

Their pizza arrived, and conversation ceased while they devoured the pie.

After dinner, they walked out into the parking lot holding hands. Between the wine and the euphoric emotions of newfound love, Avery was floating on a pink cloud of serotonin. How long had it been since she'd felt this way? Even the fact that she hadn't come out didn't tarnish the feeling.

"This is me," Avery said when they reached her rental.

"Wow, it's so tiny."

"Yeah, goth help me if I get in an accident. Probably crumple like a soda can."

"Hopefully, you can get the Gothmobile back soon."

"I had a great time tonight." Avery gazed up into Roz's face. Her heart was beating like she'd just run a fifty-yard dash. Their lips were inches apart.

"I did too." Roz's voice was a whisper filled with promise. "I'm glad you accepted my offer."

"Just hope you don't regret dating someone on the rebound. You don't know what a dumpster fire it left me."

"We all have baggage. And if you feel you're not ready to date again, that's okay. I won't be offended. No pressure. I just like you. And maybe I can help you work through the pain. My last girlfriend dumped me for some overweight ex-Marine. A guy, no less. And that was two years ago. It still hurts."

"Well, as fucked up as I am, I'm very loyal. I don't cheat. So you don't have to worry about that. I just hope you're not looking at me as something you gotta fix."

Roz brushed a strand of hair out of Avery's face. "Definitely not. I'm not here to fix you. You're not here to fix me. But maybe through loving each other, we heal ourselves."

"Shit. That's deep. You sure you're not some psychologist?"

"I majored in psych in college with a minor in philosophy. How about you?"

Suddenly, Avery felt small and out of her league. "Never went to college. Not even high school. Got my GED when I was seventeen."

"Oh, right. Homeless teen. Sorry, I forgot."

"Bobby and Melissa encouraged me to apply. Even offered to pay for it. But I'd had enough school. All the cliques and bullying, not to mention studying things I'd never use in my adult life, like trigonometry and the War of 1812 and diagraming sentences and shit."

"I hear you. I hated high school. Being Jewish and goth didn't exactly earn me a spot on the cheerleading squad. But college was different. Yeah, some of the intro courses were boring. But I really dug psychology and philosophy."

"You didn't go on to become a therapist?"

"I applied for graduate school, but my dad died a month before classes started. I dropped out and ended up taking over the store. I still think about going back. But honestly, I enjoy running the store and meet a lot of interesting people."

"And psychoanalyze them."

"Oh, no, I'd *never* do that," Roz replied wryly.

"You'd have a field day with me." Avery again felt the urge to come out as transgender to her but couldn't push past her resistance.

"If anything, studying psychology and philosophy taught me that most of us are just doing the best we can with what life has thrown our way."

"It's thrown me a helluva lot."

"Sounds like it has. But right here, right now, we have each other. And you have friends like Kimi and Chupa. And you have Bobby. And you have a promising career as a tattoo artist."

"Yeah, my life's gotten a lot better. Except for losing Sam. And now Hatchet."

"Anytime you need to cry or talk about what happened to your ex-girlfriend, that's okay. I won't be offended or jealous. I promise. And I won't psychoanalyze you or try to fix you. I'll just love you and be there for you."

"Shit. You're, like, too good to be true."

"Nah, I just know what a shitty world it can be sometimes."

"But why pick me to be your girlfriend?"

"Why not you?"

"I'm afraid."

"Why? That I'm going to dump you?"

Her chest felt tight. She was ashamed of holding in her secret from this beautiful, kind woman and terrified the curse would strike again. "So many people I've cared for have been killed. The kids I knew when I was homeless. My foster mom, Melissa. And then Sam, my former girlfriend. Someone even shot Chupa because they were trying to get to me."

"Kimi mentioned he'd been shot. That was because of you?"

The expression on Roz's face felt like a knife in the gut. "Sam worked for the Desert Mafia and stole a bunch of their money. They tortured and killed her to get it back, then they came after me when they thought I had it. And when they couldn't find me, they went after the people close to me, starting with Chupa."

Roz didn't speak right away. "What happened to the money?"

"I found it in one of Sam's bags. I gave it to the Mexican cartel. It ultimately belonged to them." That was half true. She'd kept half for herself. Much of the stacks of hundred-dollar bills were still deep in her bedroom closet.

"What about Melissa? How did she die?"

"That bomb that went off a few years ago at Bolin Plaza downtown."

"I remember. That domestic terrorist group White Nation was responsible, right?"

Avery nodded, feeling too choked up to speak.

"Wow. I'm so sorry. You have been through some serious shit."

"I'm cursed. Anyone who gets close to me is at risk."

"All due respect, Avery, that's a whole lotta bullshit. You're not cursed. No more than my family was during the Holocaust. Sometimes, shit just happens. Awful people do awful things. It's a shonde. But it's not a curse."

"Just thought I should warn you. Especially since we're looking into who killed Hatchet and Boze."

"No worries. I think we should be okay. And if not, I've got Avery the Avenger to protect me."

Avery chuckled sardonically. "Yeah, right."

"You want to follow me back to my place?"

"Sure. Where do you live?"

"Camelback and Fortieth Street. Stonewall Apartments."

"Stonewall? I hear those are nice."

"They are. Not cheap either. But it's gated. And most of the residents are queer. The few that aren't are queer friendly."

"Sounds nice. I'll follow you. Where's your car?"

"Right over there. The tan one." She pointed to a tan vehicle that looked like a cross between a convertible VW Beetle and a World War II army jeep.

"What the hell is that?"

"I call it Thing, after the character in the Addams Family."

"Cute. What kind of car is it?"

"Officially, it's a 1973 Volkswagen Type 181, but most people call it a VW Thing. So I just call it Thing."

"Wow! Very distinct-looking. I guess it will be easy to follow you back to your place."

CHAPTER 27

A LITTLE COLOR

It took Avery a moment to realize where she was when she woke the next morning. The sheets were softer than the ones on her bed. She rolled over and saw Roz laying beside her, eyes open and watching her.

"Morning," Avery whispered groggily.

"Good morning, lover," Roz replied with a smile then kissed her. "Last night was amazing."

It had been. They'd made love three times. Avery was sore, but her body still tingled from her last orgasm. A part of her felt guilty for still not coming out about being trans.

"You sure you want me as your girlfriend?"

"You kidding? I have no regrets. You're a helluva lover." Roz kissed her again, deeper this time, leaving Avery breathless.

"What… are your… plans… for the day?" Avery managed to ask between kisses.

"Technically…" Kisses. "I'm supposed to open the shop." More kisses. "I'll call Polly. Ask her to fill in. That is, if you'd like to spend the day together."

Kisses. "I won't object."

"You have any clients today?"

"Schedule's clear." Avery pulled back and gazed into Roz's beautiful eyes. "Tonight, the Sonoran Crows have their final race night of the season."

"Sounds like an exciting night of street racing and sleuthing."

"My thoughts exactly."

"Wait a minute! Stop the presses!" Roz held up her index finger to emphasize her point. "You do have a tattoo client scheduled for today."

"I do?" Avery searched her sleep-deprived brain for a forgotten appointment. Bobby would have a conniption if she blew off another client. "Who?"

"Me! This poor mermaid needs some color." Roz pointed to the outlined tattoo on her bicep.

Avery inspected the tattoo. The initial pinkness had faded. No signs of infection. The scabs were gone. "How's it feel?"

"Like it needs color."

"Okay then. We will start the coloring."

"And afterward, we could just hang out or see if Kimi and the band are doing anything fun this afternoon. There's a new horror flick, *Shadow Monster*, that's playing in theaters. Getting decent reviews."

"Or do a little digging into Jude Fischman, find out how he fits into all of this mess. Might give us an edge for when we start asking questions at race night."

"Good thinking."

Avery stared into this amazing woman's eyes. Roz was everything she'd ever wanted in a girlfriend. Beautiful, kind, funny, and smart. But every time Avery got to the point of telling Roz she was trans, shame strangled the words in her throat.

Roz would find out eventually. Someone would let it slip or assume Roz already knew. And then the whole relationship would collapse in a torrent of humiliation and possibly violence.

"Avery, is something wrong? Why are you crying? Did I say something wrong?"

She hadn't realized she was crying. "No, you're amazing. It's… It's me. I'm just afraid that when you get to know the real me that you'll run screaming."

"Does Kimi know the real you?"

"Yes. But she and I… We never…"

"No, but if you were really as horrible as you say, she wouldn't be your friend. She's very picky about who she lets into her world. So what is so horrible about you that it would send me screaming away?"

Avery held her gaze for what felt like forever. But the words would not come. "Nothing, I guess."

"You feeling guilty about us having sex so soon after your ex died?"

"I guess that's it."

"We can take it slower for a while if it would make you feel more comfortable. There's no rush. Oh shit, now you're crying more."

"I've never had someone as kind as you. I mean, Sam was great. But you… You're so goddamn caring and compassionate."

"I learned it from my folks. You ever see that movie *Kissing Jessica Stein*?"

"I saw about half and turned it off. Too awkward. The whole intimacy-avoidance thing. So frustrating."

"Yeah, a lot of awkward scenes in there. And honestly, the ending felt contrived. But there's this one amazing scene three-quarters through the film where Jennifer Westfeldt, who plays Jessica, is sitting on the porch with Tovah Feldshuh, who does an absolute bang-up job as Jess's mom. And Jessica is so desperate to come out and at the same time terrified how her mother will react. It's…"

Emotion filled Roz's voice, and her eyes glimmered with tears. "Oy, it's a real gut punch. But just so beautiful, you know? And Jessica never actually says she's gay. But her mom somehow knows anyway and says, 'I think she's a very nice girl.'"

"That's sweet."

Roz wiped away a tear. "I bawl like a baby every time she says that line. Because you can tell this is a stretch for Jess's mom. Not how she envisioned her daughter's life. But she loves her and accepts her and embraces her for exactly who she is. That's how my folks were. And how I hope I'll be if I ever have kids, no matter who or what they turn out to be."

Avery wondered if this was Roz's way of saying she already knew Avery was transgender. "Sounds really nice. Sure better than getting kicked out on the street."

"No doubt. But Bobby seems like a great foster dad."

"He is. When he and I first met, I had broken into his tattoo shop downtown looking for stuff to pawn."

"You're kidding. You did that?"

"Not proud of it, but yeah. Only instead of turning me in to the cops, he and Melissa took me in. And he's been more of a dad than my bio father ever was. Even if he is a dorky *Star Wars* geek. I sometimes call him Obi-Kwon Kenobi because he's always quoting the shows, imparting silly Jedi wisdom."

"He must've seen something special in you."

"Or took pity on me."

"You really think that's why?"

"I don't know."

"I think he could tell you were remarkable. Maybe he felt it in the Force," Roz teased.

"Maybe."

"And I think you're remarkable too, Avery. You've had a shitload of trauma in your life. I know that. And maybe you've done some shit you're not proud of. Things you had to do to survive. I won't judge. But I'm here for you. And I'm not going anywhere."

You say that now, Avery thought. "Thank you" was all she could say.

Roz stood up. "Okay, come on. Time for me to get some more ink. Mind if we take your car?"

"Sure."

They showered, inhaled a quick breakfast, and got dressed. Rather than put on the dress from the night before, Avery borrowed a shirt and black jeans from Roz, though they were a little long.

“Morning, Avery!” Frisco was tattooing a man’s chest when they walked into the shop. “Didn’t expect you in today.”

“Last-minute appointment. Frisco, this is my girlfriend, Roz Fein. Roz, this is Frisco Stuart. She’s worked at the shop almost as long as I have.”

Frisco grinned like the Cheshire cat. “I had a feeling about you two. Nice to meet you, Roz. Avery here’s a keeper.”

“Pleasure to meet you too, Frisco. And I agree.”

“Gah! Would you two stop! You’re embarrassing me. Come on, Roz. Let me get you prepped.”

Four hours later, the mermaid was practically exploding off Roz’s arm in living color. Roz had started to squirm in the last half hour, while Avery worked on the tail on the underside of the arm.

“You okay?” Avery asked.

Roz offered a pained smile. “Fine. We almost done?”

“Almost. You need a break?”

“Nope! Just do it.”

“Okay.”

When Avery was finished with the coloring, Roz again couldn’t stop staring at it in the mirror.

“It will look even better in a few weeks, once I add some shading. I could also add some other sea creatures around her for a more panoramic scene. But only if you want.”

“Oh yes. I want.” Roz kissed her.

“Okay, I’ll wrap it, and then we can go.”

“Let’s see.” Frisco was wiping down her station after her client left.

Roz modeled it for her.

“Damn fine work, girl!”

“Thanks.” Avery was pleased with how it turned out, but she was emotionally drained.

CHAPTER 28

FISCHING EXPEDITION

After they got back to Roz's apartment, Roz opened her laptop and logged in to SkipTrakkr. Avery sat next to her, feeding her what she knew about Fisch, so they were sure they had the right guy.

"Okay, Judah Isaac Fischman worked as an electronic engineer for Tesla for ten years," Roz said, reading the report on the screen. "Three years ago, our guy moved to Phoenix, where he started working for Quasar Motors. Then last October, he got a job as an auto mechanic at Classic Auto Repair. I bet that was a pay hit."

"Fisch worked for Tesla and Quasar? They're both cutting-edge auto manufacturers. Quasar's CEO, Guy Thorne, was named *Time Magazine*'s Most Influential Person last year. How's an engineer who worked for Guy Thorne end up as a grease monkey in an auto repair shop?"

"That's the ten-thousand-dollar question," Roz replied. "Maybe he got caught doing something unethical. Sexually harassing a coworker. Stealing. Dissing the company on social media."

Avery studied the credit report. "Look at this. In the past year, he's been late several times paying his mortgage, his car loan, and his credit card bills. But in the past month, he's brought everything current, though he still has a helluva lot of debt. Run his criminal record."

"Your wish is my command, m'lady." Roz clicked the button to generate the report.

Avery frowned when the screen refreshed. "Nothing. Not even a speeding ticket? So whatever he did to get shitcanned at Quasar wasn't criminal."

"But you don't know for sure that he was fired. Maybe he got sick of the job and quit. A lot of those high-tech corporations are real burnout mills, requiring eighty-hour work weeks, on call twenty-four seven. It can be a living hell after a while."

"Maybe. But he's an electronics engineer. If he quit, you'd think he could find a position with a company that doesn't treat their talent like shit. Their major competitor, Zeiber, also has a facility here. Why take a job as a mechanic?"

"Maybe someone at Quasar gave him a bad reference. Who knows?"

"I still think Quasar fired him. Just not sure why." A memory popped up in the back of her mind. "Mind if I check something?"

"Go ahead." Roz slid the laptop over to Avery.

Avery ran a news search for Quasar Motors. The first few stories were about the corporation's latest financial news, the rising stock price, and opening a new plant in Colorado. But then she found a story that she'd vaguely recalled from the previous September. "A prototype car was stolen from their Arizona testing grounds. No arrests. Vehicle not recovered."

Avery looked for more recent articles but didn't find any follow-ups. "I think Fisch was involved in stealing this prototype."

"Wouldn't Quasar have had him arrested?"

"Unless they couldn't prove it."

"So if he stole this prototype last year, what would he have done with it? Doesn't look like he sold it. Financially, he was struggling until this past month."

Avery considered Roz's question. "Maybe he waited until the heat died down or he could have had trouble finding a buyer. I imagine something like a bleeding-edge car prototype could be hard to unload. Let's look at his bank accounts."

Fisch had a little over two grand in his checking account. Avery pointed to a transaction on the screen. "Four weeks ago, he made a cash deposit of nine thousand dollars. Just below the limit where the bank has to report it to the IRS. And then another nine thousand two weeks later. Just yesterday, he deposited another two grand in cash. Where's all this money coming from?"

"It's going out just as fast as he gets current on his debts," Roz replied. "Doubling up on his mortgage payment, three payments to GM for his car loan. And a big payment on one of his credit cards."

Something clicked in Avery's brain. "Mendez."

"What about Mendez?"

"Fisch starts making big cash deposits around the time that Mendez shows up to the race nights with this new engine he won't show anybody. Fisch sold the stolen prototype to Mendez."

"Okay, that tracks. But then why kill Boze and Hatchet?"

Avery didn't have an answer to that. "I don't know. Maybe Hatchet found out that Fisch, a friend he'd hired, had stolen a prototype car from Quasar and sold it to Mendez, Hatch's biggest rival. And since Mendez and Hatchet were already butting heads over the whole Old Schooler-versus-Innovator beef, maybe Hatchet felt betrayed and threatened to turn Fisch in. Only Fisch and Mendez killed him before he could talk to the cops."

"That's a lot of conjecture there, Agatha Christie."

"It's the only thing that makes sense. Unless you can think of anything else. Maybe there's something in his texts that would confirm one way or another."

Roz pulled up the report for Fisch's SMS log for the past month, but there was nothing.

"Let me try for the past three months." Roz changed the search parameters, but the results were the same. "Maybe he doesn't text. Some people don't."

"Or he's using a burner."

"Okay, let's say you're right, and that Fisch and Mendez conspired to kill Hatchet and Boze. How do we prove it? And what are we going to do once we can? Especially if Valentine refuses to reopen the case."

"If Fisch and Mendez murdered Hatchet and Boze, they deserve to be punished."

"You mean they should die." Roz's expression grew deadly serious. "Okay, but we have to be absolutely sure. I don't want to find out later they were innocent."

Avery had considered that before. The people that she'd punished in the past had been guilty beyond any doubt. Vinnie D, the abusive pimp. Paul Andrews, the pedophile running the Samariteen shelter. Chloe Howard, the slumlord who forced her tenants to live in squalor while she lived the high life. And of course, the members of the Desert Mafia who had murdered Sam and tried to pin it on her.

"Agreed. We don't do anything to them until we have absolute proof."

"Like what? A confession? How would you get that? Beat it out of them?"

"Maybe I can get one to turn on the other."

Before they could continue the conversation, Avery's phone rang. It was Classic Auto Repair.

"Well, I've got good news and bad news," Emily said. "The good news is that the problem is a failed thermostat, which isn't expensive. Only about twenty bucks."

"That's a relief. What's the bad news?"

"Supply-chain issues. It may take a week or more to get one in."

"Crap. Okay. Go ahead and order it."

"Will do."

"Will you be at tonight's race night?" Avery asked.

"No, I need to take a break from all things Sonoran Crow for a while."

"I understand. I'm still looking into what happened." Avery was tempted to tell Emily what she'd found out about Fisch but decided to hold off until she knew something definitive.

"Honestly, Avery, maybe you should let it go. It won't bring Hatch or Boze back. And if the cops are sure it was an accident, maybe it was."

She felt the wind go out of her sails. "You sure?"

"Fisch is right. It's better for me to let it go and focus on moving forward."

"It's Fisch's idea to leave it alone?"

"It is, but I agree with him."

"Yeah, okay. Whatever you want. Let me know when the Gothmobile's ready."

Avery hung up. She wanted to respect Emily's wishes. But something inside her couldn't let this go. Not until she knew for sure.

CHAPTER 29

RACE NIGHT

At nine o'clock that night, Avery and Roz pulled off the two-lane highway southwest of Phoenix between the towns of Hassayampa and Arlington. There were so many cars, trucks, and trailers on the side of the road that Roz had to park her VW Thing a quarter mile from the starting line.

Taking Roz's car had been Avery's suggestion. Showing up at the Sonoran Crow race night in a modern subcompact just seemed wrong. At least Roz's Thing was retro and had a lot of character, though not all of it was good.

Despite the sun having been down for a couple hours, the car's after-market air conditioner had trouble fending off the sweltering summer heat. Its anemic engine sounded like a leaf blower on steroids and still struggled to keep up with traffic.

No padded leather interior aside from the seats. Only bare metal with a few analogue gauges that glowed from the dash. No stereo of any kind. And the floorboards were actual boards that looked like they'd been cut from a wooden pallet.

"I don't know how you drive this thing during the day in summer," Avery said when they got out.

Roz shrugged. "You get used to it after a while. It's a quirky car, I know. Slow, loud, and extremely spartan. But as soon as I sat in it, I absolutely fell head over heels in love with it. What can I say? I have a thing for the weird and out of the ordinary."

"So that's why you wanted to date me." Avery met Roz by the driver's door, and their fingers intertwined as if it were the most natural thing in the world. A rush of happiness flooded through her, almost pushing away the nervousness she felt about her desire to track down Boze and Hatchet's killer or killers.

They walked to where dozens of classic cars sat idling in the road, revving their engines, and doing last-minute preparations for the races. The air was heavy with the odors of burned rubber, gasoline, nitrous, and creosote.

"So this is street racing," Roz said. "How is this not illegal?"

"Technically, it is. But Major Tom—the guy over there in the black '69 Impala—is a commander with the Phoenix PD and has friends in the sheriff's office. Somehow, he keeps his buddies in blue away."

"But if the cops did show up, we could get busted."

"We're not racing, so at worst, we might get a ticket for illegal parking."

"Aw, I was hoping for something dangerous." The corners of Roz's mouth curled in a devious grin.

"Well, we are looking for a killer amongst these adrenaline-addicted gearheads. That's dangerous enough for me."

"Fair enough."

As they mingled with the crowd, a voice called out Avery's name. She turned and recognized Fisch's wife, Carolyn.

"Hey! How's it going?" Avery said a little stiffly.

Carolyn shrugged. "Been a rough year since Jude lost his job at Quasar, you know? It's really taken a toll."

"I can imagine."

"Jude really loved that job. And the noncompete clause in his contract made it so he couldn't take on a similar one for a year." Carolyn's eyes glimmered in the dim glow of headlights. "Fortunately, he's started winning some races. That's helped."

"What races did Jude win?" Last Avery remembered, Jude had been on an uninterrupted losing streak, though she had missed a couple of race nights after Sam was killed.

"At the Duel in the Desert with the 388s a couple of months ago. And a few of the recent race nights. Brought home twenty grand all told. It helped us catch up on our bills and pay off one of our credit cards. Finally have some breathing room. I just hope Emily keeps the shop running now that Hatchet is gone."

Avery remembered the Duel in the Desert meet. The 388s were a rival street racing club in the Valley, though their cars were more modern. There had been so much trash talk between the two clubs you could nearly taste the testosterone in the air. But Fisch hadn't won any races. He got the money elsewhere. Most likely from selling the stolen Quasar prototype to Mendez, who had beat all comers that night.

"I'm happy for you, Carolyn. I'm sure the shop will stay open. They seemed busy the other day when I dropped my car off."

"That's good to hear. Once Fisch can get his career on track again, I know we'll be okay. I hate to say it, but Hatchet's death may be the push he needed to apply for some engineer jobs again after those idiots at Quasar tried to pin that prototype theft on him."

Fisch approached, took one look at Avery, and scowled. "Carolyn, what the hell are you talking to her for?"

"Don't be rude. Just a little friendly girl talk." Carolyn turned to Roz. "I'm sorry, I didn't get your name. I'm Carolyn Fischman."

"Roz Fein." They shook hands.

"Fein? Not Abigail's daughter, are you?"

"I am. You know my mother?"

"From temple. I was at your father's unveiling. I'm so sorry."

"Thanks."

"You two need to mind your own fucking business." Fisch glared at Avery.

"And you're a fucking liar. I was at the Duel in the Desert. You didn't win shit unless you were betting against yourself."

Carolyn gave her husband a questioning look. "Jude, what's she saying?"

Avery continued. "You got that twenty grand from selling that stolen Quasar prototype to Mendez, which is why he refuses to let anyone see it. Then you murdered Hatchet and Boze when they found out about your dirty dealing."

His eyes widened in a mixture of shock and rage. "You nosy fucking bitch."

With shocking speed, Fisch threw a punch that caught Avery on the chin.

She fell onto her back. Before she could get back up, he was on top of her, his fists pummeling her mercilessly.

At once, her street-fighting instincts kicked in. She pinned one of his arms against his body, throwing him off balance, then flipped him onto his back.

She managed to deliver a few furious blows to Fisch's groin before Rocket Man appeared and pulled her off him.

"Fucking psycho," Avery spat, gasping for breath. Her head throbbed, and blood dripped from her nose and mouth.

"What the hell's going on?" Rocket asked looking back and forth between the two of them.

"Fucking psycho attacked me. I just defended myself."

Rocket's eyes blazed at Fisch. "That true?"

Fisch stood hunched over, holding his belly. "Bitch accused me of stealing that car from Quasar and then of killing Boze and Hatchet."

"Everybody knows you didn't win that twenty grand at the Duel in the Desert," Avery replied. "And you clearly have a violent temper."

"All right, that's enough outta both of you. Avery, quit making wild accusations. And, Fisch, if I ever see you lay a hand on any woman again, I'll tear you a new one. You got me?"

"You're one to talk."

"I mean it, Fisch. This is the last race night of the season. Let's keep it civil."

"Shithead," Avery muttered under her breath as she walked away.

"You okay, babe?" Roz caught up to her and examined her bloody face.

"I'll live. Asshole caught me off guard with that first punch."

"Let's go home and get you cleaned up. Or do you need to go to the ER?"

Avery shook her head, setting off another wave of vertigo. "I'm okay. I'd rather stay and watch the races."

Rocket reappeared and offered a handkerchief. "What the hell were you thinking, Ave?"

Avery wiped the blood from her face. "Me? Fisch is the violent psycho who murdered his own friends."

Rocket shook his head. "Avery, I know you want to hold someone responsible for their deaths. But all you're doing is stirring up a hornet's nest of trouble. You're gonna get yourself hurt if you don't stop. And I'm not talking a bloody nose and a fat lip."

"I can take care of myself."

"I don't care. We've got a couple producers from the Velocity Network here. Walrus is hoping to convince them to start that *Speed Demons* spinoff series about the Sonoran Crows. And you getting into a fist fight with Fisch isn't helpful."

"But he did it, Rocket. He's a murderer. Him and Mendez."

"That's crazy talk."

"Then why would he attack me like that?"

"When Quasar framed him over the missing prototype and threatened to sue him if he violated the non-compete clause, it hurt him deeply. He's very sensitive about it. Have some compassion, girl."

"Ever consider maybe he really did steal that car? Why else would they fire him?"

"The higher-ups at Quasar couldn't figure out who was responsible, but they needed a fall guy to appease the shareholders. Fisch had the least seniority on the team, so they pinned it on him. I'll admit, he can be an asshole at times, but he's no thief. And sure as hell ain't no killer."

"Then where the hell'd he get all that cash suddenly?"

"What cash?"

Avery realized she was at risk of saying too much. But this was Rocket Man. She trusted him to keep his mouth shut. "Rocket, this is my girlfriend, Roz. She runs the Spy Gal store."

The two of them said hello to each other.

"We ran a background check on Fisch. Turns out, he was getting behind on his bills while working for Hatchet. Then a month ago, he deposited twenty grand from out of the blue into his bank account. Carolyn even confirmed this unexpected influx of cash. Doesn't that sound the least bit suspicious to you? Like maybe he stole the prototype and finally managed to sell it to Mendez. But when his friends got wind of the deal, he□—"

"Avery…"

"He told Carolyn he won it at the Duel in the Desert against the 388s. But you and I know he only had two runs and lost both of them."

"I don't know anything about any cash. Maybe he bet on some of the other races that night. Either way, please, for the love of Chrysler, before something worse happens, let it go. You're a cute kid. And everyone raves about your skills as a tattoo artist. As a friend who truly cares about you, I am begging you to stop before you get yourself into serious trouble." He turned to Roz. "Talk to your girl here. Help her see reason."

"Maybe we should just go," Roz suggested, putting a hand on Avery's shoulder.

Avery pulled away. "No, I want to watch the races." What she really wanted was to continue to look for anything that might point to Fisch and Mendez's guilt.

To Rocket Man, she said, "I appreciate your concern, Rocket. It was stupid of me to accuse Fisch. But if he was involved Boze and Hatchet's deaths, I will find out." *And I will make them pay for their crimes.*

Rocket gave an exasperated sigh. "Well, watch your back."

"I intend to."

"Well, I better get back to it. I'm racing Vlad the Impala against Mendez's Satellite in twenty minutes. That is assuming he doesn't murder me first." He gave her a wink.

"You sure you want to stay?" Roz asked. "Your face looks like a raw brisket."

"I'll be okay."

Two cars motored slowly up to the starting line—a 1953 Oldsmobile Rocket 88 driven by Mikey Eberhardt and a 1966 Ford GT40, driven by Charms, one of the few female Sonoran Crows.

Avery always cheered for Charms whenever she raced, but this past season, she'd run into a number of engine problems.

Walrus stepped between the cars with a flashlight in hand. He gave a ready signal first to Mikey then to Charms. Both cars revved in response. Walrus raised the flashlight and flicked it on.

The desert air shook with the thunder of the engines and the squeal of tires as both cars shot off into the night. Mikey gained an initial lead when Charms's front end lifted at the start. But she quickly got her GT40 under control and narrowed the gap between them. By the time they hit the finish line, it was impossible to tell who had won from where Avery stood.

Walrus called into his walkie-talkie. Drifter, another member of the Crows, called back a moment later. “Charms, by a bumper.”

“Yeah!” Avery shouted, along with much of the rest of the crowd.

Major Tom and Big Eddie lined up next. Before Walrus had flicked on his flashlight, Big Eddie’s car jumped the start. Both cars flew down the road, but even before they reached the finish, Walrus called the race for Major Tom.

“This is exciting,” Roz said. “I can see why you enjoy it, despite it being so goth-damn hot out.”

“You get used to it after a while,” Avery replied with a grin.

“How’re you feeling? Looks like your lip stopped bleeding.”

Avery had been having so much fun watching the races, she’d pushed the pain to the back of her mind. “My lip feels like a balloon, and my ribs ache. But I’ll live.”

When Big Eddie and Major Tom returned from the finish line, Big Eddie got into an argument with Walrus, disputing claims he’d jumped the start. Fortunately, someone had recorded the race on their phone, and the evidence proved Walrus’s claim. Big Eddie stormed off cursing.

“A bit of a sore loser,” Roz commented.

“Yeah. He hates getting disqualified, but he knows he jumped.”

A few minutes later, Rocket Man’s Chevy Impala was revving its engine at the starting line next to Mendez’s Plymouth Satellite.

On the outside, the Satellite looked standard and as pristine as the day it rolled off the assembly line. But something about the engine noise seemed off. It sounded tinny, missing the deep subsonic rumble Avery expected to feel when it revved.

Could the stolen Quasar engine be under the hood? She had seen videos online about people who had installed electric engines in classic cars then connected up a sound system to give it that classic engine roar.

Walrus stepped between the cars, flashlight in hand. He gave each driver the ready signal. Both cars revved in response. Walrus raised the flashlight then switched it on.

The two cars roared off into the distance. Mendez's Satellite gained a solid lead on Rocket's Impala. But then the Satellite fishtailed and abruptly veered left into Rocket's path, missing the Chevy by a hair.

A gasp rose from the crowd.

The taillights of Mendez's Satellite looked like a tilt-a-whirl in the dark as the car tumbled end over end into the pitch black desert. When it came to a brutal stop, a flickering glow appeared from under the crumpled hood, followed by a burst of flames.

"Shit!" Avery grabbed one of the fire extinguishers kept near the starting line and raced at full speed toward the car while the flames rose higher. She could hear Mendez shouting for help from inside the car.

Unseen bushes tore at her legs as she followed the car's trajectory into the dark. Voices echoed behind her. When she reached the Chevy Satellite, she saw that it had collided with a twenty-foot saguaro. The impact had broken the cactus, sending it crashing down across the length of the vehicle, crushing the passenger side. Furious flames engulfed the crumpled engine compartment.

Avery pulled the pin on the extinguisher and sprayed the fire, hoping the car no longer had a gas-filled tank that could explode.

"Mendez! Hang in there! We're gonna get you out!" Walrus shouted as he, Fisch, and Major Tom struggled to pry open the driver's door.

Mendez shouted in reply, but Avery couldn't make it out. Despite her aiming the extinguisher at the worst of the flames, the blaze was growing, engulfing the fallen saguaro.

"Hurry!" she shouted. "The fire's not going out."

Between the lingering heat of the day and the growing furnace before her, Avery's body poured sweat. Mendez's shouts grew into frantic screams.

"He's pinned," someone said after they got the door open.

The intensifying heat burned Avery's face, forcing her back.

"Give it here!" Drifter appeared beside her and grabbed the extinguisher. She let him have it and stepped away.

Terror wrapped around Avery's heart as Mendez's shrill screams rose above the roar of the blaze that had now reached the passenger compartment with a terrifying flash. Just as she feared the worst, Walrus and the other men pulled Mendez's body from the fiery wreckage.

Avery stood there, numb, wondering if he was still alive. Someone called her name, though they sounded a million miles away.

She jumped when Rocket Man's hands clasped her shoulder. "Avery, are you hurt?"

"What? No." Focusing on his face seemed to center her.

"We gotta get out of here. Come on!"

She ran behind him, back to the starting line, where she found Roz. In the distance, sirens rose above the roar of the vehicle fire, which now continued unabated.

"Hey," Avery said dully, embracing her.

"Get her outta here," Rocket Man said to Roz.

"Come on, Ave."

CHAPTER 30
DAMAGE ASSESSMENT

"Ave?"

She sat there feeling as numb as a stone. The intense roar of the fire and Mendez's piercing screams of agony still echoed in her mind.

"Avery? We're here. We're at my place."

Roz's voice pulled Avery out of the daze. The car door next to her opened. Roz stood there with her hand extended. "Come on, sweetie. Let's go inside and get you cleaned up."

The next thing Avery knew, she was sitting at Roz's kitchen table. Her body trembled uncontrollably. She felt hot and cold at the same time. Her hands shook so badly, they reminded her of the essential tremors her nana had before she passed.

Roz offered her a bag of frozen peas. "Put this on your chin."

Avery obeyed and winced at the icy pain. "Shit, that's cold."

"I know, but it will help with the swelling. Okay now, stand up for just a sec, so I can get your jeans down."

"Trying to get in my pants?"

Roz smiled at the stupid joke. "Technically, they're my pants, since you borrowed them from me. And the right leg is torn and bloody. You must have brushed up against a cactus when you were running to put out the fire."

"Sorry." Avery stood and unfastened her jeans with her free hand.

Roz pulled down the pants, exposing a mess of bloody cuts on the outside of Avery's right thigh.

"Don't be sorry. You were running to save someone's life. But we don't want these cuts getting infected. I'll be right back."

Avery sat back down when Roz stepped into the other room. The memory of the car fire burned brightly in her mind. Mendez's screams of fear and pain cut her to the core despite her suspicions about him. Even if he had killed Hatchet and Boze, this sure as hell didn't feel like justice.

Roz returned with a first aid kit and a damp washcloth. She pressed the warm moist washcloth against the lacerations on Avery's thigh, dabbing and wiping away the blood.

Avery hissed in pain. "Fuck that hurts."

"Sorry. Needed to clean it up a bit." Roz dabbed more gently. Her other hand rested on Avery's knee, warm and calming. Her gentle touch anchored Avery against the wave of trauma pulling her toward the all-too-familiar emotional darkness. An emotion Avery could only call love poured into her soul where, until recently, there had been only raw, ragged grief.

"I'm s-sorry. I shouldn't have…" Avery muttered.

"Shouldn't have what?" Roz asked.

"Brought you to race night. Didn't think it would go like that."

"Actually, the races were a lot of fun. Up until the crash, that is. I get why you enjoy going."

"Don't understand what happened. Mendez is an excellent driver. Never saw him lose control like that."

"Who knows? Maybe he started using again. Or something mechanical could have gone wrong." Roz covered the wound with a large rectangular bandage and secured it with medical tape. "They are older cars. Things break."

"Or someone sabotaged it."

"Oh, Avery." Roz sat next to her, leaning on the table with her elbow. Their gazes met. "No offense, but you sound paranoid."

"I'm not paranoid. This is the third Crow to die in about as many weeks."

"Who would have sabotaged his car?"

"Fisch."

"Seriously? Why? I thought they were in on the stolen engine thing together."

"I did too." Avery stared down at her soot-covered hands. The intense heat from the engine fire had left her skin raw, as if she had a bad sunburn. Her face felt the same way.

"Maybe Fisch was afraid Mendez would turn himself in and throw Fisch under the bus."

"Why would Mendez confess? And how would Fisch have gotten to the car to sabotage it?" Roz asked.

"I don't know." Avery's eyelids drooped, and her mind drifted. Exhaustion gripped her, body and soul.

"Hey," Roz whispered. "Let's get you to bed."

"I'm dirty and sweaty," Avery said, though the thought of water pounding on her scorched skin made her wince. "You don't need me stinking up your bed. I should go home."

Roz leaned in until their noses were touching. She smelled so good, even with the added scent of dried sweat from an evening at race night.

A surge of attraction arose inside of Avery despite the fatigue and pain. She longed to feel this woman's lips and fingers on her body, and not just patching up her wounds. Her body ached as much from craving as from the night's tragic events.

"I don't care if you smell." Roz's honey eyes twinkled.

"Sure you do. You're just being nice."

"Can I confess something to you?"

Avery stared at her, enthralled. "Sure."

"I don't have a sense of smell."

"Seriously?" Not what she was expecting.

"It's true. I was born without one." Roz giggled, and it was the sexiest sound in the world. "It's weird, I know. I've always been self-conscious about it."

"But you always smell so good. Like jasmine."

"It's just body wash and my natural scent. I don't bother with perfume or anything like that. I'd probably pick something that smelled like a cheap hooker. But this…disability made me diligent about hygiene, I'll tell you that."

"You can't smell anything? I don't stink to you?"

"No, you don't stink. Not to me. I can smell a couple of things, like when someone is cooking onions or if I stick my nose in a bag of freshly ground coffee. But otherwise, nada."

"Must cut down on your enjoyment of food."

"Food is mostly about texture for me. I can taste sweet, bitter, spicy, sour, and salty. But things like fresh herbs just taste like plants."

"Wow." Avery managed a sad laugh. "So I could let rip with a big old fart, and you wouldn't smell it?"

"Farts are just a funny sound to me. No smell. And your shit literally does not stink. At least not to me."

"Huh. Does your doctor know why?"

"Nope."

"That is weird."

"Yep. That's me. Your weird girlfriend. You got anything weird about you? Aside from having been a homeless teen?"

Avery wanted so badly to open up to Roz about being transgender, to be completely open and transparent. No secrets. Keeping this truth from Roz felt like a vise around Avery's heart.

But Avery already felt so fragile and vulnerable that if she came out and Roz rejected her, she would shatter into a million pieces.

"Just a weird goth girl who tattoos people for a living and is into other chicks" was all Avery could manage.

"You're a goddamn freak, you are, Avery Byrne of Seoul Fire." Roz kissed Avery gently on the lips.

"Ow."

"Sorry! Still sore from where that guy hit you?"

"A little. But I don't care." Avery kissed her back harder. Before she knew it, they were in the bedroom with Roz helping Avery out of her clothes then undressing herself.

Avery knew it was all kinds of wrong to be sleeping with Roz while keeping her gender history a secret. But she couldn't stop herself.

The passion and the pleasure were so intense, she didn't notice her burns or scrapes or bruised ribs. Only this amazing, beautiful woman who was so into her, who was helping to heal all the broken pieces inside her.

CHAPTER 31

GOTH DATE NIGHT

Avery woke the next morning to the sound of her phone ringing. "Hello?"

Her body ached, but not in the good way it had when the two of them had slept together that first night. Her jaw and ribs hurt from where Fisch had beaten her. Her skin was as dry as sandpaper and tender to the touch. Roz lay beside her, still asleep.

"Morning, Avery. It's Rocket."

"Rocket Man! How's Mendez?" She sat up and noticed her reflection in the dresser mirror. Her face was bright red from the burns.

"He's gone, kid." His voice sounded choked with emotion. "Died an hour ago. I'm with Felicia and Gabriela at the hospital."

"Fuck! I'm so sorry. I… I tried to put the fire out."

"I know you did. We all tried to save him. Walrus, Fisch, and I all got burned from pulling him outta there. It was those goddamn lithium batteries. Once they catch fire, there's no putting them out."

"So he was using an electric engine."

"So it seems."

"The same one that was in the prototype Fisch stole from Quasar."

"Avery, don't go there. No more conspiracy theories or playing amateur detective. We're having enough trouble as it is convincing the Velocity Network to green-light the *Speed Demons* spinoff. You going around asking loaded questions will ruin everything."

"That's all you care about? A stupid TV show? Three people are dead. We're talking about human lives, Rocket."

"I know we are. This was an accident, pure and simple."

"You don't know that."

"Fisch loved his job at Quasar too much to steal that car. And he sure as hell wouldn't have sabotaged Mendez's Satellite, if that's what you're thinking. He suffered second-degree burns on his arms trying to pull Mendez out. Does that sound like something a murderer would do?"

"Maybe Fisch had second thoughts afterwards."

"Avery, stop. Do you even hear yourself? I don't blame you for being suspicious. After what you went through with your girlfriend and the cops chasing you all over creation. But, kid, this ain't that. What happened to Boze, Hatchet, and now Mendez, it's horrible and tragic. But it's not murder."

"What if it is?"

"I can't listen to this anymore. Felicia and her daughter need me right now. But I wanted you to know Mendez didn't make it, since you tried so hard to save him."

"Are the police at least investigating?"

"Yes. Sheriff's deputies have interviewed a bunch of us, which is all the more reason for you to stay out of it. You don't need to get dragged into this mess."

She considered that for a moment. "Is there going to be a memorial?"

"Probably."

"Am I invited?"

"Of course. To pay your respects. Not to turn this into some half-assed, amateur-hour murder investigation. Felicia, Emily, and Grace are still grieving their respective losses. We don't need you making them feel worse."

"Yeah, okay. Let me know where and when."

"Will do."

After Avery hung up, Roz said in a sleepy voice, "Morning, lover."

"Morning." Avery lay down beside her.

"You face looks sunburnt. You must've been really close to that fire when you were trying to put it out."

"Not that it did any good."

"How are you feeling?"

"Lousy. Got a call from Rocket. Mendez didn't make it."

"Oy! I'm so sorry."

"Rocket thinks I should drop this whole investigation into Boze and Hatchet, since the cops are investigating the car crash."

"Not a bad idea. Then you and I can focus on more important things." Roz kissed her, and Avery felt her body respond.

After a coolish shower to wash the dried sweat and grime off her scorched, scratched body, she borrowed more clothes from Roz. They were a little tighter in the waist, but they fit.

"How's your chest?" Roz asked when they were both dressed. "Those bruises looked serious."

"Only hurts when I laugh. Or breathe deeply. Or move."

"Well, I could kiss it some more and make it better."

Avery laughed and immediately clutched her torso in pain. "Ow, don't make me laugh."

"I checked the showtimes last night before we went to bed. *Shadow Monster* is playing at the Esplanade starting at eleven. They have a full menu of food, which they bring right to your seat. Care for brunch and a movie?"

"If it means hanging out with you, I'm all in."

The movie turned out to be a dud, but the food was good. Avery loved having someone to hold hands with during the few scary parts.

After the show, they bummed around Biltmore Fashion Center for a few hours then grabbed dinner at the "gay Denny's" on Camelback and Seventh Street.

Avery kept struggling with the urge to come out to Roz. But the timing never felt right. Too many people who might overhear were nearby. Roz was too busy giving her take about the parts she liked about the movie. Roz was busy eating. At the same time, this unspoken truth felt like an invisible wall between them.

"You are under no obligation to tell anyone you're trans until you're ready," Melissa had once told her. But would she ever be ready to tell Roz?

She had already come out to Dana, who was practically a complete stranger. Why was this so much harder?

At nine that evening, they were back at Roz's apartment.

"I had a great time with you, well, except for what happened at race night. But I really should head home."

"You could stay the night again."

Avery was torn. She wanted to, but the more time she spent with Roz, the worse the tension grew between wanting to come out and the abject terror of what would happen if she did.

"A night alone in my own bed would do me some good, I think," Avery said. "I got a lot of processing to do."

"I hear you. But I'll miss not seeing your face next to me all night long." Roz clasped Avery's hand. "I know there's something you're afraid to tell me. And that's okay. Whenever you're ready. No pressure."

Tell her, a voice in the back of Avery's mind shouted. But she couldn't bring herself to do it. "Thanks. My history's just… complicated."

Roz kissed her. "I understand. Just know that I will love you no matter what."

The words shocked Avery. So few people in her life had ever said that to her. And yet she found it easy to reply, "I love you too." And she found she meant it.

She drove home as if floating on air, trying to ignore the horrible secret she was holding back from Roz, still fearing her judgment. But for now, Roz loved her. And that was enough.

She slept remarkably well despite her recent injuries. And her vengeance on the college kids and their nightly pool parties seemed to have done the trick. Maybe they'd found someplace else to party.

Monday was routine, much to her relief. Her clients were all regulars who loved her work. Bobby grew concerned when Avery told him about what had happened at race night, but he was glad she was letting it all go. At least for now. And he was delighted that Avery and Roz were officially dating and was eager to meet her.

The news coverage of the accident was minimal. Much of it focused more on the dangers of street racing and the risks associated with lithium-ion batteries.

She half expected to get a call from the Maricopa County Sheriff's Office, wanting to question her about the incident. When it didn't happen, she considered reaching out to tell them what she knew and why she suspected Fisch of sabotaging Mendez's car. But for the time being, she let it go.

That night, Avery called Roz but kept the conversation light, focusing on their favorite goth bands. No talk of the Sonoran Crows.

On Tuesday, Rocket Man called. "Mendez's funeral is scheduled for Thursday night at seven. Salazar Funeral Home on Thunderbird near Thirty-Fifth Avenue."

"I'll be there. How are Felicia and her daughter doing?"

"Felicia's trying to be strong for Gabriela, but I know this is crushing her. They're facing a mountain of debt between the ambulance, hospital, and funeral expenses. We're asking everyone to contribute a few hundred dollars or whatever you can to help defray the costs."

"Sure, whatever I can do to help."

"Also, I heard that Major Tom has been suspended pending an investigation after Phoenix PD found out he was a member of the Crows and was paying off his buddies at the sheriff's office to steer clear of race nights."

"Damn."

"And, Avery, I know you're convinced this wasn't an accident, but I'm begging you not to say anything at the funeral. For Felicia's sake."

"I promise not to."

"And just so you know, Fisch will be at the funeral. So whatever misgivings you have about the guy, set them aside out of respect for Mendez's family."

"Have the cops talked to Fisch about the accident?"

"They interviewed all of us who were here at the hospital when Mendez was brought in. They also talked to everyone on Mendez's crew and at Valley View Auto Repair, since they were the only ones with access to the car."

"Did you tell them Fisch sold Mendez the engine he stole from Quasar?"

"Mendez did not get his engine from Fisch or anyone at Quasar."

"Then where did he get it? And why was he so secretive about it?"

"Zeiber Motors developed the engine. He couldn't show it to people because he'd signed an NDA."

"How do you know that?"

"Felicia told me. Mendez was test driving it for them. Fisch didn't have anything to do with it."

This didn't fit with any of her assumptions. Could Fisch really be innocent? Had Mendez killed Boze and Hatchet on his own? Or with Big Eddie's help? Or had Valentine been right about the accidental overdose all along? If so, why did Fisch get so defensive about her asking questions about it? Emily and Grace deserved to know the truth.

"Fisch is involved somehow. I can feel it."

"Even if you're right, which you're not, please don't start anything at the funeral. Just pay your respects, avoid Fisch, and don't play amateur sleuth. Okay? For Felicia's and Gabriela's sake."

"Yeah, all right."

That afternoon, Emily Yazzie called to let Avery know that the part had come in, and the Gothmobile was running cool.

After she finished her last client of the day, Avery dropped off her rental and caught a ride to Classic Auto Repair.

"You going to Mendez's funeral?" Emily asked as Avery was paying for the repairs. Fortunately, Fisch was nowhere in sight. She wasn't sure she could restrain herself from throttling him after he'd attacked her at race night.

"I'll be there. How about you?"

Emily shook her head sadly. "I just keep thinking about what you said. About Mendez bringing the ginger beer laced with fentanyl. I know the police tested the remaining bottle, but…"

Avery felt a pang of guilt. "I hate to think something I said is keeping you from attending."

"But if you're right…"

"At this point, I don't know what happened. And I'm sorry for stirring up suspicions."

"But the only other explanation is that Hatch knowingly took the drugs. And I don't see that happening, no matter what Fisch and the other Crows say. Someone did this to them. And if it was Mendez…"

Avery resisted the urge to point the finger at Fisch. She'd caused enough trouble. Best to leave it to the cops to sort out. "I understand. If there's anything I can do to be there for you…"

Emily gently placed her hand on Avery's. The brief human contact from someone she didn't know well felt alarming. But she resisted the urge to pull away.

"Thanks, Avery. I think you're one of the few who understand what I'm going through."

The words made her think about Bobby, Kimi, and Chupa, along with a few other select friends who had been there for her when her own life was turned upside down not long ago.

"Thanks for fixing the Gothmobile."

That night, she called Roz. "You want to come with me to Mendez's memorial?"

"If you want me there, I'm there for you. Are we investigating or just paying our respects?"

"Rocket specifically asked me to lay off the sleuthing for now, out of respect to Mendez's widow. And maybe he's right. The cops are looking into the crash. So we're just going to show up and offer our condolences."

"Count me in, sweetie."

"Thanks."

"No need to thank me. I enjoy spending time with you. Even at a funeral for someone I didn't really know. As far as date nights go, it's pretty goth."

"Doesn't get much gothier." Avery managed a chuckle. "If that's even a word."

"If it's not, it should be. I'll see you then, sexy girl."

A wave of heat and embarrassment flooded through Avery's body. She was glad Roz couldn't see how much she was blushing.

CHAPTER 32

ANOTHER CROW FUNERAL

At quarter to seven on Thursday night, Avery was standing outside the Gothmobile in the Salazar Funeral Home parking lot when Roz's VW Thing came rattling in. The sunset reflected off the boxy vehicle, bathing it in warm colors.

Avery's heart swelled when Roz emerged from the car, dressed in a black suit. She was falling hard for this woman.

"I like your dress." Roz kissed her on the lips.

Avery had chosen a simple pencil dress with cap sleeves. She pressed her forehead against Roz's. "Thanks. No shortage of black dresses in my closet. By the way, I would have brought the clothes I borrowed, but I haven't washed them."

"Keep them. They look good on you."

"Speaking of hot, it's sweltering out here. Let's get inside to the air conditioning."

Their fingers intertwined, they entered the funeral home, and Avery caught a few sidelong glances.

Two women holding hands! Oh, the horror.

They signed the register outside the room where Mendez's funeral was being held and stepped inside. Again, seeing these people dressed up felt surreal.

Flowers cascaded over a closed casket at the front of the room. A mixture of anger and sorrow rose in Avery. *Is this what karma looks like? Did Mendez deserve his fate?*

A stoic Felicia Mendez stood in a corner of the room, speaking with another woman Avery recognized as Tiffany Floyd, Rocket Man's wife. Gabriela, a girl of about eight, sat nearby, surrounded by extended family members. Avery hadn't seen the girl since before Sam died. A fretful expression that made her look like a skittish rabbit had replaced her usual beaming smile.

"Tiffany," Avery said as she and Roz approached. "How's your sister?"

Tiffany turned at the sound of her name, her eyes wide and wary. "Avery. Hey. Sorry, I gotta go. I'll see you around." She gave Felicia a quick hug and rushed out of the room.

Avery watched her disappear out the door. Had she done something to elicit such a reaction?

She turned back to Felicia. "Something I said?"

Felicia dabbed her eyes with a tissue and shook her head. "No, chica. It's not you. Tiff had to leave because Rocket will be here soon. She was just here to help me set up."

"Wait. Did she and Rocket split up? I thought Tiff was helping her sister recover from surgery."

"That's what he's been telling everyone. She's been staying with her sister ever since she got the restraining order against him."

"A restraining order? What for?"

"Long story," Felicia replied. "And not my place to talk about."

"Of course. I'm really sorry about Carlos. I tried my best to put out the fire."

"Walrus told me. Thank you. I understand you lost someone recently, too. Your girlfriend, Sam. Is that right?"

Avery squirmed a bit, even as she was holding Roz's hand. "Yes."

"I'm sorry for your loss as well. It's hard." Felicia appeared to just notice Roz. "Sorry, but I don't think we've met. I'm Felicia. Carlos Mendez's wife, er, I mean widow."

"Nice to meet you. I'm Roz Fein. I'm truly sorry for your loss."

"Thank you."

Avery bit her lip as she considered the question that had been pressing on her mind. "I don't understand how the crash happened. One second, Mendez was in the lead. The next, he veered into Rocket's lane and then off the road."

"The sheriff's office is saying the steering failed. Natural wear and tear. A risk racing old cars like that."

"Natural wear and tear? They're sure?"

"Ave," Roz whispered. "Don't."

"What else would it be?" Felicia asked.

"Maybe someone tampered with the steering."

"What are you saying?" A flicker of anger appeared in Felicia's eyes. "You think someone sabotaged my husband's car? Who would do that?"

Roz squeezed Avery's hand hard.

"I, uh… nothing. Forget I said anything. Sorry." Avery glanced to the room's entrance where Tiffany had disappeared. "This whole thing has me rattled. Again, I'm sorry he's gone."

"Thanks. I guess a lot of us have lost someone recently."

"Seems so. Maybe we should form a club," Avery said with a dark chuckle. "The Sonoran Widows."

Felicia managed a weak smile. "We should. Well, take care, and thank you for coming."

"We should find some seats," Roz told her.

"Sorry about bringing up Sam. I know we're not supposed to talk about our exes when dating someone new."

"It's fine. I'm not jealous when you talk about Sam. What kind of girlfriend would I be if I didn't allow you time to grieve?"

"Thanks." They found a couple of seats near the back.

"What bothered me was you suggesting the crash was due to…"

"I know. I promised not to, but I did anyway."

Soon after they sat down, Rocket walked in. His face also looked like he'd suffered a horrible sunburn.

"Rocket." Avery wasn't sure what else to say, considering what she'd learned about him and Tiffany.

"Avery! How are you doing?"

"Managing. I saw Tiff earlier."

"Yeah?" His expression went blank.

"I understand she got a restraining order against you. What the hell, dude?"

He shook his head dismissively. "Just a stupid misunderstanding that got blown way out of proportion."

"Really? I mean, getting a restraining order is pretty serious."

"It is. And I want to give her space. It's why I'm just now getting here. She and Felicia have been real close, and I was told she would be here to help set up. I wanted to respect that. But really, she shouldn't be airing our dirty laundry in public."

"She didn't. But you've been lying to me, saying she was helping her sister after surgery."

"I just didn't want everyone to think she'd overreacted. She does that sometimes. She'll come around. She always does."

Avery wasn't sure how to respond.

A man with a thin face, a five o'clock shadow, and a priest's collar stood at the front of the room. "If everyone will please take their seats," he said, his voice accented. "We're going to start the service."

For the next thirty minutes, Avery half listened to the priest going on about the brevity of life compared to the glory of an eternal afterlife.

Bored, Avery let her gaze drift absently around the room. She spotted Fisch's head of dark curly hair on the other side of the room. He looked as restless as she felt.

She was still convinced Fisch was involved somehow. She just couldn't prove it.

When the priest wrapped up his sermon, Felicia and others got up to share their thoughts and memories.

At one point, Roz whispered, "You want to get up and say something?"

"Got nothing to say." Even if she did, the thought of speaking in front of a group of people terrified her. She much preferred the shadows.

When everyone with a burning desire had said their piece, Felicia thanked everyone for coming and invited them to her home afterward.

"You want to go to Felicia's?" Roz asked when everyone stood up to leave.

Avery shook her head. "I've had enough. I'd probably drink too much and say shit I shouldn't. Maybe get into another fight. Especially if Fisch will be there."

"Fair enough. You want to come back to my place?"

"I've got an early client tomorrow, and I'm wiped. Wouldn't be very good company. But I'd love to spend the weekend with you. If you don't mind. I'd invite you over to my apartment, but I only have a single bed."

"Ooh, sounds very intimate and cozy," Roz teased.

"Until one of us falls off the bed and cracks her skull."

"That would put a damper on things. But I'd love to have you for the weekend."

As they approached their cars in the oppressive heat of the dark parking lot, a voice called from behind. "Avery, hold up! We need to talk."

Avery turned to see Fisch hustling toward them. Her fists balled, ready for another fight with this asshole.

CHAPTER 33

FISCH COMES CLEAN

"You come for round two? 'Cause I'm ready for you, asshole. No more sucker punches."

"Just piss off, you little putz," Roz added. "Or we'll both kick your ass."

Fisch held up his hands in surrender. They were bandaged. "I just want to talk. There's something you should know."

"Why should I listen to anything you've got to say?" Avery asked. "You lied to your wife about that twenty grand, and then you attacked me. I should have you arrested for assault."

"I'm sorry about that. You were right about some things but wrong about where I got the money."

"So you and Mendez did murder Hatchet and Boze, and then you tied up loose ends by killing Mendez?"

"What? No. I didn't kill anyone. But I do believe someone killed Hatchet and Boze. And possibly Mendez too."

"Who?"

Fisch glanced around at the people milling about the parking lot. "There some place we can talk in private?"

"We can talk at my place," Roz suggested.

"No," Avery countered. "Don't need this dipshit knowing where you live."

"Look, I'm here to come clean. But there are certain people I don't want overhearing what I say to you."

"Fine. We can talk inside the Gothmobile. Get in."

The three of them piled into her Caddy with Avery in the driver's seat, Roz next to her, and Fisch in the back.

"So spill. What do you know?"

"When Mendez showed up with his new engine, Hatchet, Boze, and me grew suspicious. Everyone knew the sounds it made were fake and that the engine was all electric, which violated the bylaws. At least before Mendez changed them. Nitrous and fuel injection are one thing, but engines that run on lithium-ion batteries don't belong. We're the Sonoran Crows. We race classic hot rods, not state-of-the-art sports cars."

"So you killed him over it?" Avery asked, not sure she was going to believe his answer.

"No, we didn't. When Mendez refused to let anyone see under the hood, the three of us broke into his garage. That engine was nearly identical to the one I helped develop at Quasar."

"Nearly identical?" Roz asked.

"The engine was bigger, with more cells, and it had the Zeiber logo on the cover where the Quasar logo had been. But essentially, the same breakthrough technology. I could explain it, but it would go over your head."

"And…" Avery said impatiently.

"I sent photos to my former boss at Quasar, telling them what I'd found and confirming that Zeiber had indeed stolen the prototype, modified it, and was now testing it. But he blew me off, saying that I should let it go, and if I didn't, he'd use this as proof of my involvement in the theft and pursue criminal charges against me."

"Sounds like he was the inside man," Avery replied.

"That's what I'm thinking, but I can't prove it. One thing I noticed was that the connecters on the Zeiber engine weren't robust enough to handle the current that engine would produce. It was a fire risk, even without crashing. I tried to warn Mendez, but he told us to go fuck ourselves. Threatened to have us arrested for breaking into his shop."

"What's this have to do with Hatch and Boze and Mendez getting killed?"

"Hatch, Boze, and me were all short on funds lately. So we used the photos of Mendez's engine to blackmail Zeiber, threatening to expose them for corporate espionage and grand theft auto if they didn't pay us. Boze and Hatchet met with some bigwig at Zeiber. I was supposed to go with them, but I had jury duty that week. Not sure who they met with, but a week later, Big Eddie showed up at Classic Auto with a package. Sixty grand in cash, twenty for each of us."

"Big Eddie? What's his part in all this? Isn't he on Mendez's crew?"

"Technically, he works for Zeiber's security division."

Avery let that percolate through her brain. "So if Zeiber paid you off, then who killed Hatchet and Boze?"

"They did pay us. But then…" Even in the dim car's interior, Avery could see guilt darken his expression. "We asked for another sixty grand."

"You got greedy," Roz replied.

"Between my mortgage and the debt I'd accumulated since getting canned from Quasar, it was going to take more than just twenty grand to get me out of the hole. Boze was buried in medical bills from his back injury. And Hatchet was struggling to keep Classic Auto afloat. So were we greedy? We were just trying to keep our heads above water."

"But instead of paying you this time, they decided to kill you instead," Avery said. "How are you still alive when your buddies are dead?"

"I don't know. But Big Eddie beat the ever-loving shit out of me that night." He pressed a hand to his face. "Damn near broke my jaw. Still got bruised ribs."

"So do I, thanks to you," Avery replied.

"Sorry." He actually looked like he meant it.

"How did Big Eddie drug Boze and Hatch?"

Fisch shrugged. "I'm guessing with the ginger beer that Mendez brought. The only other things he had that night were a pizza we had delivered and some cupcakes Boze brought for dessert. So it must have been in the ginger beer."

Roz met Avery's gaze. "So Mendez was in on it."

Avery rubbed her temple. "Wait. I'm trying to understand the timeline. Mendez brought a four-pack of ginger beer. One was left in the shop fridge, so that's one for each of you. So why didn't it affect you?"

"I was drinking Budweiser. The two of them split the four-pack. I think Hatchet had a couple. Boze had one."

"The police tested the remaining bottle that was in the fridge and didn't find any drugs."

Fisch shrugged. "I can't explain it. Maybe Mendez only put the dope in a couple of them. Or maybe Big Eddie switched out the remaining bottle after he beat me up. I don't know."

"What happened after they drank the ginger beer?" Roz asked.

"Boze was the first to be affected. Said he wasn't feeling well. Then he fell and hit his head on the side of a car. Hatchet offered to call an ambulance, but Boze told him no. He was afraid of the cost. So Hatchet drove him. Hatch seemed okay when they left."

"But you didn't go with them?" Avery pressed.

"I stayed behind because Big Eddie was supposed to show up with the next twenty grand."

"Which he obviously didn't do."

"No. He just beat me with those mallet-like fists of his and left me for dead."

Roz leaned closer. "Why did Big Eddie even show up at all? Wouldn't he assume you were all dead from the laced ginger beer?"

"I don't know."

Avery thought about it. Eddie hadn't been one of the guys trying to free Mendez from the burning car. Had he sabotaged the car? She glanced outside into the parking lot but didn't see him.

"Did Big Eddie cause Mendez's accident? Could he have sabotaged the car?"

"I can't prove it, but he had access to the car and could have easily tampered with the steering. But thermal runaway in the lithium-ion batteries started the fire and made it all but impossible to put out."

"You tell the cops what you know?" Roz asked.

"Hell no! I don't want to go to jail for extortion or breaking and entering."

"Even if Big Eddie murdered three of your friends?" Anger rose in Avery's voice. "What's to stop him from killing you now? Or another member of the Crows? And why bother telling us?"

"I'm telling you because you seemed interested in making things right somehow. Not that there's much you could do. Big Eddie would wipe the floor with the both of you. And the people at Zeiber have a lot of friends in powerful positions. I don't know how far up the chain the corruption at Zeiber goes. Possibly all the way up to the CEO, Guy Thorne. Tech billionaires like Thorne don't have to live by the same rules the rest of us do. Even if I went to the cops, I doubt they'd do anything. But you wanted the truth. So now you know everything I do."

"Who at Zeiber authorized the first blackmail payment?" Roz asked.

"I don't have a name, only a phone number that Hatch had for his contact at Zeiber." Fisch gave them a phone number. "I never called it myself."

Avery tried to think of anything else Fisch might know. "What about a number for Mendez?"

"Why? He's dead."

"Do you have his phone number?" Avery pressed.

Fisch coughed up that number as well. "There, I've shared all I know. Try not to get yourself or your girlfriend here killed. And don't mention my name to anyone."

With that, Fisch opened the back door and disappeared into the night.

"Oy vey," Roz said. "That was a bombshell. What are you planning on doing with this information?"

"I plan to make Big Eddie pay for his crimes. But before I do, I want to double-check the facts. I'm not taking Fisch's word on anything."

"Could get rough. Big Eddie doesn't sound like the kind of guy you could take in a fight."

"Not a fair fight, no. But one thing I learned on the street is not to fight fair. Everybody's got a weakness. We just have to find what Big Eddie's is and exploit it. And right now, we have the advantage of surprise. He doesn't know that we know."

"What about Zeiber Motors?"

"My first impulse would be to let Quasar Motors know who stole their prototype. But sounds like Fisch already did that. I want to focus on Big Eddie for now. Maybe I can find a way for him to tell me who at Zeiber was calling the shots."

"Makes sense. You want to grab a drink before heading home?"

Avery shook her head. "I need time to process. But I'll see you tomorrow night."

They kissed good night and parted ways.

Avery drove home, reflecting on what Fisch had told them. Her gut told her he wasn't lying. There wasn't much point.

If Mendez and Big Eddie were working together, how did they make sure Boze, Hatchet, and Fisch would drink the bottles laced with fentanyl if at least one bottle didn't have any drugs in it? Or did Big Eddie switch it out with a clean one?

And if Big Eddie showed up to tie up loose ends, why let Fisch live? Why leave it at a beatdown? And was Big Eddie acting on his own, or was this mysterious executive at Zeiber giving the orders?

She hoped she would find answers tomorrow.

CHAPTER 34

VANDALIZED

That night, Avery dreamed she was driving down Thomas Road toward the Central Corridor, only to find the buildings around her ablaze. Even from the safety of her car, she could feel the flames scorching her skin. Smoke filled the air, choking her.

Suddenly, she was no longer in the Gothmobile but dashing through the burning building on foot, searching desperately for an exit.

By the time she found a door, it was engulfed in flames. Roz stood in the way, a blowtorch in her hand. "You should have told me."

Avery woke with the smell of smoke still in her nose. She glanced around her dark bedroom. Nothing was on fire, thankfully. *Just a fucking nightmare.*

The next morning, as she was walking to her car on the way to work, she discovered someone had spray-painted the driver's side of the Gothmobile with the words "nosy bitch" in large red letters.

"Fuck!" She dropped her keys as anger exploded inside her.

Jaden the jock came strolling by with his arm slung over his girlfriend's shoulders.

"Nosy bitch," he said with a chuckle. His girlfriend laughed.

Avery lunged at him, grabbing him by the collar and slamming him hard against one of the carport's metal supports. "You do this?"

"Chill out, bitch. I didn't do shit."

"Liar." She glared at him but couldn't tell if he was lying or not.

“If I’d done it, it would’ve read ‘psycho freak.’ Guess you just piss everyone off, bitch.”

“Asshole.” She picked up her purse, climbed into the Gothmobile, and squealed the tires as she tore out of the parking lot.

She wasn’t sure if she could wash off the graffiti without damaging the paint job underneath. And she didn’t have time to drop the car off at Classic Auto before her first appointment. So she just drove to Seoul Fire, fuming the entire way.

Who could have done this? Who knows where I live? Did someone follow me after the funeral? Was this Big Eddie’s doing?

When she arrived, she sat in the parking lot for a few moments to meditate and let go of the anger, as Bobby had taught her.

She was still pissed when she let herself in Seoul Fire’s back door but was no longer shaking with rage. A moderate improvement, at least.

Her first appointment was a longtime friend and client. Avery had been working on a back piece for her for a month, and it was finally looking like something more than line art.

Even when everything else around her was going to shit, her art always made her feel connected. Like she was a part of something permanent. At least as permanent as her clients.

When she was done coloring and shading a few hours later, her client gasped at her reflection. “Wow! Avery, that’s so amazing. Thank you. Can I give you a hug?”

For once, Avery didn’t mind and found the embrace comforting.

After the woman settled up and left, Bobby approached her. “I saw what someone did to your car.”

“Please, Appa, no lecture. I am so not in the mood.”

“No lecture. I’m sorry that happened to you. Are you still looking into these Sonoran Crow deaths?”

"No," she lied. "I'm letting the police handle it. At least, they're investigating Mendez's crash."

"We haven't really talked since that night. How are you feeling?"

"I'm fine."

"Fine? As in 'fucked up, insecure, neurotic, and emotional?' Talk to me."

"I don't know. Still processing it, I guess."

"And how are you and Roz doing?"

"Still haven't come out to her, if that's what you're wondering. I keep wanting to, but every time I think I'm ready, I get tongue-tied."

"You'll figure it out. Trust your feelings."

"Okay, Obi-Kwon Kenobi," she said with a smirk.

"I know you probably have plans for tomorrow night, but I would really like you and Roz to join Dana and me for dinner tomorrow night at the Poké Bar. Give you a chance to make up for the previous time."

Avery nodded. "I'll ask her."

A woman Avery didn't recognized walked into the shop.

"Can I help you?" Bobby asked.

"I have an appointment with Avery," she replied. "I'm Mandy Alvarez."

"I'm Avery."

After a brief discussion, it became apparent that Ms. Alvarez couldn't decide what she wanted. "Just do something creative."

"I'd rather not."

"Why not?"

"I don't want to start inking a design, only for you to change your mind halfway through. Best bet is to wait until you're sure. Your tattoo should be an extension of you, not me."

Ms. Alvarez protested, but Avery held her ground. Finally, the woman marched off in a huff.

When Avery caught Bobby's eye, she replied, "What? You think I was wrong to send her away?"

"Just the opposite. I think you made the right call."

"My next client's not for another couple of hours. I'm going to drop my car off at the shop."

Avery arrived at Classic Auto a little while later.

"Back again?" Emily asked. "Is it still overheating?"

"No, the radiator's fine. Some asshole spray-painted the side of my car."

Emily leaned over the counter to see the Gothmobile in the parking lot. "Oh, no! How awful. Who would do such a thing?"

"No idea." Not the complete truth, but Avery didn't want to upset Emily. "I considered removing it myself but was worried about damaging the finish. Hatch did such a great job of restoring it, I'd hate to ruin it."

"I'll see what we can do, but we'll probably have to send it out to our paint shop."

"Whatever it takes. How you holding up?"

She shrugged. "One day at a time. You?"

"Same."

"Was that your new girlfriend at Mendez's funeral?"

"Yeah," Avery replied, feeling awkward. "It's so soon after losing Sam, I almost said no. But I'm just so…"

"Lonely? No need to explain. I get it. Life's too short not to seize love when you can. Don't let anyone judge you for taking care of yourself."

"Thank you. You too. How long do you think it will be before I get the car back?"

"If we can't do it ourselves, it depends on how backed up the paint shop is. Maybe a week."

"Okay, thanks."

She once again called for a rental car and got into another vehicle with all the roominess and solidity of a tin can. This one also reeked of smoke with a hint of weed. She'd been willing to pay for a larger vehicle or at the least one that didn’t stink, but apparently, they’d all been rented out, despite the lot being half full.

Avery couldn’t help but wonder if it was because she’d declined their damage protection scam, because she was goth, or because they’d figured out she was trans. But she wasn’t in a mood to make a scene, since her next client would soon arrive at Seoul Fire.

CHAPTER 35

DIGGING INTO BIG EDDIE

When the end of the day came, she rushed out of the shop with barely a goodbye to Bobby, Butcher, or Frisco. All she could think of was spending more time with Roz. And finding out more about Big Eddie if Roz was on board with it.

She arrived at Roz's apartment a little earlier than expected and was disappointed when Roz didn't open the door after Avery knocked.

Avery sent her a text.

Avery:
I'm at ur apt. Where R U? :-(
Roz:
Running late. B thr soon.

Avery felt awkward standing outside the door, dressed in a revealing black lace top, miniskirt, and knee-high buckle boots. A Victorian-style cross hung from a choker down to her breasts. And her makeup, which was on the verge of washing away in a flash flood of sweat, was pale bisque with black lipstick, heavy eyeliner, and mascara.

Even in this predominantly LGBTQ+ apartment complex, she stood out like a sore thumb. A couple of guys wearing muscle shirts and holding hands gave her the side-eye but didn't say anything.

"Sorry I'm late." Roz appeared just as Avery was about to text her again. "Figured I'd pick up some wine to go with dinner."

Flashes of the dream from the night before flickered in her memory, as did the scent of smoke. Avery felt a sudden awkwardness. The voice in the back of her mind screamed at her to tell Roz she was trans.

But as the two of them made a dinner of pan-fried salmon and oven-baked French fries, Avery's courage to come out once again faltered. Instead, she told Roz about the day's clients. Roz shared about the quirky people who came into Spy Gal. She had a marvelous way of telling stories that made Avery laugh at even the stupidest situations.

"These two were seriously tweaking," Roz explained. "Pupils like pinpoints. Scabs all over their faces. Goth only knows what they smelled like, but judging from their greasy hair and crumpled clothes, I guessed they hadn't bathed in a month. And of course, what were they interested in buying? Electronic bug detectors."

"Don't want the government to find out about their secret meth lab." Avery chuckled.

"They kept asking over and over if I sold anything that would alert them if the cops were tapping their cell phones. Even offered to pay me in drugs if I did. As if. I told them no, there's not any hardware that can detect a tapped cell phone. They didn't want to hear that and started accusing me of working for 'the Man.'" She said the word *man* in air quotes. "Got super paranoid, especially when they spotted my security camera. Accused me of being a Fed posing as a clerk in a spy store."

"These guys sound like a couple of winners."

"Finally, I explained that the best way to determine if their phones were being tapped was to listen for unusual noises on the line or excess battery drainage. Or better yet, to stop paying the cell phone bill. If the phones still worked after a couple months past due, they were being tapped."

"Is that true?"

Roz shrugged. "Honestly, I don't know. Something I saw on an episode of *The Wire*. Probably wouldn't work in real life unless they were really gunning for you. These idiots were clearly low-level meth heads who consumed more of their product than they sold."

"Wow, and I thought my clients were weird."

Roz smiled and stared deeply into Avery's eyes. After a moment, Avery grew paranoid herself. "What? Is my mascara smeared?" *Did you figure out I'm trans?*

Roz laughed. "No. You just look beautiful, and I enjoy looking at you, looking at my girlfriend."

"How come no one's snatched you up already? You must get hit on a lot in bars."

"I dunno. Maybe I'm picky. I've been single for a year and a half. I kinda like it. My ex, Cassandra, was super weird."

"Weird how?"

"Lots of ways. For example, she'd send me to Sonic to get a cup of crushed ice, but only if they got it from the ice machine at the back of the store, because it was supposedly softer. Mind you, this is the same woman who dumped me for a guy who claimed to be an Iraqi vet. But the joke was on her. She found out later he'd lied about that. He never served in the military. Oh, and the real cherry on top is that he eventually got her pregnant, and she didn't realize it until she was giving birth."

"No way! You're making that up."

"I would have thought so too, but I ran into her at L Street a year after we broke up, and she told me. Apparently, he dumped her not long after she had the kid."

"How could a woman not know she was pregnant?"

Roz shrugged. "She was always a bit of a big girl, so she just thought she was gaining weight."

"But wouldn't she be suspicious after she missed her period a few months in a row?"

"Hers were always irregular. Some hormonal issue. And like I said, she was quirky. And get this—she had the audacity to ask me to go out with her again."

"What did you tell her?"

"I told her I didn't need her cheap drama in my life."

"And yet you asked me to be your girlfriend. Why?"

"I dunno. There's something special about you."

Avery shifted in her chair and stared at her now empty plate. "Guess it's not every day you meet a psycho vigilante."

"You're no psycho. Cassandra was a psycho. You are passionate about protecting innocent people and making sure predators get the justice they deserve. You're like a one-woman A-Team."

Again, Avery felt the overwhelming urge to come out, but the proper words wouldn't form in her head.

"Roz, you'll probably hate me, but I'm transgender." No, that's no good. "Roz, my parents kicked me out for being trans." No, not that. "Roz, I know we've already slept together a few times, but I used be a boy." No, I was never really a boy. "Roz, please don't go all Crying Game *on me, but I used to have a penis." No, no, no.*

"Never watched that show" was all she said. "And really, I'm not all that special."

"I know there's something you're afraid to tell me. I can see it in your eyes. But when the time is right, I hope you'll trust me enough to tell me, whatever it is. I won't judge you."

That's what they all say, Avery thought. *Until they know.* "Just give me time."

"You got it. Meanwhile, let's clean up the kitchen then maybe get a little hot and sloppy in the bedroom."

Avery wanted to say yes. Roz was such a generous lover. But the thought of sleeping with her again without coming out felt wrong. "Or maybe we can start digging into Big Eddie's background."

Avery half expected Roz to be disappointed at the suggestion. Instead, a sly grin spread across her face. "You sure know how to show a girl an interesting time."

The two of them sat in front of Roz's laptop and plugged Eddie Myles's details into the SkipTrakkr app. The basic report appeared on the screen.

“Okay, looks like he’s divorced, lives in north Phoenix, decent credit scores, no criminal history in the past five years. Served in the Marine Corps.” Roz clicked on a button for his military record. “That’s interesting. Got a bad conduct discharge along with a court martial. Served nine months in jail back in 2010. Assault, larceny, drug trafficking.”

“Drugs, huh? That’s interesting. Pull up his employment report.”

When the report appeared, Avery pointed to the screen. “Look at this. After the Marines released him from jail, he worked for a security firm.”

“Seriously? How’d he get a security job with a big chicken dinner on his record?” Roz replied.

Avery choked back a laugh. “A what?”

“It’s what marines call a bad conduct discharge. Had an uncle in the Corps. Someone he knew got busted for stealing a truckload of cash in Iraq.”

“Is a bad conduct discharge the same as a dishonorable discharge?”

“Not quite as serious. Dishonorable discharges usually involve murder, treason, or rape. Still, how’s a guy like Big Eddie get a security job with a BCD on his record?”

“Good question. Maybe he pulled some strings,” Avery suggested. “Run his full criminal background. Let’s see if he’s been busted since.”

Roz pulled up the report, which again showed the court-martial, but nothing else. “Guess he’s kept his nose clean after they booted him from the Corps.”

“Or he got better at covering his ass. Go back to his employment report.” When Roz did, Avery studied it. “So he worked for Big Wolf Security for six years. Then got a job working at Zeiber Motors Corporation as a security specialist. Nothing here suggests he was involved with stealing the prototype from Quasar or drugging Boze and Hatchet.”

“Maybe Fisch was wrong about him.”

Avery thought about it. “Maybe. But why would Fisch come clean to us about blackmailing Zeiber? Run his phone and text message logs.”

Roz ran the report. “Nothing really pops out on the phone log. A lot of calls back and forth between Zeiber Motors and him, but the last four digits are 1700. Probably the main switchboard number.”

“Any way to know which extension he called?”

“No.”

“And no text messages. Zeiber’s not one of your clients, by chance, is it?” Avery asked, hoping for a break.

“Nope. I mostly work with mom-and-pop businesses.”

“What about that number Fisch gave us for Hatchet’s contact at Zeiber? Can you run that?”

“Your wish is my command.” Roz opened a new window and ran the phone number. “Well, this looks promising. No phone calls, but a lot of text messages.”

Avery pointed to the screen. “Pull up that conversation, dated May 16.”

The full conversation appeared, and Avery’s jaw dropped, causing her to nearly spill her glass of wine.

CHAPTER 36

A PLANNED HEIST

Avery read through the conversation. The number they'd queried was the mysterious contact at Zeiber. The other matched the phone number she had for Hatchet.

> Hatchet:
> We want another $60K.
> Zeiber:
> Just gave you 60K. No more.
> Hatchet:
> Then we tell everyone what you did. Quasar. The police. The press. This will end you and your company.
> Zeiber:
> Don't be stupid. We have you on video breaking into Valley View garage. And you'll go down for extortion. You willing to go to prison for this? Be smart. Let this go.
> Hatchet:
> We both know you'll lose more than we will if this all goes public. Or you can pay us another $60 grand. Your choice.
> Zeiber:
> Fine. But this is the final payment. No more. It ends here. Agreed?
> Hatchet:
> It ends when we say it ends.
> Zeiber:
> It will take a few days to gather the funds. Our courier will be at Classic Auto Friday 8pm.
> Hatchet:
> Smart move.

“Wow,” Roz said.

Avery again pointed to the screen. “How about this other conversation a couple of days later?”

> Zeiber:
> Your friends are asking for more money.
> Unknown:
> What U want me 2 do?
> Zeiber:
> Send them a message: No more money. Keep quiet or else.
> Unknown:
> Will do.

Avery guessed the unknown party must be Big Eddie. Roz pulled up another conversation between the two numbers from just a week ago.

> Big Eddie:
> Mendez could be a problem. Acting all righteous since rehab.
> Zeiber:
> Eliminate the problem. Make it look like accident. No loose ends.
> Big Eddie:
> Copy that.

They both stared at the screen for a moment in silence. Avery felt a surge of adrenaline. The missing pieces, at least some of them, were falling into place. If the cops were really interested in prosecuting these murders, this would be the linchpin of the case. But Valentine had ignored what she’d brought him before.

“Assuming this unknown number belongs to Big Eddie, let’s see who else he’s been talking to,” Avery said at last.

Roz ran a search on the new number they suspected was Big Eddie’s.

There were several other conversations on the SMS report. One from just the day before caught Avery's eye. "Pull up that one."

Big Eddie:
Yushan is go. Fri nite. 2130 hrs.
Unknown:
What about alarms and cameras?
Big Eddie:
All covered. Gate code is 7690. Card key for door. No alarms. My contact says cameras will be off 20 min. Enough time if we move fast.
Unknown:
Won't cameras off alert guards?
Big Eddie:
Guards told software w/b updated during window. Shld be no problem
Unknown:
Then lets get paid

"Sounds like they're planning some sort of heist. Tonight!" Avery re-read through the texts. "What the hell's Yushan?"

"Let me check something." Roz ran a search for "Yushan" in a new browser window. The first few hits were about a mountain in Taiwan. After that were news stories about the new Yushan microprocessor plant that had recently opened north of Phoenix.

"That's got to be it," Avery said. "But why would they steal microprocessors? Is there a black market for that?"

"They put microprocessors in everything these days. And with the increasing tensions between China and the US, it's gotten crazy. There've been some serious supply chain issues lately. This new Taiwanese-owned manufacturing plant north of town could solve the problem. But if Big Eddie and his partner in crime steal a bunch of their inventory, they could make a shitload of money on the black market. If this is going down tonight, we should inform the police."

"Or use it as leverage."

Roz did a double-take. "Leverage for what?"

"I'm thinking we use your super surveillance equipment to catch these bozos in the act of robbing the Yushan plant. Then we use that evidence to put pressure on Big Eddie to tell us who at Zeiber ordered Hatchet, Boze, and Mendez killed."

"That sounds dangerous."

"Not if we do it right. Trust me. I'm Avery the Avenger. Remember?"

"And when we find out who at Zeiber was calling the shots, then what?"

"We could turn everything we know over to the police. But we know how that turned out last time. Fucking Valentine practically laughed in my face."

"What about Major Tom? You said he's a commander with Phoenix PD. You could talk to him. Maybe he could get Valentine to reopen the case."

"He got suspended for participating in illegal street racing and bribing the sheriff's office."

"So if we're not going to turn everything over to the cops, then what are we going to do with it? I saw Big Eddie at race night. He's huge. And whoever he's working for at Zeiber probably has a lot of clout. I know you've brought down a lot of folks who deserved it. But, babe, these guys are heavyweights. What if things go sideways?"

"We could use a little muscle. Let me call Rocket, see if he'd help us."

Avery dialed the number.

"Yello," replied Rocket Man's baritone voice.

"Rocket? It's Avery."

"Hey, kid. How's it going?" He didn't exactly sound excited to hear from her.

"I figured out who killed Hatchet and Boze. And Mendez too."

"Oh, for the love of Chrysler, Avery. You gotta let this go."

"It's Big Eddie. I've got proof. And he's pulling a heist at the Yushan plant tonight."

"What's a moo shu plant?"

"Not moo shu. The Yushan plant. The new factory in the north valley, where they make microprocessors for computers. Big Eddie's planning a heist there. Roz and I are planning on catching him in the act and then pressuring him to tell us who at Zeiber gave the order to kill Boze and Hatchet."

"Avery, stop this. You're not a superhero. If Big Eddie's planning to rob some factory, call the cops. But I don't want to hear any more of your wild conspiracy theories. You sound like those QAnon wackos. You're going to get yourself killed. I know you feel Boze and Hatch deserve justice. Hell, I do too. But neither of us are cops. Let's just leave it be."

"I tried that, and now Mendez is dead."

"Mendez was driving an old car, and the rack-and-pinion steering gave out. That shit happens. It had nothing to do with Hatch and Boze."

"Fine. Be that way. But, if you change your mind, meet us at Roz's apartment around eleven tonight." Avery gave him the address. "We really could use you."

"Hard pass. Be safe, kid, and try not to get yourself into too much trouble."

"Thanks, Rocket Man." Avery hung up and turned to Roz. "Looks like it's just you and me."

CHAPTER 37

SECRETS IN THE DARK

Roz pulled up a satellite map of the area around the Yushan plant to determine the best place to park for surveillance. The plant sat on the north side of Carefree Highway, a two-lane road five miles west of the I-17 and surrounded by scrub desert. There were no other signs of humanity for miles in any direction. The place was far enough north of the bustling metropolis of Phoenix to avoid much traffic late at night.

"Switch to a street view," Avery suggested.

Roz dragged the icon to the plant on the map. A street-level photo of the Yushan entrance replaced the satellite image.

"Move a little ways past the entrance."

Roz clicked the arrows on the screen to travel virtually down the road. "What are you looking for?"

"That." Avery pointed to a green-barked palo verde tree growing near the south side of the road. "That tree should give us enough cover that we won't be easily spotted but can still watch for Big Eddie when he shows up."

"Smart."

"My guess is they'll come from the I-17 and leave the same way for a faster getaway."

"Makes sense." Roz switched back to the satellite image. "Though they could head the other direction and cut south on New River Road a couple miles and pick up the Loop 303."

"The 17's closer."

"True. Another possibility is that they could try to vanish into the desert on one of these little side streets. Or even the labyrinth of roads around Lake Pleasant. Anywhere they can lie low for a bit."

Avery studied the map. "Shit, you're right."

"But I think your initial guess is most probable. Late at night, their headlights would be easy to spot from a police helicopter on the side roads. Not much traffic. Even on the 303. Whereas if they get to the I-17, it'd be easy to hide amongst the throng of people driving north to escape the weekend's summer heat."

Avery pointed to a spot near the entrance. "Either way, if we park here about thirty minutes prior, maybe they won't notice us. When they show up, we can start taking photos and get the proof we need."

"Sounds like a plan. Until then," Roz said, giving her an alluring glance and whispering into Avery's ear. "How about you and I slip into the bedroom for a little pre-espionage fuck? I wonder how many times we can make each other come before we have to leave?"

An uncontrollable need in Avery pushed aside all guilt, sending a flood of heat to her core. "Yes, please."

A few hours later, they both lay exhausted in Roz's bed. The answer to Roz's earlier question was five: three for Roz and two for Avery. More than anything, Avery wanted to spend the rest of the night lying next to this remarkable woman. But if they did, they would miss their chance to nail Big Eddie.

She forced herself up into a sitting position. "We better get cleaned up and dressed if we're going to get to the plant before Big Eddie."

"But, Mom, I don't wanna go to school today," Roz joked wearily, and they both laughed like goofy teenagers.

Avery glanced at her phone and noticed a text from Bobby she'd missed from a few hours earlier.

Bobby:
R U and Roz joining us for dinner tomorrow nite?
Avery:
Lemme ask her.

Avery's pulse quickened. She wasn't sure why she felt so awkward. "Hey, Roz?"

"Yeah, babe?"

"Bobby invited us to dinner with him and his girlfriend tomorrow night. You interested?"

"Ooh, like a double date?"

"Yeah, I guess. You can totally say no. He asked, so, I, uh, just…"

"I'd love to."

Avery was surprised. "Really?"

"Sure. Why not? Bobby seemed cool when I met him briefly the first time I was at the studio. What's his girlfriend like? Another *Star Wars* geek?"

"Worse, she's, like, this very straitlaced, stick-up-her-butt accountant type."

"And you don't like her?"

"We had a bit of an argument the first time we met."

"Over what?"

"She was asking too many questions. Felt very intrusive, like she was judging me." Avery took a deep breath. "Although, honestly, I think maybe subconsciously, I was trying to sabotage things."

"Afraid she was trying to replace Melissa?"

"Pretty stupid, huh?"

"Feelings aren't stupid. They're just feelings. But you acknowledged it."

"Yeah."

"Have you spoken with her since? Or is this going to be a really awkward dinner situation?"

"No, I talked to her. I think we cleared the air." Avery remembered coming out to Dana. Why could she come out to a near stranger but not her own girlfriend?

"Two goth lesbians, a *Star Wars* nerd, and a bean counter. Sounds like an all-American date night to me."

"We're going to the Poké Bar. Is that okay?"

"Poké Bar? Is that a bar for Pokémon players?"

Avery laughed at the image. "No, not as far as I know. They specialize in poké bowls. It's Hawaiian, I think. Like a mix of sushi and salad. It's great, actually. Do you eat sushi?"

"You kidding? I love sushi. What are lox but Jewish sashimi?" Roz winked at her. "I just don't eat shellfish, so no shrimp or squid or octopus."

"Shouldn't be a problem." Avery replied to Bobby's text, though she wasn't sure if he was still up this late.

Avery:
She's coming to dinner.

To her surprise, Bobby responded despite the late hour. He was much more of a night owl than she was.

Bobby:
Cool. Anything she can't eat? Jewish, right? She keep kosher?
Avery:
Yes, Jewish & keeps kosher. Poke Bar s/b OK.
Bobby:
See U 2 love birds tomorrow nite.

Avery blushed at the phrase "love birds," but it filled her with joy.

Thirty minutes later, they were both dressed in gothic all-black.

"You want to take my rental car or Thing?" Avery asked, when they stepped into the dark parking lot. A near-full moon was approaching its zenith. "And before you answer, know that the rental reeks of smoke and weed."

"Like I said earlier, I don't have a sense of smell, so that won't bother me as long as it doesn't get into my clothes. As much as I love Thing for all of its quirkiness, I don't think it'd be good for surveillance."

"Why not?"

"For starters, if we want to keep the A/C on, the engine's a little noisy."

"It does sound a bit like a riding lawn mower."

"And almost as fast."

"The stinky tin can they rented me isn't much faster. And the rental is bright red, whereas Thing is the color of sand. I know it's dark, but the less conspicuous, the better, I'm thinking."

"Yes, but at least you can take the rental on the highway."

"But not Thing?"

"If I gun it all the way through the gears—and I mean 'balls-to-the wall, pedal-to-the-metal' gun it—it might make it up to sixty-five miles an hour with a good tailwind and when I'm alone in the car. With two people? Probably won't top sixty."

"Seriously?"

"Afraid so. I never drive it on the highway."

"Then why'd you get it?"

Roz shrugged. "I like weird. What can I tell you?"

Avery sighed, dreading the idea of spending hours sitting in the stinky rental car. "Maybe you can't smell anything, but if I have to sit in that rental for more than thirty minutes, I'll be sick to my stomach. It's that bad."

Roz shrugged. "Okay, Thing it is. We'll stick to the surface streets."

Forty-five minutes later, they turned onto Carefree Highway from Lake Pleasant Parkway.

Avery spotted the glow of the brightly-lit Yushan plant right away and pointed. "There it is."

The three- or four-story industrial building sat far back from the road, separated by a parking lot the size of a football field and dotted with security lights. A ten-foot fence topped with concertina wire surrounded the grounds. Uniformed guards manned the front gate.

Roz slowed, staring at the facility as they approached it. "Looks a lot bigger in person."

"I think it was still under construction when the satellite images were last taken."

A little before they reached the security shack guarding the front entrance, Roz pulled off the road behind the large palo verde tree they'd seen on the street view.

Roz turned off the headlights. Faint moonlight lit the sprawling desert outside of the glow of the manufacturing plant.

"Should I kill the engine? It's still almost ninety-five degrees outside."

Avery debated. *Loud engine or unbearable heat?* "Kill it," she said reluctantly. "If they hear the engine, this whole thing is for nothing."

Roz turned off the ignition. Avery immediately felt a push of warmth seeping through the rag top.

A coyote's cry pierced the sudden quiet. It sounded only twenty feet away from where they sat. Several other coyotes joined in, yipping and howling in a furious chorus. Goose bumps rose on Avery's arms at the pack's primal cries. They must have made a kill. A rabbit, possibly a deer.

Avery took a deep breath and stared out at the illuminated facility. Even in the middle of the night, the parking lot was a third full. They must be working multiple shifts. But not a person in sight. Just the harsh shadows from the security lights, the empty parked cars, and the sounds of the desert. Something about the tableau made her feel lonely.

From the back seat, Roz grabbed a canvas bag and pulled out what looked like a pair of high-tech binoculars.

"What's that?" Avery asked.

"Night-vision binoculars. Brought a pair for you too if you want. Switch is on the front."

Roz handed her a pair.

Avery switched it on and held it up to her face. "Holy shit! This is so cool!"

"Also brought this."

Avery lowered her binoculars. Roz retrieved what looked like a small satellite dish.

"What the hell is that?" Avery whispered. "Satellite Wi-Fi?"

"No, it's a parabolic mic. It channels distant sounds and amplifies them so you can hear conversations from far away." Roz flipped a latch at the top of the windshield. "Get the one on your side."

Avery unlatched the one above her head. "Now what?"

Roz pushed back the convertible roof then pulled the window out of her door, storing it in the smallish backseat. Their bubble of cool air dissipated, though the dry heat wasn't unbearable since the sun was down.

"The window just pulls out like that? You don't roll it down."

"Weird, huh?"

Avery removed the window on her side and placed it next to Roz's.

Roz plugged the parabolic mic into her phone and pointed the dish toward the guard shack.

"I'm telling you, Mac, this girl was into me. And looks? We're talking supermodel," said a man's voice coming from Roz's phone.

"That's the security guard?" Avery asked.

"One of them."

"A supermodel type was into you?" asked a second male voice. "What was she, a hooker?"

"Hell no, she wasn't a damn hooker. She was nice. She even liked my jokes."

"Now I know she was a hooker. Your jokes are a one-way ticket to a cringe fest."

"We should have picked up some cold drinks. We really worked up a sweat earlier." Roz winked at her.

Avery replayed the amazing sex in her mind. And again, her dreaded secret weighed on her. *Why am I making this so hard? Fuck it! I'm telling her.*

"Roz…"

"Yes, my sexy girlfriend?"

Avery swallowed hard. The term of endearment only made this harder.

"There's something you should know. About me. Something that… I probably should have told you before. Like, right when you asked me to be your girlfriend. I don't know, maybe before that even."

"Okay."

She braced herself, her heart hammering in her chest.

CHAPTER 38

THE YUSHAN HEIST

"Roz, I'm transgender."

Holy fuck balls! I said it. It's out there. Trigger pulled. Relationship over. Let the humiliation begin.

"You're transgender?"

"Yes."

"Which way?"

"What?"

"I mean, are you planning to transition to being a guy? Or are you nonbinary?"

"Um, no, I…" Avery's mind felt like a swarm of bees was buzzing inside it. Not the nice, friendly domestic honeybees. No, these were angry-as-fuck Africanized killer murder hornet bees.

"I transitioned when I was thirteen. Or at least that's when I started. It's why my old man kicked me out of the house. Why I ended up on the streets before Bobby and Melissa took me in. I had surgery when I turned eighteen."

"You were assigned male at birth?"

Avery was surprised that Roz was familiar with the proper terminology. "Yeah. "

Roz's expression was impossible to read in the dark. Avery waited. And waited. She resisted the urge to keep explaining.

After what felt like forever, Roz finally replied. "Wow. That's a lot to take in."

Her words were bitter.

Fuck, Avery thought. Not the response she was hoping for. But she wasn't surprised. The angry murder bees in her brain cranked everything up by a factor of ten. She should ask Roz to drive back so she could go home alone and get plastered.

Twin circles of light appeared in the distance. Avery checked the time on the phone. It was 11:29.

"That must be them," Roz said matter-of-factly, as if their previous exchange had never happened.

The approaching vehicle stopped short of the Yushan driveway then turned off onto a side road that ran parallel to the security fence.

Avery looked through the night-vision binoculars. "That had to be them. That road they turned down must be new. It wasn't on the map."

"What do you want to do?" Roz didn't sound as excited as she had before Avery came out to her.

"I'm guessing that road leads to the backside of the plant. We should follow them."

"What if they spot us?"

"They won't. Come on."

Roz started Thing again and followed the other vehicle down the side road. Avery could see the taillights in the distance before the vehicle turned left around the back side of the facility.

"I don't like this," Roz said.

"It'll be okay. I promise."

On the far side of the Yushan campus, they reached a sliding security gate that was closing. There was no way they could get through in time. The other vehicle, a black panel truck, cruised past a fleet of parked semitrailers and a cluster of forklifts toward a loading dock at the back of the plant.

"Shit." Avery watched the truck back up to the dock.

"Maybe we should call it a night."

"No, I'm not letting them get away with this."

Avery grabbed her phone, opened her camera app, and switched it to low light mode. When she zoomed in, she could see two men climbing out of the truck. Their faces were too blurry to make out from this distance, but from his considerable size and cheesy eighties-style mullet, she recognized the driver as Big Eddie. She had no clue about the guy with her.

"Point the parabolic mic at them."

Roz did so.

"Grab the equipment bag," Big Eddie said, his voice a deep Texas drawl. "Our window opens in thirty seconds."

Avery continued to take photos of the men.

"You got the card key?" his buddy asked.

"In my pocket."

"You sure the cameras are off?"

Big Eddie pointed at something above the door next to the dock. "You see any red lights? Quit dawdling, or we'll lose our chance."

"You recording this?" Avery asked.

"Yes."

Big Eddie approached the door. "Let's do this thing."

He pressed a white card to a sensor next to the door, and the two men disappeared into the building.

"You get what you needed?" Roz asked.

"I need a photo of them with the stolen goods if I'm going to get him to tell me who he's working for. Right now, all we got is a blurry image of him getting out of a truck."

"Avery, be sensible. There's a gate. How are you going to get through that?"

"I remember the gate code from their texts."

"Ave… this is crazy. We could get busted for trespassing. Or worse, shot by these guys."

"I won't be long. Just be ready to take off when I come running. It'll be okay. Trust me." Avery stepped out of the car.

"You just now told me you're transgender, and you're asking me to trust *you*?" Roz's words felt like a knife in Avery's gut. "Where was your trust in me? Why did you wait until after we slept together. Not just once but several times?"

"Look, can we talk about this after?"

"Whatever. Go play Avery the Avenger."

Avery stepped up to the keypad and punched in the code. A buzz sounded, and the gate clanked open. The second there was enough room, she slipped through and hustled past several parked semitrailers, a small brigade of forklifts, and a dumpster to where Big Eddie's truck idled.

She took photos of the license plate and the side of the truck then crouched behind a stack of shipping crates to wait for Big Eddie Myles and his accomplice to return.

Avery sent a text to Roz. "Should be back in 10." There was no immediate reply.

As she waited, she replayed her coming out to Roz, followed by her final words. *"Why did you wait until after we slept together?"*

It was over. She should have told Roz the truth when they first met for brunch at Essence Bakery.

The night air suddenly felt smothering, her throat choked with dust. Roz was probably long gone by now, having left Avery's sorry ass behind to deal with Big Eddie and his partner. Not that Avery blamed her. Who would want to be with her? She was a dumpster fire to the nth degree.

After what felt like hours, the sound of a metal garage door opening caught her attention. Big Eddie emerged, pushing a dolly laden with a crate of what she guessed was microprocessors and loaded it into the back of the truck. His partner followed with another dolly of stolen goods.

Avery felt a surge of adrenaline as she snapped photo after photo, documenting the heist in progress. Just as Big Eddie was approaching the truck with another crate, her phone pinged, and the screen flashed with a text alert.

Shit! Avery slipped her phone into her pocket.

Big Eddie stopped and scanned the area.

"Glen, we got company," Big Eddie whispered.

"I'll take care of it." Glen stepped out of the back of the truck. He drew a pistol with a silencer and pointed it in Avery's direction. "There!"

The top of the crate next to her exploded.

"Fuck." Avery took off running, zigzagging between semitrailers, forklifts, and dumpsters. Bullets zipped past her, ricocheting off the vehicles she was dodging past.

Avery ducked behind a trailer, staring at the closed security gate. She wanted to make a run for it, but knew she wouldn't have time to enter the code before she was shot in the back.

She cursed herself for not listening to Roz. *Why did I think I could get away with this?*

A shadow charged her. Before she could react, she was thrown to the ground.

"Gotcha!" Glen wasn't as big as Eddie, but he moved fast.

He tried to shoot her as they grappled, but she knocked the gun out of his hand. She raked her nails across his face and slipped out his grasp, jumping back to her feet.

"Kitten's got some claws." Glen flicked open a knife. "I got a claw too."

He lunged at her with the blade, slicing open her right arm. She kicked him in the nuts and pressed her other hand against the wound.

"Fucking cunt," he growled, half bent over. He still held the knife and was shuffling back toward her.

Avery risked glancing away for a split second and spotted what she was looking for.

When he lunged at her again, she made a rolling dive and came up with his pistol. She put two in his head before the slide locked back. The gun was empty.

"Glen, what's your status?" Big Eddie called.

She spotted him approaching through the shadows. Her instincts told her to run, but she was trapped. The gate was still closed, and Big Eddie was no doubt armed as well.

His steps grew closer. "Glen, where the fuck are you?"

Heart pounding, she snatched up Glen's knife and braced herself for the fight of her life against a man twice her size.

A clanking sound caught her attention. The gate was opening. Confused but grateful, Avery raced toward the exit despite a series of pops from behind her. Eddie was shooting at her.

As Avery reached the gate, Roz shouted from behind the wheel of Thing. “Get in!”

Avery dove into the passenger seat and slammed the door.

Tires screeched against the pavement as Roz floored the accelerator, and they sped down the side street toward Carefree Highway.

Avery and Roz exchanged a look of relief, their hearts pounding in unison. They'd made it. As they disappeared into the night, Avery grinned like a madwoman, knowing she had the evidence she needed to bring down Big Eddie Myles and his criminal empire.

CHAPTER 39

THE GETAWAY

"You get what you needed?" Roz's voice sounded angry and cold.

Avery looked down at her hands and realized she still held Glen's pistol. "I think so."

"Holy fuck! Is that a gun?"

"It was Big Eddie's partner's." She tossed it into the passing desert. The effort made the slash in her arm burn. "Shit."

"Are you shot?"

"No. Knife wound." She pressed against the cut, hoping to stop the bleeding. "Sorry for putting you at risk."

"I agreed to come on this adventure. You got your precious photos. That's all that matters, I guess." Roz said it all so matter-of-factly that the message was abundantly clear. This relationship, if it could be called that, was over.

Avery wanted to say something, anything, to salvage their friendship. But no words came. Instead, she stared out at the road ahead.

Roz took a hard right onto Carefree Highway, heading toward Lake Pleasant Parkway. Thing's engine whined and strained as Roz floored it to the limit.

Avery glanced out the back and spotted two pinpoints of light. "Shit. That's gotta be him."

"We can't outrun them. Not in Thing."

"I'm… I'm so sorry I got you into this."

"Don't be sorry. Just hold on."

"Hold on? Hold on to what?" Avery found a bar above the windshield and clung to it for life.

Roz braked suddenly and took a hard right. Avery fell toward the gearshift, but held on despite the fierce pain. As more side roads appeared, Roz randomly turned onto them.

Did she know where she's going? Avery didn't have a clue.

Eventually, the road they were on came to a dead end. Roz killed the engine.

"Where are we?" Avery dared to ask.

"Somewhere around Lake Pleasant. How bad's your arm?" Roz was panting. A flashlight appeared in her hand and she shined it on Avery's arm smeared with blood.

"Oh, shit! Avery! That looks bad." Roz grabbed a first aid kit from the floor of the back seat and pressed a large sterile pad over the wound. "Keep pressure on it."

Avery followed her instructions while Roz wrapped it tightly in gauze and tied it off.

"Thanks."

"You're welcome."

"We can't stay here," Avery suggested. "If he finds us, we got no way out. We'll be cornered."

As she said it, the sound of a truck engine approached. A moment later, a pair of headlights appeared behind them.

"Maybe you shouldn't have tossed that gun."

"It was empty. Got any weapons in that bag of tricks of yours? A stun gun? Baton? Maybe a bazooka?"

"No."

Avery took in a deep breath. Do or die time.

"Stay here," she said as she opened her door. "Get ready to turn around and leave on my signal. Without me."

"Avery, no."

Avery stepped out of the car and stood trembling but defiant in the glare of the headlights.

"I'm the one you want. Come and get me, motherfucker!" She balled her fists, ready to strike the instant Big Eddie stepped into range.

Flashing blue and red lights washed over her.

"Ma'am, get back in the car," said a stern male voice. Not Big Eddie's baritone.

She stood her ground.

"Ma'am, I'm not going to ask you again. Get back into the car. Do it now!"

A cop. Probably a sheriff's deputy. Or a park ranger. Not Big Eddie coming to kill them. She climbed back into Thing. Every muscle in her body shook from adrenaline overload, pain, and exhaustion.

A Maricopa County sheriff's deputy appeared outside Roz's door and shined a flashlight in their faces. "Evening, ladies. Can I see some IDs?"

Avery and Roz handed him their driver's licenses. He examined them then handed them back. "So, Ms. Fein and Ms. Byrne, what are you two doing parked here?"

"Enjoying the meteor shower," Roz said without missing a beat. "All the light pollution from the city makes it hard to see most of them."

As if on cue, a shooting star zipped across the sky, followed by another. Maybe someone up there was looking out for them.

"You have a camping permit?"

"No," Roz replied.

"Well, I'm afraid you'll have to find someplace else to enjoy the show. This section of the park's closed after hours."

"Yes, sir."

He shined the light at Avery, and she squinted in the glare.

"Ma'am, do you require medical assistance?"

"I cut myself opening a bag of chips with my knife."

"Uh huh." He clearly wasn't buying it. "I suggest you two go home and take care of that injury before it gets infected."

"Yes, sir."

"Okay, ladies. You have a good night now." He backed away and returned to his truck.

"That was fun," Roz said in a humorless voice. "Not."

The ride back to Roz's apartment seemed to take forever—in part because they had to stick to the surface streets. But it seemed longer because neither of them spoke.

The Thing had no radio, so there was nothing to break the silence other than the strained drone of the engine. The searing pain in her arm grew more intense as the adrenaline wore off. On the plus side, there was no sign of Big Eddie.

When they at last pulled into the apartment complex, Avery said, "I'm sorry. For everything."

"I know." No offer to come inside. No words of understanding or terms of endearment.

Avery held out her injured arm. "Thanks for the rescue and for patching me up."

"You should go to the ER. Might need stitches."

"Yeah. Maybe I will."

They climbed out and stood staring at each other for the longest time.

"Well, good night," Avery said at last.

To Avery's surprise, Roz cradled Avery's head in her hands and gave her a peck on the lips. "Goodbye, Avery Byrne."

CHAPTER 40

THIRD WHEEL

When Avery got home, she unwrapped the gauze and peeled back the blood-soaked pad. The wound was about three inches long and still bled a little.

She probably should have taken Roz's advice and had it stitched up at the ER. But she wasn't in the mood to be sitting around a hospital for hours and then have to cough up a few grand because of her lousy insurance. As a former cutter, she'd treated similar wounds in the past.

She turned on her shower and rinsed it for a few minutes under scalding water, gasping at the pain. She then put some antiseptic ointment in the wound, closed it with Steri-Strips, then covered it with a large bandage.

Her sleep was fitful and haunted by nightmares of shadowy figures chasing her as she dodged bullets coming from every direction. The next day, she opened her phone and spotted an unread message from Roz. Her heart rose. Had she reconsidered? Did she still want to be her girlfriend?

Avery opened it, only to realize it was the text sent the night before. The one that had alerted Big Eddie and his partner in crime to her presence down by the loading docks.

Roz:
Should I open the gate?

Her heart sank. Roz had punched in the code and saved Avery's life. But now she wanted nothing to do with her.

Avery spent the next hour studying the photos she'd taken of the heist. She was amazed by the quality, considering the low-light conditions. Both men's faces were visible in a few of the shots.

Having the audio from Roz's phone and the reports from SkipTrakkr would've sealed the deal. And that thought took all the joy out of Avery's victory. She'd gotten the dirt she needed on Big Eddie, only to lose her relationship with Roz.

"That's a lot to take in," Roz had said when Avery finally told her the truth. "Why did you wait until after we slept together to tell me you're transgender?"

Translation: "You're not who I thought you were. I can't trust you and don't want to be with you anymore."

Ignoring Roz's concerns and running off to follow Big Eddie hadn't helped the situation. She could have gotten them both killed.

She sat in her apartment, staring at the walls, going over and over in her mind how she could have done things differently. Why had she waited so long to tell Roz truth of who she was? Then again, fuck Roz for judging her. It wasn't like she chose to be trans. It didn't make her less of a woman.

She spent most of the day in a funk. She had the urge to call Kimi and tell her what had happened but didn't want to put her in the awkward situation of choosing sides. Avery had no one left to hang out with and complain about life to.

Around three o'clock, Bobby texted her.

Bobby:
U want to meet @ the house or the restaurant?
Avery:
House is fine.
Bobby:
OK. C U 2 @ 5pm.

Avery didn't have the heart to tell him Roz wouldn't show. Still, she didn't like how they had left things. So she mustered her courage and called her. After a few rings, the call went to voicemail.

"Hey, Roz. It's Avery. I… I'm sorry about last night. I'm sorry I'm not who you thought I was. I don't blame you for not wanting to see me again. But in the unlikely chance you still want to join Bobby and his girlfriend and me for dinner, we're meeting at his house around five." She gave his address. "I can pick you up in the rental if you'd rather not drive Thing. I'd really love to hear from you."

She hung up. The rambling message she'd left made her seem like a desperate, clingy, blathering idiot.

She checked the news feed on her phone and saw a news story about the break-in at the Yushan plant, though the details were scant. The story said that three hundred thousand dollars' worth of state-of-the-art microprocessors had been stolen. One armed suspect had supposedly been killed by security.

The armed suspect they were referring to was no doubt Big Eddie's partner, Glen. *Well, if they want to take credit for shooting the bastard, let them.* At least the cops wouldn't be pounding on her door, asking questions.

Avery still hadn't heard from Roz when she showed up at Bobby's, fully gothed out.

As soon as Bobby saw her walk into the house, his expression darkened with obvious concern. He stared grim faced at the large bandage on her arm. "What happened, kiddo?"

"Accidentally cut myself with a knife opening a package from Amazon. Those plastic clamshells are a bitch."

"Ave." He put a hand on her shoulder. "Be honest with me, kiddo. Are you cutting again?"

The genuine concern in his voice ripped at her self-control. She held back the tears in her eyes.

"No, Appa. It was an accident. I swear." She met his gaze, hoping he didn't ask for more of an explanation.

"Okay. But if you're struggling again, I'm here for you."

"I know."

"Where's Roz?"

Avery's heart sank. "Not coming. We kinda broke up after I came out to her last night."

He pointed to her injured arm. "Did she do that to you?"

"What? No. We just broke up."

"Oh, kiddo, I'm so sorry."

Avery shrugged. "She was mad that I didn't tell her until after we… you know."

Bobby hugged her and turned to Dana. "Well, I guess it's just the three of us."

Avery considered bailing, not wanting to be a third wheel. But Poké Bar had been a favorite of hers and Bobby's. And for once, she needed to be around people.

At the restaurant, she picked at her food and barely participated in the conversation between Bobby and Dana. Every so often, she caught them making googly eyes at each other like a couple of lovesick teenagers. She wanted to sink into the floor and disappear.

Repeatedly, she checked her phone for any reply from Roz. But there was nothing.

When they returned to Bobby's house after dinner, Avery wanted to go straight home. But Bobby and Dana talked her into staying and playing video games with them.

Avery reluctantly agreed and played a multiplayer *Star Wars* game where they were fighting the Empire, first in X-wings, then with laser pistols, and finally with light sabers. Dana seemed to have the most fun despite her avatar getting killed most frequently.

After a few hours, Avery had had enough, and Bobby walked her to the door.

"Good night, Appa."

He gave her a farewell hug and a peck on the forehead. "Sorry things didn't work out with Roz. She seemed like a keeper."

"She deserves better."

"Bullshit." Bobby rarely cursed, and the word shocked her. "Don't ever talk that way about my beloved daughter."

She hung her head. "But…"

"No buts. You are a beautiful, talented, funny, smart young woman. The fact that you're trans only ads to your beauty. It's a feature, not a bug."

"That's not true."

Dana approached the two of them. "Bobby's right, Avery. I don't know much about what it's like to be transgender, but all my life, I've dealt with anti-Asian hate and ignorance. One thing I've learned is that the parts of ourselves that make us unique only add to our worth. These are the qualities that shape us and bring out our strength and beauty. Like a rare orchid or a precious gem. And if Roz can't see it, then that is her failure, not yours."

Avery stood there, surprised by Dana's encouragement. Until recently, she had seen this woman as competition for Melissa's memory and Bobby's attention. Dana would never replace Melissa, but it felt good to have her as a friend and ally.

"Thanks, Dana. That means a lot."

Bobby asked, "You going to be all right tonight?"

"I'm okay, Appa. Just take some time to get over her." She knew he understood.

"There are a lot of fish in the sea, kiddo. Eventually, you'll find a keeper."

They hugged again, and Avery took off.

CHAPTER 41

NOISY BROS ARE BACK

As Avery approached her apartment building, she caught the sounds of splashing, laughter, and hip-hop coming from the pool area. According to her watch, it was just after ten thirty. Jaden the Jock and his college bros were back.

"Fucking assholes," she muttered.

She took out her phone, hoping to hijack Jaden's Bluetooth speaker again. It didn't work, since the speaker was already connected to Jaden's phone. She settled for covertly recording them on video.

"Fucking Ms. Patterson," Jaden said. "What a dingbat. She was so impressed with my term paper, she read the first page aloud to the class. I kept a straight face, but inside, I was laughing my ass off at her. Can't believe generating that essay off that AI site got me an A on that shitty assignment. She thinks I'm the next Ernest Hemingway."

The group laughed.

"Fucking teachers," Jaden's girlfriend said. "They're so clueless. I did the same thing last semester in Mr. Warren's American history class. Same results. Where'd they get their teaching degrees? A vending machine?"

More raucous laughter followed.

"Those who can't do, teach, am I right?" another male jock said.

Jaden caught her gaze and shouted, "Hey, look! Vampira's back! Hey, goth girl, you wanna brew, or do you only drink blood?"

Again, the group thought he was so funny and followed with a barrage of taunts.

"What I want is for you assholes to respect the rules. Pool closes at nine. So go the fuck home! Unless you'd like another early-morning punk rock wake-up call."

All humor drained from Jaden's face. He stormed out of the pool, splattering water onto the pavement, and stopped on the other side of the fence. He was a good six inches taller than her and at least fifty pounds heavier, all of it toned muscle.

"You do this," Jaden growled. "You hijacked my speaker and played that shit you freaks call music."

"Prove it, asshole."

The two of them glared at each other for what felt like hours.

Finally, Jaden broke the silence. "You do that shit again, I'll have my father's lawyers put your freaky white ass in jail."

"Your daddy's lawyers? Is that who you have fight your battles for you? Poor little Jaden has to hide behind daddy's skirts?"

"Oh, you wanna go, little girl?" He turned back to his friends. "Bitch thinks she can take me."

They laughed.

"You looked pretty scared when I slammed you against the post yesterday morning."

Avery knew he could probably wipe the floor with her. But she didn't care. She held her ground and glared at him like she wasn't worried in the least.

"This girl took you, man?" one of Jaden's buddies asked. "Dude!"

Fury blazed in Jaden's eyes. He banged on the fence. "You're lucky I don't hit girls."

"Well, I have no problem hitting arrogant assholes. Keep pissing me off, Jaden. You'll learn just how far I'll go." She extended her arms, revealing the countless lacerations. "You should see the other guy."

Jaden seemed to notice the scratches. She could see the wheels turning as he no doubt wondered what she'd done to get them.

"Fuck off, bitch."

"Tell me something. How come you're at a community college? Were your grades so bad that even your rich daddy couldn't get you into a real college? Not even on an athletic scholarship?"

He pounded on the fence so hard, she flinched but held her ground.

"Guess I was right." She walked away and climbed the steps to her apartment without giving Jaden another look.

Once she'd turned the deadbolt, she downloaded the video she'd taken to her laptop, deleted the part where she admitted to slamming him against the post, and uploaded it to the web.

On the Glendale Community College website, she located the teachers Jaden and his girlfriend had mentioned duping with AI-generated term papers and sent them a link to the video.

Still no response of any kind from Roz. Avery could handle an outright rejection, but the uncertainty and silence was driving her crazy. At some level, she knew that this was a rejection. But she couldn't stop herself from sending a text.

> Roz, I really miss you. I understand why you don't want to see me. But I thought we had something. I didn't choose to be transgender, but that doesn't make me any less of a woman. I've got all the same parts you do, except maybe the baby factory. You sought me out because you said you saw something special in me. You said you'd love me no matter what. Please let's talk.

She couldn't think of anything else to say, so she turned on the TV and started re-watching the TV series *Wednesday* until she fell asleep.

CHAPTER 42

RETALIATION

There had been no response from Roz when Avery got up on Sunday morning. Not that she was expecting one. The relationship was over. Time to move on. More importantly, time to exact a little revenge for Boze, Hatchet, and Mendez.

She needed to know three things. First, how had Big Eddie drugged Hatchet and Boze so that it looked like an accidental overdose? Second, what specifically had Big Eddie done to the steering of Mendez's Plymouth Satellite. And finally, the name of the person at Zeiber who had ordered the murders.

Even without the audio from Roz's phone, she had enough dirt on Big Eddie that she should be able to coerce him into telling her what she wanted to know.

But how should she approach him? Should do this over the phone? Or should she meet him someplace? If so, where?

Her first instinct was to meet somewhere private, away from prying eyes. But if things went sideways, Big Eddie could beat her to death. She'd be nothing but the latest in his string of victims.

So, someplace public. But not where other people could overhear. The last place she'd done something like this was Grumpy's Bar and Grill. And while she'd successfully taken down the Desert Mafia, she'd also been banned from the restaurant for life.

She eventually settled on Elbie's, a local chain of restaurants offering mediocre American fare and abysmal service. The locations she'd been to in the past were rarely more than a third full, even at peak hours. The lazy servers wouldn't be pestering them every five minutes for a drink refill. And they had booths that offered a little privacy from the rest of the tables.

Now, how to get Big Eddie to meet her there? She didn't want to tip him off that she was onto him. Maybe she could claim she was still grieving about Mendez's death and wanted to spend time with someone on his team.

As she pondered this, her phone rang. The caller ID said it was Kimi.

"Hey, girl, what's up?" Avery asked.

"It's Roz. She's been attacked."

Kimi's words felt like a punch to the solar plexus. "Attacked? Oh my goth! By whom? Is she okay?"

"She's in the ICU at University Medical Center. Her mother says a neighbor saw her attacked in the wee hours of Saturday morning outside her apartment. She's in surgery now."

Guilt and shame hit Avery like a punch to the gut. This was all her fault. She'd insisted on going after Big Eddie. He must have followed them back to Roz's apartment complex and gotten through the gate.

"Where's University Medical Center? Tempe?" Avery guessed it was near the ASU campus.

"No, it's in Phoenix. The hospital that used to be called Good Samaritan—the one on McDowell that looks like a giant beehive."

"I know the one. I'll be right there."

Twenty-five minutes later, she walked into the ICU waiting room. Kimi and Chupa were sitting with a woman in her fifties. She looked like an older, less-goth version of Roz. Again, the guilt hit her. This woman's daughter might die because of Avery's misguided need for revenge.

Kimi's face lit up when Avery approached. They rushed toward each other and embraced.

"Do they know anything?" Avery asked, desperate for good news.

"Still in surgery last we heard."

"Did the police catch who did this?" Avery fantasized about blowing a hole in Big Eddie skull.

"A Detective Calderón was by earlier talking to Abigail, Roz's mom. He said the neighbor who witnessed the attack described the guy as a large white man, over six feet tall. Didn't get a good look at him because it was too dark. But he drove off in a red older-model car when the neighbor started shouting."

"I swear it wasn't me," Chupa said, followed by his goofy Seth Rogen laugh.

Kimi glowered at him.

"Sorry. Just trying to lighten the mood."

"Did Roz have her phone with her?" If the cops recovered it, it could be used to bring down Big Eddie.

"Her phone? I don't know. Why?"

"Maybe she caught a photo of her attacker."

"I don't know. If it was with her, the police probably took it as evidence," Kimi paused a moment. "Avery, let me introduce you to Roz's mom."

They walked over to the older woman. "Abigail Fein? This is Avery Byrne, Roz's girlfriend."

Avery didn't have the heart to mention the breakup. "I'm really sorry, Ms. Fein."

Ms. Fein stood and embraced her. "I'm sorry too. Roz told me a lot about you. And please, call me Abigail."

"Thanks, Abigail."

"I hear you're quite the artist. I saw the tattoo on Roz's arm before they took her into surgery. Is that your work?"

"Yes, ma'am."

"A bare-breasted mermaid?"

Avery squirmed. "Yes, ma'am."

"I suppose it's the duty of every generation to shock and embarrass the one before. My mother hated when I married a private investigator instead of a doctor or lawyer. Of course, when she was young, she dropped acid at Woodstock and followed the Grateful Dead around for a few years. And her father was a Nazi hunter."

"Oh."

"You are talented."

"Thank you."

"Ms. Fein?" A diminutive Latinx man in surgical scrubs appeared in the waiting room doorway.

Abigail approached the surgeon. Kimi gripped Avery's hand, but they kept their distance to afford Roz's mother some privacy. When Abigail began to sob, Avery's heart sank.

After the surgeon left, Abigail returned to her seat and let out a deep breath. "Doctor Gutierrez says she's stable. They were able to relieve the pressure on her brain, and the swelling is already going down. They're cautiously optimistic, though they don't know the extent of any brain damage."

"When will they know?" Avery asked.

"Just have to wait, I'm afraid. They will bring her up to her room shortly." Abigail took a deep breath and let it out slowly. "As Roz's girlfriend, you're family, as far as I'm concerned. So when they bring her up to her room, you're welcome to come with me to see her if you'd like."

Emotion choked her words. "I'd like that a lot. Thank you. I'm really sorry this happened."

"It's not your fault, dear."

Abigail explained she had wanted to contact Avery right away but hadn't known how to reach her. It had taken more than a day to get in touch with Kimi, who then called Avery.

As they waited, Avery sent a text to Bobby, letting him know Roz was in the hospital. Bobby replied a little while later, offering his condolences.

A nurse stepped into the waiting room. "Ms. Fein, Roz is in her room. You can come see her now."

"Thank you." Abigail turned to Avery. "You ready?"

Avery wasn't sure all of a sudden. It was her fault Big Eddie had done this to Roz. Still, what would it look like if she refused? "Yes."

She and Abigail walked hand in hand into the unit. Abigail introduced herself at the nurses' station and said Avery was her daughter's fiancée, which only added to Avery's growing mountain of guilt.

Abigail's grip tightened when they entered Roz's room. Avery barely recognized her swollen, bruised face and the crown of bandages atop her head. Every conceivable monitoring device filled the small room, beeping and dinging incessantly.

Avery's knees buckled, and she grabbed a nearby chair in time to avoid falling to the floor.

"Roz," she whispered as tears fell. Memories of finding Sam's broken body strapped to their kitchen chair played on repeat in Avery's mind. This was her curse. To see the people she loved most murdered in the most brutal ways. The Lost Kids. Melissa. Sam. And now Roz, who clung to life.

"Who would do this to you, my sweet girl?" Abigail asked her unconscious daughter, having taken a seat on the other side of the bed.

Avery wanted to tell her but held back. She would make it right. She would bring Big Eddie Myles and his boss at Zeiber to justice. Even if it cost her freedom and meant a lifetime in prison, facing goth knew what horrors trans women endured in those places. Even if it cost Avery her life.

As the minutes turned to hours, dragging the way they always did in hospitals, Avery found herself studying Abigail's face. There was strength and resilience in the older woman's golden-brown eyes. She had buried a husband. And now faced losing a daughter .

And yet she'd barely shed a tear. Not for lack of compassion or lack of sorrow. No, Avery could clearly see the love and heartbreak in this woman's eyes. It was something else. Something Avery envied even as she herself turned into a blubbering puddle of misery.

She took a deep breath, drawing in strength and resolve, just as Bobby and Melissa had taught her over and over. *Breathe in peace. Release fear.* But she wasn't really interested in peace now. Only revenge.

CHAPTER 43

ASKING FOR BACKUP

"What happened to your arm, Avery?" Abigail asked after a long silence.

Avery stared down at the bandage. "Cut it opening one of those plastic clam shell packages. Something I'd ordered for work."

"I see. How did you get started in the tattooing business? Is that the correct term?"

"Close enough. I liked to draw as a kid. When my foster father took me in, he taught me. He's had his own studio for years."

"Foster father? What happened to your birth parents? Were they killed?"

"No, they kicked me out of the house when I was thirteen."

"For being gay?"

Avery was not about to share any more than was necessary with this woman, especially after how things had gone with Roz. "Yeah, for being queer. My foster dad, he's been more of a father than my birth father ever was."

"Well, I'm glad you found someone who is supportive. Family is important. When Roz came out to us, we already suspected. She was never into dresses or dolls or girly things. Preferred playing sports with her older brothers. We didn't care who she loved so long as she was safe and didn't get into drugs."

They continued to talk. And although it was mostly small talk, Avery didn't feel as uncomfortable as she usually did chatting with strangers.

When her phone rang, she saw it was Bobby and stepped out of the room. Once past the nurses' station, she answered. "Hey, Appa."

"How's our girl doing?"

Avery wasn't sure if he meant her or Roz. "She's out of surgery. Doctors are hopeful, but she's still asleep."

"Does she have family there? You want Dana and me to come by?"

"Her mom's here, as are Kimi and Chupa. No need to come down right now. I'll let you know when there's an update."

"Please do, kiddo. We're here for you. And for Roz too."

"Thanks, Appa."

She hung up and glanced back at Roz's hospital room. It was time for Big Eddie to pay for his crimes. But she would need help. She called another number on her phone. It was a long shot.

"Hello?"

"Rocket, it's Avery."

"Hey, girl! How's it going?"

"I need your help."

"What with?"

"Taking down Big Eddie."

He sighed. "Geez, Avery, we talked about this."

"That was before he put Roz in the hospital, Rocket. Beat her to shit. She may die. That, on top of the fact that he killed Hatchet, Boze, and Mendez. We can't sit on our hands any longer."

"Girl, Mendez's crash was an accident. The cops said so. Rack and pinion was worn out. You know these old cars. Same thing happened to Drifter a few years back. Those teeth wear out after a while, then next thing you know, you got no steering. Not great when you're going a hundred miles an hour."

"Do you seriously believe that? Just like Boze and Hatchet just accidentally overdosed. And I suppose you think my girlfriend just accidentally got herself bludgeoned nearly to death."

"Avery, listen…"

"No, you listen! Fisch told me everything about how he, Hatch, and Boze were blackmailing Zeiber Motors."

"What are you talking about?"

"They found proof that Zeiber stole the prototype from Quasar—the one Fisch got fired for. Zeiber put that engine in Mendez's Satellite. Then when Boze, Fish, and Hatchet threatened to blow the lid on the entire scheme, someone at Zeiber paid them off, using Big Eddie to deliver the money. But when the guys asked for more money, Zeiber used Mendez and Big Eddie to shut them up permanently. And then he sabotaged Mendez's car to take care of loose ends."

"You can't really believe that."

"It's the truth, Rocket. Not only that, you remember I told you Big Eddie was planning on breaking into the Yushan microprocessor plant? Well, he did. And I've got the pictures to prove it. I was there when it happened."

"I did hear something on the news about a burglary at the plant."

"All I'm asking is that you be my backup when I get Big Eddie to confess how he poisoned Hatchet and Boze and then sabotaged Mendez's ride. Oh, and who at Zeiber was pulling the strings. Maybe you'll finally believe me when you hear from his own lips."

Rocket didn't respond right away.

"I need your help, dude. If nothing else, to give me a little protection. He fucking killed our friends."

"Avery, I love you like a kid sister. But right now, I got enough problems in my own life. Tiff is accusing me of violating the restraining order and beating her up again."

"Again? You beat up your wife?"

"No. Just a stupid misunderstanding. A month ago, I pushed her out of my way so I could go to work. She wouldn't let me out of our own house, just wanted to stand there and scream at me. But it's been blown way out of proportion now that she's got this shyster of a lawyer who just wants to make my life miserable with these insane accusations."

"I'm sorry, man. That sucks. It really does. But, Rocket, I need you. Unless you want me to be the next to die."

"Nobody else has to die, Avery. Just walk away. Let the police handle it."

"I can't. Maybe I could when it was just Hatchet and Boze, but he then hurt Roz. Someone's gotta stop him. And if you're too chickenshit to help, then I guess it's all on me."

"Avery, I understand what you're saying, but I can't be a part of that. Not right now. And I'm real sorry about your girl. Hope she pulls through."

"Fine. Be that way." She hung up and called Big Eddie on the phone number that had come up on the background check.

"Myles here."

"Big Eddie? It's Avery Byrne." She tried to keep her voice light and friendly, even though she felt like she was going to throw up. Did he suspect she was onto him?

"How'd you get this number?"

Shit, shit, shit! "Um, one of the guys gave it to me a while back. Hatchet, maybe? I forget."

"Oh. Well, whatcha want?"

"I was hoping you and me could grab a bite to eat. After what happened to Mendez, I want to do something special for Felicia and Gabriela. You were part of his crew, so I thought you could help me with some ideas. You doing anything this afternoon?"

"I'm free. Where you want to meet?"

"There's an Elbie's Restaurant at Glendale and Twelfth Street. Meet me there in about a half hour?"

"Sure, why not? I'll see you then."

She hung up, her heart thundering.

CHAPTER 44

CONFESSIONS

Avery returned to Roz's ICU room, where Abigail sat quietly.

"I've got to go out for a bit, but I'll be back." Assuming Big Eddie didn't kill her too. "Is there anything you need me to pick up while I'm out? Some late lunch, maybe?"

"A cup of coffee would be nice. Doesn't need to be fancy. Just black is fine."

"Okay. I'll be back soon." Avery turned to go.

"Avery…"

She paused and looked back at Abigail. "Yes?"

"Thank you."

"For what?"

"For loving my daughter."

Avery blushed, guilt crushing her chest. "She's a good person and didn't deserve this."

Avery arrived at Elbie's twenty minutes later and nabbed one of the corner booths. Since it was the middle of the afternoon, the place was empty.

She ordered a coffee and said she was expecting someone.

Big Eddie arrived a few minutes later. Damn, he looked even bigger than he usually did at race night. His shoulder-length mullet looked like it hadn't been washed in a week. He immediately spotted her in the empty restaurant and sat down in the booth opposite her.

"How's it going?" he asked casually.

"Okay," she lied.

"What happened to your arm?"

"Cut it." She opened her photos app on her phone and located the first of the several pictures of Eddie and Glen at Yushan. "I wanted to show you something."

“Yeah? What’s that?”

She handed him the phone. “Just FYI, all of this is backed up to the cloud. A friend of mine has copies too.”

“Okay.” He looked down at the screen and his gaze narrowed.

She studied him as he flipped through the photos. His face colored, and a blood vessel throbbed at his temple. “How’d you get these?”

She held out her hand. “My phone back, please?”

He held it out of her reach. “How?”

“I followed you. You and your buddy. Glen.”

His nostrils flared. “That was you. At the loading docks. You killed Glen.”

“Nonsense. Didn’t ya hear? Security guards say they shot him.”

“Bullshit. They’re just trying to cover their asses. Make it look like they were trying to stop it. So that leaves you who killed him for real.”

“In self-defense.”

“Bitch.”

“Relax. I’m not turning you in to the cops, provided you give me what I want.”

“Oh yeah? And what the fuck is that?”

“My phone back, for starters.” When he didn’t offer it, she added, “Like I said, I’ve got it all backed up to the cloud. You keeping the phone won’t stop me from reporting to the cops. And if anything happens to me, my friend has copies of it, including texts between you and Glen and your boss at Zeiber. So, my phone?”

He handed it back to her.

“Thanks.”

“So what the fuck you want?”

“Information.”

“What information?”

"How you drugged Hatchet and Boze the night they died. Was it you or did Mendez put the fentanyl in the ginger beer?"

Big Eddie let loose an explosive laugh. "You're fucking kidding, right?"

"No, I'm serious. Deadly serious."

"Boze and Hatchet were a bunch of junkies who OD'd. Ask the cops."

"The cops are idiots. Hatchet would never touch drugs in a million years. Boze could have slipped, but he wouldn't have taken Hatchet down with him."

"Don't know what you want me to say," Eddie growled. "If someone drugged them, it wasn't me. Maybe Mendez. He and Hatchet had some bad blood between them. Course, he's dead now, ain't he?"

Avery wasn't sure she believed him. "Let's say for the moment you didn't kill Boze and Hatch. But you did kill Mendez. Fisch told me how he discovered the stolen Quasar engine in Mendez's Satellite. Only Zeiber had put their name on it. I have texts from you agreeing to kill Mendez after he got all—what was the word you used?—righteous. I'm guessing you filed down the teeth off his rack and pinion that it failed completely when he raced. That's murder. "

"Fisch! That scrawny little Jew boy. I had fun kicking his ass."

"Who at Zeiber ordered you to kill them?"

He sat there, looking like a bull readying to charge. "Didn't kill nobody. My boss asked me to send a message to those punks trying to blackmail him. And I sent it."

"Who's your boss?"

"Nunya business."

"I'm making it my business. You beat the shit out of my girlfriend. Tell me or you go to prison for stealing those microprocessors. And since Glen was killed during the heist, whether by me or the guards, you also go down for felony murder. That's on top of the murder charges for sabotaging

Mendez's ride and drugging Boze and Hatch. Probably get the death penalty."

"Thorne."

"What?"

"Guy Thorne. He's my boss."

Avery sat there, staring at him. Zeiber's multibillionaire ubergenius CEO was the one behind this whole business? Avery had figured it to be some midlevel manager, not Zeiber's top guy. "I want a meeting with him."

"Not gonna happen."

"Make it happen."

"Thorne told me to rough up Hatch, Boze, and Fisch to send the message that Zeiber wasn't paying no more blackmail money. When I got to the garage, Boze and Hatch were already gone. So I gave Fisch a beatdown and left. Figured he'd pass along the message."

"So I guess it was Mendez who killed Boze and Hatch."

"I don't know what Mendez did or didn't do."

"But you sabotaged his ride after he got that Twelve Step religion. No loose ends, right?""

Big Eddie glared at her for a few minutes. "He was just supposed to crash. Crows crash all the time. We got safety equipment. Helmets, neck braces. No one ever got seriously hurt until now. Didn't realize the batteries would catch fire like that."

"That sounds like a confession to murder. Or at the very least, manslaughter. And then you tried to murder my girlfriend."

"What? You're delusional. Ain't laid a hand on your girl."

"Right. She's in the hospital right now. The person who found her identified you as her attacker."

"You don't know shit."

"I know a lot, actually. I have enough evidence for the state of Arizona to stick a needle in your arm."

"Bitch!" Big Eddie pounded the laminate table so hard, it left a dent.

Avery jumped and wished again she had Rocket with her. She steeled herself, remembering Abigail's remarkable strength. "Who was the inside man at Quasar? The one who orchestrated the theft of the prototype."

"You really expect me to tell you?"

"Maybe you're so low in the pecking order that your boss doesn't tell you the important details."

"Bullshit. I know everything. I just ain't gonna to tell you."

"Right." She pressed some buttons on her phone and put it to her ear.

"What are you doing?"

"Calling Detective Valentine in Phoenix PD's homicide unit. Ask him who's running the investigation the Yushan plant robbery."

"Wait."

Avery simply glared at him. "I'm waiting. Line's ringing."

"Vincent Foster. He was Fisch's boss at Quasar."

She hung up the call. "What's his phone number?"

"Beats the hell out of me. I never called him. Anything else?"

"Yeah, I want a sitdown with your boss. Make that happen, this all goes away."

"Why you wanna meet with Thorne?"

"That's my business. Your job is to get me an appointment with him."

"How do I know you'll keep your word?"

"You don't. But it's him I'm after. You're just the small fish doing his dirty work."

He snorted a few times. "Fine. I'll talk to him."

"Be very convincing. Or else. And in case you get any ideas, remember…"

“Yeah, you got it all backed up, and a friend’s got a copy.”

Big Eddie stood up so suddenly, he tipped the table toward Avery. She let him storm off before leaving a few bucks for the coffee. When he was out the door, she pulled out her phone and ended the recording she’d made.

CHAPTER 45

BACK IN THE GOTHMOBILE

Avery drove off, keeping an eye on her rearview for Big Eddie or anyone else following her. Her friend Jinx Ballou had once told her that whenever she suspected she was being followed, she would circle the block and watch for any vehicles still behind her.

She turned north instead of south onto the Piestewa Freeway, exited at Dunlap, and got back into the highway's southbound lane. As far as she could tell, no one was following her.

When she arrived back at the hospital with a tray of coffees, she offered Kimi and Chupa each one in the ICU waiting room.

"Any change?" Avery asked.

"Not that we've heard. Ms. Fein's still in there. We're not allowed in since we're not family."

Avery stared down at her cup. "Neither am I, technically."

"Almost. You're her girlfriend."

"Not anymore."

"What are you talking about?"

"I came out to her Friday night before she got hurt. It didn't go well."

"Oh, Avery. I'm so sorry. I can't imagine why she would see you any differently just because you're trans."

"Maybe because I came out after we slept together."

"Still, she's had trans friends before."

"Maybe it's different when it's someone she's dating."

"I will talk to her when she wakes up."

"If she wakes up."

"*When*. Let's stay positive."

"It's my fault she's here."

"How so?"

Avery explained about the events at the Yushan plant.

"That still doesn't make it your fault, Avery. If this Big Eddie did this to shut you up, well, you and I both know he messed with the wrong gal."

"I met with him a half hour ago. That's where I was."

Kimi looked worried. "Why? What are you planning, girl?"

"I convinced him to get me a meeting with his boss, Guy Thorne. He's the one responsible for the murdered Crows."

"Guy Thorne? Are you serious?"

Avery nodded.

"So you meet with him. And then what?"

"I'm going to make sure they don't hurt anyone else ever again."

"Do I want to know what all that means?"

"Probably not. But I want to send you what I've got just in case."

"Ave…"

"If something happens to me, give it to the cops. Okay?"

"No convincing you otherwise?"

Avery shook her head. "I better go see how Roz is doing."

After a quick hug, Avery returned to Roz's room and handed Abigail her coffee.

"Thank you."

"How is she?"

"No change, really, but I think she's got a little more color in her cheeks. How'd your thing go?"

Avery shrugged. "Okay."

They spent the next several hours sitting vigil at Roz's bedside. She would have been bored if she hadn't been brainstorming ways to exact revenge against Big Eddie and Guy Thorne.

She considered turning over the information to Walrus and the rest of the Crows. Maybe they would exact their own revenge, keeping her hands relatively clean. It's what she'd done with the Desert Mafia.

But the Sonoran Crows, for all their flaunting of traffic safety laws, weren't a bunch of bloodthirsty gangsters. They were ordinary people with a love of classic cars and a need for speed.

What she needed was to dig into Guy Thorne's background, to find his weak spot and exploit it. But with Roz unconscious, she had no way to log into the SkipTrakkr account.

"Avery…"

Avery jolted awake. Abigail stood beside her. She hadn't realized she'd fallen asleep. Her watch said it was after ten o'clock.

"Visiting hours are over. Why don't you go home? Get some rest."

"What about you?"

"I grabbed a few winks while you were at your meeting. I'll be fine."

"I can be back in the morning."

"If you'd like. Do you have work tomorrow?"

"A few clients. I can reschedule."

"Take care of your clients. If anything changes, I'll call you, okay?"

Avery felt like she was letting Abigail—and Roz—down. Yet she was right. Avery had blown off too many clients. Bobby would understand, but he would worry about it impacting her career.

"I'll call you in the morning, okay?"

"Okay. Get some rest, dear."

At the apartment complex, she was surprised to find that the college kids weren't at the pool. She thought about the email she'd sent to their professors and wondered if it would do anything. Probably not.

The next morning, she got a call as she was leaving for work.

"Avery, it's Emily over at Classic Autos. The Gothmobile is all shiny and new."

"Oh, thank goth! I'll be right over."

She dropped off the rental and caught a ride to the shop. Fisch was manning the front desk when she walked in.

"I met with Big Eddie," she told him.

His eyes went wide. "Did he confess?"

"To beating you up? Yeah. And to sabotaging Mendez's car."

"I knew it."

"But I don't think he drugged Boze or Hatchet."

"Probably Mendez who did that. Guess he already paid for his crimes. Just wish I could get my job back at Quasar."

"Big Eddie told me that Vincent Foster was the inside man at Quasar who orchestrated the prototype theft."

"Foster was my boss. I should've known. They'd never take my word over his."

"Maybe I can get proof for you. Help you get your job back. I'm trying to get a meeting with Guy Thorne. He's been the one calling the shots."

"You'd do that?"

"Might as well."

"I'd appreciate that, Avery. You need anything from me?"

"I may need an alibi after all this shakes down."

Fisch stared at her, and she hoped he understood the message. "Whatever you need."

"How much I owe for the paint job?"

"On the house."

"No, I know the shop is struggling, especially with Hatchet gone. And you're strapped too. I got money." She put down her card.

"I wish you were wrong, but you're not. Maybe I can buy you a beer sometime."

"I'd like that."

On the drive back to Seoul Fire, she allowed herself the joy of once again riding in the comfort and smoke-free luxury of the Gothmobile. She cranked up Siouxie and the Banshees on the stereo as part of the celebration.

Her phone rang as she was getting into downtown Glendale. She answered it once she stopped at a red light.

"Avery? It's Abigail." She sounded out of breath and emotional.

Avery braced herself for bad news. "What's going on?"

"It's Roz..."

CHAPTER 46

ROZ AWAKENS

"What's happened?" Avery braced herself for the bad news.

"She's awake. And she's asking for you."

The driver behind Avery laid on their horn. She glanced up and realized the light had turned green. "Say that again?"

"Roz is awake. It's a miracle. And she's asking to see you. How soon can you be here?"

"Give me thirty minutes. I'm in downtown Glendale."

"I'll let her know you're on your way. See you soon, dear."

Avery called Bobby. "Hey! I need you to reschedule my appointments."

"Avery, we've talked about this. You can't keep cancelling and treating your clients this□—"

"Roz is awake, Appa. She's asking for me. I gotta go."

"Okay, okay. Go be with her. I'll make some calls. Give her our best, okay?"

The drive to University Medical Center should have taken her a solid half hour, especially during morning rush hour. But the ancient gods must have been smiling upon her.

She caught each green light, maybe a few yellow lights. She didn't stop until she pulled into the parking garage twenty minutes after Abigail had called her. Then, like a sprinter from her preteen years, she flew up the stairs to the ICU. She was out of breath by the time she reached Roz's room.

Roz turned her head, and their eyes locked. Avery dreaded seeing the rejection in her eyes, the kind of rejection she'd faced so many times before. But all she saw was Roz's warm, weary smile.

Avery grasped her hand, and Roz squeezed back.

"Hey." Roz's voice was gravelly and weak, but it was the sweetest sound Avery had heard in days.

"Hey," Avery replied, just now catching her breath. "I ran."

"From the tattoo studio?"

"No." Avery managed a laughed. "From the parking lot."

"Nice to see you," Abigail said from the corner of the room.

"You too," Avery said, embarrassed at not acknowledging her presence sooner.

"I'll leave you two lovebirds to catch up while I go in search of a bagel and a schmear."

"How are you feeling?" Avery asked.

"Sore. Groggy. Confused."

"Yeah." She hesitated before asking the big questions. "What do you remember?"

"I remember… I remember you and me in my car. We were at a factory. That microprocessor plant. Someone was robbing it, I think."

"Wow, you remember a lot." Avery wasn't sure if that was good or bad.

"Did we get pulled over by the cops?"

"Sort of. We were parked on a road at Lake Pleasant. Cop told us to leave."

An embarrassed smile crossed Roz's face. "Were we making out?"

"More like hiding."

"Right. Someone was chasing us, right?"

"The man who robbed the microprocessor plant."

"Did he catch us?"

Guilt punched Avery in the gut. "He must have followed us. And he caught you."

Roz closed her eyes for a moment. Avery thought she'd slipped back asleep.

Then Roz said. "He was big—the guy who attacked me. Can't remember much. But I remember big."

"I'm sorry he hurt you."

"Do you know who did it?"

"Big Eddie Myles. The one who broke into the plant. He also killed a few of my friends on orders from Guy Thorne."

"Guy Thorne? I know that name."

"Asshole billionaire CEO of Zeiber Motors."

"Right."

"He's behind this whole thing. I'm going to make them both pay, Thorne and Big Eddie. I promise.

"I don't want you to get hurt, sweetie." Roz squeezed Avery's hand.

Avery wanted to say something, but emotion choked off her words. Instead, she let tears fall on the clasped hands.

"You're transgender."

Avery froze, unsure of what to say.

"You told me that night. Before. Before the robbery. Before the big man."

Avery braced herself for the rejection all over again.

"Yes."

"I was upset at you."

No one said anything for several minutes. The only thing worse than getting dumped was getting dumped twice by the same person.

Avery stared at the floor, unable to face the bitterness she'd seen in Roz's eyes a few nights before. "I should have told you up front. Before you asked me to be your girlfriend. I don't blame you for dumping me."

"No, I was wrong."

"What?" Avery looked into her eyes.

"I was wrong to be upset at you. I love you."

Roz's words stopped Avery's heart from beating. "You… You what?"

"Will you still be my girlfriend?"

Avery stared into the depths of Roz's rich honey eyes. "That's all I want. I'm sorry I didn't tell you before we…"

"Must be hard… to tell someone," Roz said, almost serenely. "I don't care if you're trans. I love you, Avery."

"I love you too. I really, really do. I was afraid I was going to lose you. Like I lost Sam."

"I come from a long line of survivors."

"Yeah, you do."

The two sat there, just holding hands and gazing into each other's eyes for the longest time. Eventually, Roz started drifting off again. Avery realized she probably needed more sleep. But Avery needed her help.

"Roz, the men who hurt you and who killed members of the Crows, the cops won't touch them. They covered their tracks too well. But if I don't stop them, who knows how many other people they could hurt."

"What do you plan to do?"

"I don't know. If I get into SkipTrakkr and learn more about Guy Thorne and his dirty secrets, maybe I can come up with some way to bring them down."

"You going to kill them?"

Avery took a deep breath. No more secrets with Roz. "I don't know. Maybe."

"It's findMay?22."

"What?"

"My password on SkipTrakkr. Lowercase *f-i-n-d*, capital *M*, lowercase *a-y*. Then a question mark. And the numeral twenty-two. I have a system. Username is davidfein, no space, all lowercase."

"Thank you."

Roz laughed weakly. "Guy Thorne. Having people murdered. So bizarre."

"Big Eddie all but admitted it. I've told him to get me a meeting with Thorne."

"You talked with the man who attacked me?"

"He denies hurting you, but I don't believe him. He tampered with Mendez's steering. And I've got the photos of him and his buddy robbing Yushan."

"What about the police?"

"I've tried talking to Valentine before. He treated me like I was a nutty conspiracy theorist."

"But now you have proof now, right? Don't want you getting hurt or going to prison."

Avery hated the idea of talking to Valentine again. But Roz was the victim. She should have a say.

"If that's what you want, that's what I'll do. I'm willing to tell the cops everything I know. I don't care whether Big Eddie spends the rest of his life behind bars or ends up in a shallow grave." Avery stared down at the floor. "But his boss needs to go down too. And that's where I don't trust the legal system to deliver. People like Thorne tend to get off scot-free."

Avery's phone rang and she answered it. "Hello, Eddie. We were just talking about you."

"Who's we?"

"Me and Roz. You remember her? My girlfriend. The one you beat up after we caught you breaking into Yushan. Guess what? She's awake. And she remembers you."

"I told you I didn't touch her."

"You're a lousy liar, Eddie Myles."

"Believe what you want. I'm calling to tell you that I got you a meeting with Mr. Thorne. Four forty-five this afternoon. Tell them who you are at the front desk. They'll take you to his office."

"Good boy." The call ended.

"You got your meeting."

"Four forty-five." Avery checked the clock on the wall. It was not yet ten.

"You sure it's safe?" Roz asked.

"I told them I had all of my evidence backed up in the cloud and had given a copy to a friend. If something happens to me, they're still in the shit."

"You're good at this. Avery the Avenger."

Avery thought some more about involving the police. "Maybe I'll call Detective Calderón, the one handling your assault case, and tell him everything I know."

When Abigail returned to the room, Avery stepped into the corridor and called Calderón. He told her he'd be there in an hour to take her statement.

While they waited, Avery loaded the SkipTrakkr app onto her phone and logged in. Pulling up info on Guy Thorne was a little trickier than on a laptop and involved a lot of scrolling both horizontally and vertically. But eventually, she found some juicy dirt that she could use to turn the screws on Thorne. Just in case Calderón ignored her the way Valentine had.

When Calderón arrived, Avery told him what she knew about the crimes that Big Eddie, Thorne, and Mendez had committed. She showed him the photos she'd taken the night of the heist.

"When you learned about the planned heist at the plant, why didn't you call the police then? You could have prevented Roz from getting attacked in the first place."

She hated that he was right, and the guilt weighed on her. "I was hoping to use it as leverage."

"Leverage?"

"Get him to admit to murdering my friends." Then she remembered. "I have a confession recorded on my phone."

"Really? Let's hear it."

She played the recording of Big Eddie admitting he'd tampered with Mendez's steering. Calderón didn't speak for a few minutes. She wondered if he was using the waiting game to get her to continue, maybe even implicate herself in something he could arrest her for.

"Carlos Mendez died west of the valley, didn't he?"

"Yeah."

"Unfortunately, that confession is for a crime committed outside my jurisdiction. You might want to reach out to the Maricopa County Sheriff's Office."

"Big Eddie tampered with the steering at Mendez's shop. That's inside Phoenix city limits."

He seemed to consider this. "I can certainly look into it. You mentioned he was involved with the deaths of Mr. Bozeman and Mr. Hatchet. Did he confess to those murders as well?"

"No, but he was involved. Dig deep enough, you'll find the evidence."

"I'll look into it. Send me those photos and that audio recording. I'll get the code to unlock Ms. Fein's phone, and we will retrieve the audio recording she made the night of the Yushan robbery."

At four o'clock, Avery kissed Roz goodbye and drove north to the Zeiber Motors facility.

CHAPTER 47

AT ZEIBER MOTORS

It was ten to five when a security guard escorted Avery to Guy Thorne's office after patting her down for weapons and taking her phone.

"Hey, that's mine!" she'd protested.

"Mr. Thorne doesn't allow phones in his office," the guard had insisted. "You can have it back when you leave."

The office on the building's top floor was vast and overlooked Deer Valley Airport. Sunlight glinted off the small planes as they took off and landed.

"Do come in and have a seat." Thorne stood up from his desk and approached with hand extended. He looked to be in his forties. Black sport jacket over a T-shirt and jeans. Limited edition Nikes. Perfect hair. Perfect smile. The kind of guy who had everything handed to him because of his charm and privilege.

Avery shook his hand. Her escort closed the door behind him, leaving the two of them alone. She wished for the millionth time that Rocket was here with her and that she still had her phone. Taking it from her was a clever move on Thorne's part.

"Ms. Burns, is it?"

"It's Byrne, with a *Y*. Like David Byrne."

"From the Talking Heads. Of course. Please have a seat."

His desk was remarkably large and cleared except for a blotter, a laptop, and a fancy fountain pen that probably cost three figures. He leaned back in his chair as if he hadn't a care in the world. Avery hoped to change that.

Thorne glanced at his Rolex. "I was afraid you wouldn't show."

"Traffic."

“What is it I can do for you, Ms. Byrne? Mr. Myles was rather vague about why you so urgently needed to speak with me. Are you looking for employment? I think there may be an opening for a receptionist. You don’t strike me as an engineer.”

“I’m not here about a fucking job. I want to hear you confess to ordering the murders of Hatchet, Boze, and Mendez.”

Thorne had the nerve to look genuinely bewildered. “Sorry to disappoint, but I’m afraid I have no idea what you’re talking about.”

“Then let me refresh your memory. You conspired to steal an electric car prototype from Quasar Motors. Vincent Foster, a manager at Quasar, was your inside man. The two of you pinned the theft on a junior engineer by the name of Jude Fischman. Several months later, you developed your own electric engine based on this stolen prototype and gave it to Carlos Ybarra-Mendez, a member of the Sonoran Crows, to test out.”

“Ms. Byrne, I know nothing about a stolen proto□—”

“Don’t interrupt!” Avery stood and glared down at him. “When Mendez started winning races, Dwayne Hatchet, Leonard Bozeman, and the aforementioned Jude Fischman grew suspicious. They broke into Mendez’s Valley View Auto Repair and got a look at this fancy new engine. Fisch recognized the design from the prototype he had been working on at Quasar, even if it had the Zeiber logo all over it. He knew your company had stolen the engine.”

Thorne’s gaze narrowed, but he said nothing.

“They blackmailed you, and you paid up. Sixty grand, isn’t that right? Figured it would stay nice and quiet. But then they got greedy. They wanted more. So you ordered Mendez and Big Eddie to shut them up. Mendez brought them bottles of ginger beer, Hatchet’s favorite, laced with fentanyl. Then you sent in Big Eddie to clean up the mess. Only things didn’t go as planned.”

Thorne's face was coloring with anger now.

Avery knew she was hitting the mark, so she continued. "Sure, Hatchet and Boze died. And lucky for you, the cops ruled it an accidental overdose. But Fisch didn't drink the doctored soda. So Big Eddie put the beatdown on him and told him to keep quiet. Which he did—for a while, anyway."

"Someone's been telling you tales, young lady. I never ordered anyone killed. And I've never had anything to do with fentanyl or any other drugs."

"Not true. Seven years ago, police busted you for two grams of cocaine. You got probation. No jail time. Typical for a powerful white guy like yourself. System's always looking for reasons to give you guys a second chance. And a third chance. And a fourth. Dare not bring down the patriarchy, right?"

"That was a long time ago. A youthful indiscretion. Haven't touched it since."

"You learned it was better to give the drugs to someone else to cover up your other crimes. But it didn't stop there. Mendez grew nervous. You realized he might talk, so you sent your little errand boy, Big Eddie, to tie up loose ends. Sabotaged the steering in his car. Then bam! Mendez dies in a fiery crash. Problem solved. Mendez is out of the way, and the evidence of the stolen prototype is nothing but melted metal and plastic. Cops rule it an accident due to reckless driving and a worn rack and pinion."

"Listen, you impudent little bi□—"

She slapped him.

He sat there, stunned and wide-eyed.

"You interrupt me again, I'll give you a fucking tracheotomy with your own fountain pen."

He glared at her silently.

"But you forgot about a few things. For starters, you didn't count on someone like me looking into their deaths. Plus, Fisch was still alive. And he started talking after Big Eddie killed Mendez. He confessed and gave you up, so don't bother to deny it. I have it all recorded. I also have the texts of you giving the kill order."

"There was no kill order. Mendez wasn't supposed to die. We were just trying to scare him and get rid of the engine. His death was an accident."

"The law has a term for that. Manslaughter in the first degree. But considering this is part of a greater conspiracy, I have a feeling the county attorney will bump it up to murder."

"Don't threaten me, little girl."

Avery snatched up the fountain pen and examined the tip. "I might have let this all go until Big Eddie tried to kill my girlfriend."

"And why would he do that?"

"We caught him and his buddy, Glen, stealing microprocessors from the Yushan plant."

"What is it that you want, Ms. Byrne?" All hint of humor and niceties were gone. "Money?"

Avery scoffed. "I don't need your dirty money, rich boy. What I want is you and Big Eddie dead in a shallow grave. But I'd settle for the two of you in prison for life."

She and Thorne stared at each other.

"You've got nothing but allegations. Maybe I know something about Quasar's missing motor. Maybe I don't. I certainly don't know a damn thing about anyone being given doctored beers. Sounds like your friends had drug problems of their own. And it appears the police agree."

"But—"

"Don't interrupt, Ms. Byrne. I started this corporation in my dad's garage. Today, I employ tens of thousands of people all over this country. Twice that overseas. If I accepted an offer from a competitor to purchase one of their prototypes, who was I to say no? I call that smart business. A perfect business transaction. Anyone in my shoes would have done the same."

"Yeah, right."

"We developed our own version after reverse engineering the Quasar prototype. Bigger, better. And Mr. Mendez agreed to help us with our testing. Again, all above board."

Avery wanted to say something, but let him talk.

"Then your little hot rod friends broke into Mr. Mendez's garage and had the audacity to blackmail me. Breaking and entering, trespassing, and extortion. They're the criminals. Not me. I considered turning the matter over to my lawyers, but after considering the proprietary nature of the project, I opted to keep the project confidential, and so I paid them what they were asking."

"And when they came to you asking for more, you killed them."

"Don't be absurd. I instructed Mr. Myles to inform them that there would be no more payoffs. But then Bozeman or Hatchet went for a drug-induced joyride."

"But when Mendez got out of rehab, he wasn't so keen being part of your industrial espionage conspiracy. Not after it got one friend fired from his job at Quasar and two others killed. So you told Big Eddie to get rid of him before he could talk."

"I. Never. Ordered. Anyone. Killed," he said between clenched teeth. "He was only supposed to get rid of the engine. Quasar's prototype was flawed anyway."

"Bullshit. He told you that Mendez was becoming a problem. You told him to take care of the problem. He sabotaged the car's steering and boom! Mendez is dead and your flawed prototype nothing but scrap. Just like you wanted."

"Problem solved," he replied with a smirk.

"Except I was on to him. I caught him robbing the Yuhan plant."

"What did you care?"

"I wanted justice for my friends. But then that bastard put my girlfriend in the hospital. Nearly killed her. No doubt on your orders as well."

He shrugged. "Collateral damage."

Avery wanted to make good on her threat and shove that fountain pen into his throat. "You're going to regret this. I'm going to make sure you spend the rest of your pathetic excuse of a life as someone's prison bitch."

"I doubt that. No matter what so-called evidence you think you've got, my battalion of lawyers will ensure I never see the inside of a cell. People like me never do."

"Is that so? Then you may be interested to know that shortly before I arrived here, I got word that Big Eddie's been arrested and charged with two counts of assault, four counts of murder, and one count of grand theft. Wonder what he's going to tell the cops? Who's he going to point the finger at?"

"Time's up, Ms. Byrne. Leave before I have security throw you out of here. And if you so much as whisper any of this to anyone, "

A commotion in the hallway outside the office caught Avery's attention. She grinned. "I think you're the one whose time is up, Thorne."

The door flew open. Detective Calderón appeared with several uniformed officers. He flashed his badge. "Guy Leslie Thorne, you are under arrest for the murder of Carlos Ybarra-Mendez. You have the right to remain silent."

As he Mirandized Thorne, Avery pulled the wire out from underneath her shirt. Let's see his battalion of lawyers get him out of this.

CHAPTER 48

RED VELVET CUPCAKES

After a thirty-minute debrief with Calderón, Avery drove back to the hospital.

Would the charges against Thorne stick, even with all the evidence she provided Calderón? Would he ever see the inside of a prison cell? Or would his battalion of lawyers protect him with an endless barrage of delays, motions, and appeals? Only time would tell. And if the cops or the courts dropped the ball again, all bets were off. Avery the Avenger would handle things once and for all.

She managed to reach the hospital gift shop before it closed. As she was buying flowers for Roz, her phone rang. She didn't recognize the number. "Hello?"

"Avery, it's Grace Bozeman."

"Hey, Grace, how are you holding up?"

"Managing. I'm finally calling everyone who showed up at my dad's memorial to thank them for coming. Emily gave me your number. I hope you don't mind."

"No, I don't mind. Your dad was a great guy."

"He was, once he got clean."

There was an awkward pause in the conversation.

"Avery, Emily told me you'd been looking into their deaths. That you don't believe my dad relapsed."

"I hope I didn't overstep." Avery wasn't sure what to say. "I just thought it odd, considering your dad had been in recovery, and Hatch was the son of an addict."

"That's the other reason I'm calling. And I don't even know if it's relevant. But the day they died, the guy they called Rocket Man stopped by the house. He brought my dad a box of red velvet cupcakes."

Something tickled at the back of Avery's mind, like she'd missed something obvious. "Cupcakes? Was it your dad's birthday?"

"No, Dad's birthday was in September. But he had helped Rocket's wife, Tiffany, get an order of protection against her husband."

"He what?"

"Tiffany had told me Rocket was abusing her. I was shocked because he never acted that way when I was around him. But I recognized the look in her eyes. And she showed me the bruises."

"Oh my goth! Poor Tiff."

"I told my dad. His own father used to beat on my Nana. And as much as it pained him to turn on a friend, he accompanied her to the courthouse to get the restraining order. He also went to court with her when Rocket tried to quash it. That's when Rocket learned my dad was helping her."

"Wow, that's unbelievable."

"He wanted to tell the other members of the Sonoran Crows, but Tiff begged him not to. I guess she was embarrassed about being abused."

"What happened?"

"Rocket went ballistic, pardon the pun. Accused Dad of sleeping with Tiffany, which he would never do. He was just trying to protect a vulnerable woman. Rocket can be really scary when he wants to be. I can't imagine what Tiff went through."

"So what's with the cupcakes?"

"A week later, Rocket showed up at the house and admitted he'd overreacted. Said he was going to anger-management therapy. Wanted to make peace, you know? But I got a weird vibe off him. His apology sounded… forced. I didn't say anything because it wasn't really my business."

"And you think Rocket laced the cupcakes with something? Did you eat any?"

"No, I'm trying to avoid sweets. But he took them with him when he went to meet Hatchet and Fisch at the garage. He said they were working on a secret project for race night."

Avery considered this new information. If the fentanyl was in the cupcakes, it would explain why there wasn't any in the remaining bottle of ginger beer. *But still... Rocket Man?*

"Thanks for letting me know, Grace."

"I hope I haven't caused any trouble."

"No, you did the right thing. And again, I'm really sorry for your loss."

"Thank you."

When Avery hung up, she called Fisch.

"Hey!" he said. "How goes the investigation?"

She told him about the attack on Roz and about wearing a wire during her meeting with Thorne. "But neither Thorne nor Eddie admitted to killing Boze or Hatchet. They both assume Mendez did it."

"Makes sense."

"Maybe. Did Boze show up with cupcakes the night that he and Hatch died?"

"Yeah, those red velvet ones. I passed. I'm allergic to cochineal beetles."

"Allergic to what?"

"They use the shells of cochineal beetles to make the red food dye. Kind of gross, if you ask me. But I'm allergic to them. So I don't eat anything with red food dye."

"But Hatchet and Boze ate them?"

"Yeah. There was one left over the next day, but we tossed it. Why the question about the cupcakes?"

"I think it was the cupcakes, not the ginger beer, that were spiked with fentanyl."

"Are you serious? Why would Boze have put drugs in his own cupcakes? Wait, no. He said he got them from someone."

"Rocket Man," Avery replied.

"That's right. He said Rocket Man had brought them by the house. Trying to bury the hatchet over some dispute they'd had."

Only it got Hatchet buried instead. And Boze too. She tried to wrap her head around the idea that Rocket could have murdered Boze and Hatchet. He'd seemed genuinely broken up about their deaths. Or maybe he was only upset about Hatchet's death, an unintended consequence of murdering Boze.

"Thanks for letting me know."

"Hey, did you talk to Big Eddie and his boss about clearing my name so I can get my job back?"

"They both admitted Vincent Foster was the inside man at Quasar. And now the cops know. Maybe it will help you get your job back," Avery replied.

"That'd be great. Thanks, Avery. Sorry I attacked you at race night."

"I'll talk to you later."

When she passed the ICU waiting room, she ducked inside, opened up SkipTrakkr, and plugged in Rocket Man's real name, Stephen Floyd. A number of possible matches came up but she recognized his address from when the Crows had had a barbecue at his place.

The first report she ran was a criminal background. She stared, gaping at the results.

CHAPTER 49

MURDERER CONFIRMED

According to the criminal background report, Rocket had served three years for aggravated battery and domestic abuse. That was before he and Tiffany had gotten married five years ago. Since then, there had been several domestic violence complaints but only three arrests, including one for possession of OxyContin and fentanyl. In every case, the charges had been dropped. The filing of an order of protection was also listed.

Avery wondered if Major Tom had intervened on Rocket's behalf to get the charges dropped.

The most recent entry on the report was just a few days ago, when Rocket got caught by a red-light camera on Camelback less than a block from Roz's apartment fifteen minutes after she was assaulted.

She studied the photo of his face the camera had taken. There appeared to be blood on his face. Roz's blood. He was driving his candy-apple-red 1959 Chevy Impala. Abigail had mentioned the neighbor had seen Roz's attacker drive off in an older-model red car.

But how did he know where Roz lives? And then it hit her. When she begged Rocket to join them the night of the Yushan heist, she had given him Roz's address.

The murder bees in her brain were at full swarm. Rocket had attacked Roz. It was Avery's fault he knew where Roz lived. But she was going to make it right. And he was going to pay. Only this time, she wasn't calling the cops. This time, it was personal.

Roz's face lit up when Avery walked into the room with the bouquet. "You shouldn't have."

"You're not allergic, are you?"

"Not at all. I only wish I could smell them. They're beautiful. Almost as beautiful as you."

"That's very thoughtful, Avery. Thank you." Abigail stood and gave Roz a peck on the cheek. "I'll give you girls some alone time."

"Thanks, Mom." When Abigail left, Roz asked, "How'd your meeting go with the great and powerful Guy Thorne?"

"He admitted his involvement in stealing the Quasar prototype and ordering Mendez's death. But I don't think he or Big Eddie killed Boze and Hatchet. And I don't think Big Eddie was the one who attacked you."

"No?"

"It was Rocket Man."

"Your friend? But he seemed so nice."

"Had a lot of people fooled."

"But why would he attack me? What did I ever do to him?"

"He was abusing his wife. Boze helped her get a restraining order against him. He drugged Boze to get even. Hatchet was just collateral damage."

"Shit. That's extreme. Why come after me? I barely met the man."

Avery sighed. "I think because I was looking into their deaths. He kept telling me to back off, but I wouldn't listen. I suspect he was the one who spray-painted my car, too."

"You're sure it's him?"

Avery told her about the red-light camera photos near her apartment and the blood on Rocket's face.

"How did he know where I lived?"

Avery told her. "I'm so sorry. This is my fault."

"No, it's not." Roz clasped her hand. "This is all on him. He's the one who likes to abuse women."

Avery shrugged.

"Have you told Calderón?"

"All the evidence linking Rocket to Boze and Hatchet's deaths is circumstantial. No solid proof. And the evidence proving he attacked you isn't much stronger. Plus, every time Rocket was arrested for assaulting his wife, the charges got dropped. I think Major Tom has been intervening on his behalf. Even if I told Calderón everything I knew, my gut tells me Rocket would just slither out from under the charges again."

"So what's your plan?"

"You really want to know?"

Roz nodded. Avery told her, then sent Rocket a text.

Avery:
Hey, Rocket. Feeling depressed about Roz. Could use some company. Mind if I stop by your place tonight for a drink?
Rocket:
Sure. Love to have you. Should be there around six. Remember the address?
Avery:
Yep. C U there. Ill bring the booze.

CHAPTER 50

AT ROCKET'S PAD

"Hey there, Rocket Man," Avery said in her most sultry voice when he walked in through the front door.

She was lounging on Rocket's living room couch, wearing a lacy black corset, a thong, fishnets, and not much else.

Avery suppressed a laugh when Rocket stumbled at the sight of her.

"Um, holy shit. What's going on? Am I in the right house?"

"You're right where you need to be, big man." She sat up, patted the seat next to her, then offered him one of the two tumblers filled with whiskey. "Have a drink. It's single-malt Scotch. Your poison of choice."

"Uh, thanks." He took the glass and sat beside her. "This is… unexpected."

"I know, but with Roz in the hospital, I've been feeling really lonely the past few nights. And who better to cure that loneliness than my best friend, Rocket?"

"How'd you get in here?"

"Door was unlocked." That was a lie, but he didn't need to know she'd picked the lock. "Come on! Let's party."

"Last time I checked, you were into chicks not dicks."

"You know what they say—'It's a woman's prerogative to change her mind.' And I've always been a curious girl. Figured I'd experiment with heterosexuality. See what all the fuss is about. Bottoms up."

"Bottoms up." They clinked glasses.

"Whew," he said when they'd both drained their glasses. "That's damn good shit. What is it?"

"Macallan 25. Found it in your cabinet."

Avery grabbed the bottle on the side table and poured him another three fingers, which he also drained.

"Enough drinking," he said. "Let's see about curing that loneliness of yours."

Avery steeled herself but went with the plan. She straddled his waist and began kissing him passionately. Even with her kneeling on his lap, he was a few inches taller.

She'd never kissed a man before and tried to imagine she was kissing Roz. But his face was bristly, so unlike Roz's soft skin. It took everything in her not to recoil when he firmly gripped her ass with his huge hands. She could feel his hardness pressed against her and wondered how long she would have to pretend.

When he kissed the tops of her breasts, she moaned for effect, even though it felt like someone was rubbing her tits with coarse sandpaper.

"How you get this thing off, anyway?" Rocket asked.

"Patience, baby. Don't wanna rush things. We got all night long." She laid a string of kisses along his neck, and he let out a low rumble of pleasure. With her hand, she reached down and massaged his cock.

"Oh, fuck yeah."

"You're just so hard," she sighed. "And big."

"Fuck yeah, I am." Then he blew out a breath. "Whew, that whiskey's got a real kick to it."

Avery paused and leaned back. "You feeling all right, baby?"

"Just… just a little woozy."

"Must be the fentanyl I put in your glass. Found it in your nightstand, same place it was when the cops busted you last time. You really should hide your shit better."

"Wait, what?"

She stood and took a step back. Playtime was over.

He rubbed his face wearily. "What's going on?"

She lifted the plastic bag filled with white pills, each one stamped with the letter M. "Is this the same stuff you put in the cupcakes?"

He didn't answer at first. Just sat there, glaring at her through lidded eyes.

"Is it?" She kicked his shin.

"Fuck!"

"Answer me."

"Crushed some up into the icing. Why you care?"

"And you gave them to Boze?"

"He was messing with my woman. My marriage." He was slurring his words.

"You killed him. And Hatchet."

"Just wanted him to relapse. Show everybody what a hypocrite he is." He shook his head again, as if to clear the cobwebs. "Damn, girl. How much of that shit you'd put in there?"

"Not more than six or seven pills. Okay, maybe ten. Got plenty left for the cops to find."

"Ten? Bitch, you're gonna kill me."

She held up a small cardboard box. "Good thing I got this Narcan nasal spray. Could save your life."

He reached for it but nearly fell off the couch when Avery took another step back.

"Not so fast, Rocket Man. I want you to tell me the truth. Did you attack Roz?"

"Shit, girl. Just trying… to get you to forget… about Boze and Hatch. You wouldn't leave it alone. Spray-painted your car. Wouldn't stop. So I… I, uh… roughed up your girl. Don't be mad."

"You killed Boze. You killed Hatchet. You vandalized my car. And nearly killed Roz. But I shouldn't be mad? Are you fucking insane?"

He started gripping his chest. "Hard… to breathe."

"Reckon so."

“Narcan. Please.” He began to wheeze. His face turned red, eyes wide with fear.

“Sorry, dude. Gotta put you down. Don’t be mad.”

As his moans grew quieter, she put her glass in the dishwasher and ran it. She dropped the Narcan into her purse and wiped down everything she had touched. Finally, she pulled on her pants and a light jacket.

He was slumped on the couch. Eyes bulging. Mouth agape. And dead.

“Goodbye, Rocket.” She let herself out.

CHAPTER 51

FALLOUT

A couple days later, Avery was leaving her apartment on her way to visit Roz at the hospital when a pair of professional movers emerged from Jaden's apartment carrying a couch. The asshole was moving out. She couldn't help but smile.

Her neighbor, Lucas, stepped outside. "Real shame."

"Why? You wanted him here?"

Lucas shook his head. "Naw. I hated him and his little troop of delinquents. Local news said he crashed his Mercedes into another vehicle late last night while driving the wrong way on the I-17. Killed a mother and two kids. Little punk blew a 1.6 on his Breathalyzer."

"Shit."

"Apparently, he'd just been expelled from GCC for using one of those AI apps to write his term papers. I swear, that kid was a fuckup from the word go. Just a shame about that mom and those kids."

"Yeah." Avery didn't know what else to say.

After nearly two weeks in the hospital, Roz was released, though the doctors instructed her not to return to work for at least another month due to her head injuries.

Avery sat next to her on Roz's bed, reading the latest edition of the weekly alternative newspaper, *Phoenix Living*. She opened it to the cover story, which was titled "A Murder of Crows."

"What's it say?" Roz asked.

"They're describing the Sonoran Crows as an outlaw band of hot-rodders who've been terrorizing the streets of Phoenix for years but are now imploding from the inside out."

"Wow. Give me the deets."

Avery read, “Phoenix Police are saying that Stephen ‘Rocket Man’ Floyd, now deceased from an overdose of fentanyl, is suspected of involvement in the deaths of two of his fellow Crows, Dwayne Hatchet and Leonard Bozeman. The drugs believed to have killed Hatchet and Bozeman were a match to those found in Floyd’s system the Phoenix Crime Lab confirms.”

“What’s it say about Big Eddie and Guy Thorne?”

Avery scanned the page. “A bigger scandal appears to have ensnared two other members of the Sonoran Crows as well as billionaire tech mogul Guy Thorne, founder and CEO of Zeiber Motors, and one of his competitors, Vincent Foster, VP of Development at Quasar.

“Last September, one of Quasar’s electric motor prototypes disappeared. Jude Fischman, a junior engineer at Quasar and a member of the Crows, was suspected in the theft but never charged. New evidence has led police to charge Thorne, Foster, and Edward ‘Big Eddie’ Myles with grand theft larceny. Myles, another member of the Crows gang, also faces first-degree murder charges for the death of fellow Crow Carlos Ybarra-Mendez and Glen Garrett, who was killed by a security guard during a heist at the Yushan Microprocessor plant.”

“They’re not charging Thorne with murder?” Roz asked.

“Not according to the article. Typical case of PWM.”

“Powerful white men.” Roz nodded. “Probably get a slap on the wrist for everything. And Rocket died from an overdose of his own drugs. Rather Shakespearean.”

“That fentanyl is deadly shit,” Avery said. “Just say no.”

The two of them laughed.

“Avery the Avenger strikes again,” Roz said with a serious face. “You killed the man who nearly killed me.”

“What wouldn’t I do to protect the woman I love? He also abused his wife for years, killed two of my friends, and sprayed graffiti on the Gothmobile. And after Phoenix PD reinstated Major Tom, it was highly likely Rocket would never face any charges. How many more people would he hurt or kill, just because they got in his way?"

"I'm not complaining. You did the right thing. Avery the Avenger. My own personal superhero."

"I'm glad you see it that way. I'm also glad you understand about me not coming out to you right away."

"This again? Of course I understand. Avery, you are a woman. You being trans has nothing to do with who you are or what I love about you. It's not much more than medical history. Guess what? When I was eight, I had an appendectomy."

Avery made a stern face. "An appendectomy? And you're just telling me now? After we've slept together?"

They both laughed.

"You wanna see the scar?"

"Definitely. By the way, Kimi and the band are playing The Zombie Room tonight," Avery said. "You up for going?"

"I think I could be persuaded."

They started kissing.

ENJOY A BONUS

Did you enjoy ***A Murder of Crows***? Would you like to a free bonus?

No need to subscribe. No strings attached. Just click the link below to read.

https://dharmakelleher.com/pages/a-murder-of-crows-bonus-content

AUTHOR'S NOTE
WRITING ABOUT TRAUMA, COMING OUT, AND STEPPING UP

I hope you enjoyed reading *A Murder of Crows* as much as I enjoyed writing it.

Each story I write explores a variety of issues, and this one was no different.

One of the big ones I explore in *A Murder of Crows* is dealing with the aftermath of trauma. In the previous book, Avery experienced multiple major traumas, on top of the ones she survived as a teen. In this book, I wanted to look at how that trauma changes one's outlook.

I dug deep into my personal experiences with trauma, hoping to convey more than just the pain and shame. With trauma comes a distorted worldview and a tendency to see unrelated events as part of a greater pattern. Even with a lack of religious or spiritual beliefs, it can feel like the universe is conspiring against you. A curse.

I also explored the subject of coming out. Contrary to what a lot of straight, cisgender people think, coming out is not a single event. It is something that queer people have to do over and over. Every time we meet a significant person in our lives or we change jobs or doctors or move, we face the decision of if, when, and how to come out.

It never stops being scary.

Let me repeat that. It never stops being scary. Because you never know how someone will react, especially if they have power over you. Even if they claim to be an ally.

If I go to the ER or urgent care, it's standard procedure for the medical staff to ask me when my last period was. Do I lie? Do I turn it into a joke and say, "It's been a while." After all, I'm in my mid-fifties. Or do I tell the truth? And if I do, how will the medical professionals treat me? The doctor, the nurses, the other staff?

Last year, I had to change endocrinologists because my current one viewed me as a man with breasts rather than a woman on HRT. Never mind that I transitioned over three decades ago. It was humiliating, painful, and scary.

I debated reporting her to the corporation that oversaw the medical practice. Their website claimed they didn't tolerate discrimination against patients, including on the basis of sexual orientation and gender identity.

I was shaking when I finally made that phone call, feeling the shame and humiliation all over again. They promised to investigate. But nothing ever came of it. It just got buried. No surprise.

Coming out while dating is a whole other thing, especially when you're transgender. Where do you tell—public or private? How do you tell? When do you tell? When you first meet? Before the first kiss? Before you have sex? Are you obligated to say ever? Does the other person already know? What happens if things go violently wrong?

It's terrifying, and all too often heartbreaking. And there is no right or wrong answer as to how or when or if.

I put Avery in this situation to help readers who've never been there experience what it's like. That is, after all, what story is for. To take readers on a journey of new experiences.

The final issue I touched on in the book is domestic violence. I didn't dive too deeply into it. But it served as the motive for the initial crime.

I drew on personal experience for this as well. I am a survivor of domestic violence.

And I have also had the significant other of a close friend confide that my friend was abusing them. I was surprised. My friend was the last person I would have suspected of being an abuser. But I knew that many abusers hide in plain sight.

I helped this person get an order of protection against my friend. Because I would rather lose a friend than allow someone to suffer the way I had suffered. I will never turn a blind eye to cruelty. Ever.

If you enjoyed this book, I really hope you will leave an honest review wherever you bought it. Honest reviews help readers like you find books they enjoy. And they help authors like me continue to tell stories that need to be told.

And if you like free books, giveaways, behind-the-scenes trivia, and more, I hope you'll join my mailing list. Just go to https://dharmakelleher.com/subscribe.

Peace and love,

Dharma Kelleher

ENJOY A FREE E-BOOK

Download a free copy of *Blood and Fire*, a Jinx Ballou novel, by subscribing to Dharma Kelleher's Readers Club at dharmakelleher.com.
Join now to receive special offers, exclusive behind-the-scenes details, cover reveals, new release announcements, and to **get your free e-book**.

You can unsubscribe at any time.

ALSO BY DHARMA KELLEHER

Did you enjoy *A Murder of Crows?* Then you won't want to miss these books from related series.

JINX BALLOU BOUNTY HUNTER SERIES

Chaser

Extreme Prejudice

A Broken Woman

TERF Wars

Red Market

SHEA STEVENS OUTLAW BIKER SERIES

Iron Goddess

Snitch

Blood Sisters

Road Rash

ABOUT THE AUTHOR

Dharma Kelleher writes gritty crime thrillers including the Jinx Ballou Bounty Hunter series and the Shea Stevens Outlaw Biker series.

She is one of the only openly transgender authors in the crime fiction genre. Her action-driven thrillers explore the complexities of social and criminal justice in a world where the legal system favors the privileged.

Dharma is a member of Sisters in Crime, the International Thriller Writers, and the Alliance of Independent Authors.

She lives in Arizona with her wife and a black cat named Mouse. Learn more about Dharma and her work at https://dharmakelleher.com.

ACKNOWLEDGMENTS

Even in the world of self-publishing, bringing forth a new book into the world is always a team effort.

Let me start by thanking every member of the transgender community. It is not easy for us to live as our true selves, especially these days.

It takes courage, persistence, and deep level of self-trust. But it also takes the generosity of community to reach out and lift each other up. We are stronger together.

I want to thank the many author communities I'm a part of, especially Doing Wide Wright, Rebel Authors, and Sisters in Crime.

For their brilliant editing skills, I want to thank my editors at Red Adept Editing.

Last, but certainly not least, I want to thank all my loyal fans, especially my newsletter subscribers. Enjoy!

Made in the USA
Middletown, DE
09 June 2024

55526998R00179